ISLAND HERITAGE

An Isle of Man Romance

DIANA XARISSA

Text Copyright © 2014 Diana Xarissa
Cover Copyright © 2019 Tell-Tale Book Covers
All Rights Reserved

ISBN: 1548253472
ISBN-13: 978-1548253479

❊ Created with Vellum

For Lisa – my biggest fan.

AUTHOR'S NOTE

Welcome to another romance set in the wonderful Isle of Man. The island location is an important part of the story, so I want to tell you a little bit more about it.

Man is located between England and Ireland in the Irish Sea. It is a Crown Dependency, but it is a country in its own right, with its own currency, stamps, language and government.

This is a work of fiction. The historical sites and landmarks on the island are all real, however all of the events that take place within them in this story are fictional. Manx National Heritage is real and their efforts to preserve and promote the historical sites and the history of the island are incredible. All of the Manx National Heritage staff members in this story, however, are fictional creations.

All of the modern characters are a product of the author's imagination. Any resemblance to actual persons, living or dead, is entirely coincidental. Similarly, the names of the restaurants and shops and other businesses on the island are fictional, but may resemble actual shops or businesses on the island.

The historical characters mentioned within the story (the Seventh Earl of Derby and his wife) did exist and the details of their history given in this story are as accurate as I can make them. Having said that, while the Isle of Man has its share of ghosts, spirits and Little People (fairies), to the best of the author's knowledge the ghost of Charlotte de la Tremouille does not haunt Castle Rushen.

Many of the characters in my romance series appear in more than one of the books. Each book is designed to stand alone, however. (Darcy Robinson, for example, first appeared in *Island Escape* and Finlo Quayle has turned up in every romance so far.) Additionally, some characters in the romances make appearances in my Isle of Man Cozy Mystery Series as well.

The cozy mysteries are set about fifteen years before the romances (they start circa 1998), so the characters from the romances that appear in those books do so as younger versions of themselves.

The first two romances had American heroines in them, which allowed me to use some American terms and to explain British ones when they arose. That isn't the case with this book, so I've included a glossary at the back, as well as some extra notes to help explain some of them. (As I do in the Bessie series.) As ever, a few Americanisms have probably sneaked in as well, sorry. Also in the back of the book is a list of all of the sites that Lisa visits to help readers keep track of them.

I really hope you enjoy the story and would love to hear from you. My contact details are also in the back of the book.

I

"Ah." Lisa Mylchreest sighed deeply and sank lower into the deep and bubbly bath. This is just about as good as it gets, she thought to herself. She grabbed her book and opened it, carefully placing the bookmark on the floor next to the tub. Popping a chocolate truffle into her mouth, she chewed slowly, letting the expensive chocolate melt on her tongue as she began to read.

She'd managed to read a paragraph before the phone started to ring. Instinctively, she sat up, reaching for her bookmark, before she shook her head.

"Ring as much as you like," she shouted at the phone. "I'm having a bath and I'm not getting out."

She slid back down and tried to find her place on the page. The phone stopped ringing and she sighed happily, grabbing a second truffle. Before she swallowed, she could hear her mobile phone blasting out a distinctive ringtone.

"Leave me alone, Darcy," she muttered under her breath. She'd assigned that particular ringtone to her closest friend, and usually when she heard it she was quick to answer, but whatever Darcy wanted tonight would have to wait.

Lisa grabbed a third truffle and turned the page. In less than a minute she was lost in a Regency romance, sighing over earls and lords and their pursuit of beautiful, if unsuitable, women. Fifteen minutes later, just as she was contemplating adding a bit more hot water to the tub, she heard someone knocking on her front door.

It had to be Darcy, no one else ever visited at totally unsuitable times, Lisa thought. She briefly considered climbing out of the tub and going to the door, but there was no point. Darcy would let herself in if Lisa didn't answer. Lisa wasn't giving up her lovely hot bath, not even for her dearest friend.

Moments later, as Lisa set her book aside and quickly gobbled down the last truffle before her friend got it, the sound of the front door opening reached her ears.

"Lisa? Where are you?" a voice called from the front of the small bungalow.

"I'm in the bathtub, and I want you to go away," Lisa called back grumpily.

Lisa heard her friend's throaty laugh and then the clickety-clack of Darcy's ever-present stilettos. Little black dress? Fire-engine-red gown? Midnight blue velvet frock with crystal accents? Lisa tried to guess what her friend would be wearing when she appeared in the doorway. Lisa was wrong, as usual.

Darcy appeared around the corner in a stunning dress in a seasonally appropriate autumnal orange that showcased the other woman's incredible figure. It was strapless, with a hemline that fell just above Darcy's knees and a full and swirly skirt that Lisa instantly loved. The colour shouldn't have worked with Darcy's red hair, but somehow it looked gorgeous on her.

Darcy stood in the doorway, smiling at her friend. "There you are," she said. "I've been ringing and ringing. But you need to get out of the tub. We have a party to attend."

Lisa sighed deeply and deliberately. She didn't want to go to a party. She wanted a quiet night. "I'm busy," she told Darcy, sliding deeper into the tub.

Darcy shook her head. "You're not," she countered. She bent down and picked up the book that Lisa had set on the floor by the tub. "*The*

Earl's Unsuitable Companion? Really? I think real life is more important, don't you?"

"No," Lisa said with a shrug. "Real life is dull and boring, unless you're a gorgeous redhead who gets men to fall at your feet with a single look."

Darcy laughed. "I wish," she replied. "You know men don't fall at my feet."

"Nonsense," Lisa told her. "Lots of men fall at your feet. You just aren't interested in them if they're that easy."

Darcy laughed again. "You've got me there," she admitted. "But that doesn't matter. We have a party to attend."

Lisa shook her head. "Really, Darce, I just want to stay home tonight. I had a very long week at work and I'm exhausted. The only thing that got me through today was thinking about this bath and now that I'm in it, I'm not getting out."

"What did you have for dinner?" Darcy asked.

"What does that have to do with anything?"

"I bet you didn't even bother with dinner, did you? You probably bought yourself a handful of truffles and ate those in the bath. I bet you haven't eaten anything proper tonight at all."

"So what?" Lisa demanded. "I'll eat proper food tomorrow. Besides, chocolate is good for you."

"*La Terrazza* is catering the party," Darcy told her friend, naming Lisa's favourite restaurant.

"I don't care," Lisa said, with only a hint of uncertainty.

"It's just finger foods, of course," Darcy said casually. "You know, those little garlic toasts and the tiny spicy chicken bites, that sort of thing."

Lisa growled at her friend. "I don't want to go," she said stoutly.

"And of course, their famous pudding buffet," Darcy added. "You know, with the mini-chocolate mousses in solid chocolate cups and the tiny shortbread squares with caramel sauce, that sort of thing."

Lisa grinned. "Bring me back one of each," she suggested.

Darcy giggled. "No way. If you want the goodies, you have to come with me."

"Where is it?" Lisa sighed, knowing that it didn't really matter. She very rarely said no to Darcy's requests, and she didn't have a good enough reason to do so today.

The two had become friends when they were both six-year-olds and in Year Two at school. Darcy's family had moved to the island over the previous summer, and Lisa had found Darcy sitting next to her in Miss Stone's class on the first day of school. They'd bonded over fractions, being only children, and the shared notion that boys were gross.

They'd stayed friends through school, gone to the same university in Liverpool, and even shared a flat for a few years once they'd both returned to the island after they'd finished their studies. Now, twenty-two years after that fateful September in Miss Stone's classroom, they were closer than most sisters, in spite of their very different personalities.

"The House of Manannan," Darcy replied. "They're opening a new exhibit and it's a grand opening party."

"And Finlo will be there," Lisa guessed as she reached for a towel.

"Maybe," Darcy said, looking down at her perfectly manicured fingernails.

"You need to stop chasing Finlo Quayle," Lisa told her friend for the millionth time.

"I'm not chasing him," Darcy said firmly. "I'm going tonight to show him what he's missing. I most definitely won't even be talking to him."

Lisa shook her head. Darcy was beautiful, smart, funny, and sweet, but she had terrible taste in men. She tended to fall for wealthy and attractive men who loved having the gorgeous redhead on their arms but weren't looking for more than a bit of fun. Finlo Quayle was just the latest in a long line of men who'd swept Darcy off her feet only to find their own feet quite cold once Darcy mentioned any type of commitment.

"Stop frowning at me like that," Darcy said with a fake pout. "I know he's all wrong for me. Tonight I shall be looking for a wonderful, kind, considerate, and caring man who isn't at all interested in how I look."

Lisa laughed. "You wore the wrong dress," she said dryly as she climbed out of the bath and pulled the plug.

"Ah, but what will you wear?" Darcy demanded, heading into Lisa's bedroom. As Lisa patted herself dry, she could hear Darcy flipping through the clothes in her wardrobe.

"No, no, no, definitely not, no, no, not tonight, no, hideous, no, no," Darcy's words carried through the small house.

Lisa shook her head. She probably didn't own anything that Darcy would consider appropriate.

"No, maybe, no, no, could work, no, hello, what's this?"

Lisa wrapped the towel around herself and walked into her bedroom. Darcy was holding up a little black skirt that Lisa hadn't worn since her university days.

"I didn't know you still had this," Darcy laughed.

"I didn't know I still had it either. I'll drop it off at a charity shop next week. It's much too short for me now."

Darcy shook her head. "You have great legs," she argued. "You should show them off."

Lisa grinned. "To distract everyone from the rest of me, you mean?"

Darcy frowned at her friend. "You know you're very pretty," she countered. "And you have a wonderful figure. You're unbelievably slim, in spite of all the chocolate you eat."

Lisa frowned and studied herself in the full-length mirror that hung on the bedroom wall. She had boring brown hair and dull brown eyes. Standing next to Darcy, she always felt nearly invisible. And slim sounded good, but next to Darcy's generous curves, Lisa always felt boyishly underdeveloped.

Her looks had never been much of a concern to her, though. Lisa was pretty happy with her life and her appearance most of the time. It was only when she compared her more ordinary attractiveness to her best friend's breathtaking beauty that she sometimes felt a bit let down. She never noticed how her shoulder-length hair perfectly framed her face or how her eyes sparkled when she was happy.

"Anyway, I'll wear my green dress," Lisa told Darcy. "It's perfect for this sort of thing."

"It totally isn't," Darcy countered. "Not only have you worn it to just about every event you've been to in the last five years, but it's a horrible colour and it doesn't flatter your figure."

Lisa laughed. "Are you suggesting that you don't like it?"

Darcy laughed with her. "I hate it and you know that," she replied. "I tell you that every single time you wear it."

"And I keep wearing it because it's comfortable," Lisa reminded her.

"Comfort isn't everything," Darcy answered. "Do I look comfortable?"

Lisa looked at her friend's slinky strapless dress and sky-high heels. "Nope, you definitely don't look comfortable," she told Darcy.

"Exactly," Darcy laughed. "But I feel fabulous." Darcy glanced at her watch. "We have exactly six minutes to get you to fabulous before the taxi gets here."

Lisa laughed. "Not gonna happen," she told her friend.

Seven minutes later, Lisa climbed carefully into the back of the taxi Darcy had arranged. "I don't think this is what fabulous feels like," she told Darcy as her friend settled into the seat next to her.

"So how do you feel?" Darcy asked.

"Cold," Lisa grinned. The mid-September night was dry but cool and Lisa had felt the chill of a seasonal breeze as she'd rushed into the car.

The little black skirt actually looked better than she'd expected. Darcy had dug through Lisa's wardrobe and found a gorgeous silk blouse in a deep magenta colour that looked almost like a jacket over a black lace camisole. Black tights and a pair of black high heels that Darcy had left at Lisa's house months earlier completed the look.

Darcy had done Lisa's makeup for her, something she'd been doing for her friend since they'd first started playing with makeup in their tween years.

"I have learned how to do it myself," Lisa pointed out as Darcy smoothed foundation over her face.

"You'd do ordinary makeup. This is an evening event. Everything has to be more dramatic."

When Darcy finished, in record time, Lisa had to admit the results were dramatic. Her eyes looked enormous and her lips were fuller and shinier than Lisa ever managed to get them.

Darcy had grabbed a brush and in less then a minute had Lisa's hair caught up in a messy but attractive knot on the top of her head.

"Perfect," Darcy told her. "Now we just need to find you the right man to appreciate it."

The taxi's horn had cut through Lisa's reply. Now, on their way from Lisa's Douglas home to the House of Manannan in Peel, Lisa finally managed to respond.

"I'm not looking for a man," she told Darcy. "I'm quite happy single."

"But think how much happier you'd be with a man in your life," Darcy replied.

Lisa shook her head. "I'll admit it would be handy to have a guy around to squash spiders and carry heavy stuff for me," she told Darcy. "Just occasionally there's an event that I wouldn't mind having an escort for as well, but really, it isn't worth giving up half my wardrobe or all of my privacy just for those odd occasions."

Darcy grinned. "You'd love a date for Joney's wedding, though, wouldn't you?"

Lisa couldn't stop the deep sigh that escaped her lips. "I'd love a broken leg to get me out of going to Joney's wedding," she retorted. "But yeah, I'll admit it, a date might make the day a bit more tolerable."

Joney Harrison had gone to primary school with them. She'd been a spoiled, bratty child who had turned into an over-indulged and obnoxious teen. Darcy and Lisa had made no effort to keep in touch with the girl after their school days had ended, but Joney had recently moved back to the island with a wealthy fiancé called Nigel and a professed desire to reconnect with her old school friends.

Neither Darcy nor Lisa had ever considered Joney a friend, but apparently they were the only ones from their class at school who were too polite to tell Joney that fact. Last week they'd both received their expensively engraved invitations to what was already being called "the wedding of the year" on the small island. It was clear that no expense was being spared. The invitations included an extensive menu that guests could choose from for the five-course sit-down dinner.

Lisa and Darcy had each been invited to bring a guest as well, and Lisa was already dreading what Joney would say if she turned up on her own.

"So tonight's mission is to find us both dates for Joney's wedding in December," Darcy told her.

"Why would anyone want to get married at Christmas anyway?" Lisa asked. "I can't imagine anything worse."

"Unlike you, Joney wasn't born on Boxing Day," Darcy pointed out.

"Still, December is crazy enough with Christmas and New Year," Lisa argued. "Why have your wedding anniversary in there as well?"

"I'm not going to try to understand anything that Joney does," Darcy said with a laugh.

"Yeah, well, I'll be having a June wedding, if I ever get married. You know that," Lisa said.

"I know," Darcy laughed again. "You've been saying that since you were six."

Lisa grinned. "With Christmas and my birthday all lumped together, I just want something to celebrate halfway through the year."

"Which makes perfect sense," Darcy assured her.

"It makes a lot more sense than getting married on Christmas Eve," Lisa muttered under her breath as their taxi pulled up in front of the House of Manannan.

She climbed out of the car carefully, determined not to trip in the stupidly high heels that Darcy had insisted were perfect for her outfit. Darcy had, of course, slid elegantly from the car and was now standing next to it looking glamourous.

"Let's go, then," Darcy muttered, taking Lisa's arm.

"Joney isn't going to be here, is she?" Lisa hissed to her friend.

"Why would she be?" Darcy asked.

"I don't know. I'm just really not in the mood for her tonight."

"I can't imagine why she'd be here," Darcy said with a shrug. "But if she is, we'll just steer clear of her."

Lisa nodded. Joney was okay in small doses, but she had a way of talking to Lisa that made her feel inadequate, even if they were just discussing the weather.

Inside the museum, the large "classroom" right off the foyer had been set up for the party. Lisa's mouth started watering, as she smelled garlic and tomato sauce as soon as they entered the building.

"The food smells fabulous," she told Darcy.

"I knew you'd be happy you came," Darcy told her with a grin.

Lisa smiled back at her and then winced as Darcy squeezed her arm tightly.

"He's here," Darcy whispered.

"Finlo? You said he was going to be here," Lisa replied.

"Yeah, but I was hoping he might not make it," Darcy said with a shake of her head. "We shouldn't have come. I don't think I can face him."

"Did you two break up?" Lisa asked, wondering why her friend hadn't mentioned a fight.

"Oh no, nothing as dramatic as that," Darcy said, sighing. "Breaking up requires some sort of relationship to actually exist, and with Finlo that wasn't happening. I'm sure, if he didn't bring anyone tonight, he'd happily spend the evening with me and take me home. The problem would start tomorrow when he'd suddenly be too busy again to make plans to spend time with me."

Lisa could hear the sad anger in her friend's voice. "I should go tell him exactly what I think of him," she said furiously. "He can't treat you that way."

Darcy shook her head. "He treats all women that way," she replied. "I should have known better. I've worked for him for five years and I've watched the women come and go. I should never have fallen for him in the first place."

"Why did you start going out with him, exactly?" Lisa couldn't stop herself from asking, even though this was hardly the time or the place for a long conversation about Darcy's love life.

"When he wants to, he can be unbelievably charming," Darcy said with a wry grin. "He makes you feel like the only woman in the world, and you start to believe that you'll be the one that changes him, until suddenly, you aren't the only woman in his world anymore." Darcy shrugged. "I knew what I was getting into, but that doesn't really make it any easier."

"Do you want to leave?" Lisa asked.

"You'd do that, wouldn't you?" Darcy replied. "You're the best friend in the whole world. After I've dressed you up and dragged you here and then let you smell the most glorious food ever, you'd turn around and leave if I asked."

"You'd do the same for me," Lisa told her.

Darcy looked thoughtful. "Maybe," she said, grinning suddenly. "But anyway, I'm not letting anyone spoil our night out. We need to find dates for Joney's wedding and I'm sure there are plenty of suitable candidates here, somewhere."

"I think I should start looking near the buffet," Lisa told her. "Men always hang out around food, right?"

Darcy laughed. "You go that way, then. I'm going to pretend to read the displays that explain the new exhibit. Maybe I'll learn something."

Lisa nodded, noting that the displays were about as far removed from where Finlo Quayle was standing as Darcy could possibly get. She watched her friend sway sexily away towards the large display panels that showcased the new exhibit. There was no doubt in Lisa's mind that every man in the room was watching Darcy's progress. As she turned back towards the buffet, Lisa noticed that Finlo had certainly been watching Darcy, but he didn't seem to be in any hurry to speak to her.

With a frown, Lisa headed towards the food tables that stretched across the back of the room. Maybe Darcy would find a nice man tonight who would help her forget all about the way too gorgeous, sophisticated, and wealthy Finlo Quayle.

Two minutes later, Lisa was completely focussed on food. She nibbled at spicy chicken and mini pizza squares and was just about to try some of the garlic toast rounds when she was interrupted.

"You look stunning tonight," the voice said. Lisa jerked her hand back from the plate that held the garlic toast and turned to face the speaker.

"Finlo? I suppose I should be grateful you didn't sound too surprised when you said that."

Finlo laughed and Lisa frowned. Even his laugh was sexy. He had dark hair that fell across his forehead in what Lisa could only hope was a deceptively casual way. She imagined him spending hours combing his hair and applying an assortment of products to it to achieve that perfect just-rolled-out-of-bed look. His eyes were a stunning blue that Darcy had assured her was entirely natural. At five feet, seven inches tall, Lisa wasn't exactly short, but she felt small next to Finlo who was at least six inches taller.

"Is Darcy avoiding me?" Finlo asked.

"I don't think so," Lisa replied. "Should she be?"

Finlo shook his head. "She's not really happy with me at the moment," he said in a confessional tone. "I've been really busy with work and I haven't had time to wine and dine her like I normally do."

"Work? Is that her name?" Lisa asked.

"Whose name?" Finlo countered.

"The skinny blonde I saw you with in town last weekend."

Finlo frowned. "I didn't see you in town last weekend."

"No, you were too busy holding hands and whispering with 'work.'" Lisa replied.

"Darcy and I have an agreement," he said defensively. "We can both see other people."

"That's good to know," Lisa told him. "I know Darcy's looking for a new guy right now."

Finlo flushed. "I came on my own tonight, hoping to see her," he told Lisa.

"Your blonde friend was busy?" Lisa asked.

"Not at all," Finlo countered. "I wanted to spend time with Darcy."

Lisa laughed. "Then maybe you should have rung Darcy and asked her to come with you, like as your date? Or is that too much like being in a relationship for you? Honestly, you don't deserve Darcy. She's much too good for you."

"Spoken like a true best friend," he said. "I'll get out of your way and leave you to the buffet, then. Have a nice evening."

He was gone before Lisa could come up with a suitable reply. She felt aggravated and annoyed as she watched him cross the floor. If he headed towards Darcy, she was determined to follow, but before he'd gone far, his cousin William, whom Lisa knew slightly, stopped him and the two fell into conversation. Lisa smiled as she turned back to the garlic toast.

"Lisa, darling, you must meet my new friends," Darcy gushed in Lisa's ear a short time later.

Lisa turned away from the wafer-thin Parma ham slices to smile at her friend. "That didn't take long," she muttered, more to herself than her friend.

Darcy winked at her and then smiled at the two men who had accompanied her across the room. "This is Mark Blake. He's in charge of special projects for Manx National Heritage," she told Lisa, gesturing towards the man she had her arm wrapped around. "And this is his brother, Michael."

Lisa smiled and shook hands with both men, studying them as she did so. Mark was very attractive and Lisa noted his dark hair and blue eyes seemed worryingly similar to Finlo Quayle's. While Mark didn't look exactly like Darcy's former boyfriend, there was a resemblance there that Lisa found unsettling. Michael's hair was lighter, but he had the same gorgeous blue eyes. The men were both around the same height, several inches taller than Lisa, and in excellent shape.

"And what do you do?" Lisa asked Michael, since Darcy hadn't mentioned it.

"I work for one of the off-shore banks," he told her. "I'm based in London, but I'm here for a few weeks at least twice a year to work with clients on the island."

"Interesting," Lisa murmured.

Michael laughed. "It isn't really," he told her. "But it pays the bills and it means I get to spend a few weeks with my brother every now and then, which is a nice bonus."

Lisa grinned. "As an only child, I'll have to take your word for that."

Michael smiled back. "We didn't always get along, but I really enjoy spending time with him now, even if he is obsessed with history."

Darcy laughed. "Maybe he'll find a way to make me interested in the subject, then," she purred, fluttering her lashes at Mark.

Mark flushed and looked down at the ground. "It's a fascinating subject," he said. "I probably do talk about it too much, though."

"I'm sure we'll find lots of other things to discuss," Darcy told him silkily.

"How does the new exhibit look?" Lisa asked her friend.

"Oh, well, it's, um," Darcy laughed. "I was so busy making new friends that I didn't even notice," she confessed.

"It's a terrific exhibit," Michael told Lisa.

Mark laughed. "He's only saying that because I designed it," he told Lisa.

"Maybe I should have a look," Lisa said. "I've had an awful lot of food."

"Why don't you take Michael and have a look while Mark and I try out some of the gorgeous looking canapés?" Darcy suggested, giving her friend a wink.

As if I was in any doubt as to which brother she was interested in, Lisa thought to herself as she smiled at Michael. It didn't much matter, though, Lisa decided. She wasn't interested in either brother, though both seemed nice enough. Still, she needed to get away from the food for a few minutes, or else she'd be too full to enjoy the pudding bar when they set that up.

Lisa took the arm that Michael offered and the pair headed towards the display panels. She glanced back to see Darcy giggling and flirting outrageously with Mark, who looked slightly stunned. It was already turning into a long evening, she thought to herself.

2

Michael was right. The exhibit was very well done. The House of Manannan was one of the island's very best museums, full of interactive displays. It managed to condense the fascinating and complicated history of the island into an easily understood series of chronological sections that were as interesting for adults as they were for the busloads of school children who were taken through the building each year. The new exhibit focussed on the English Civil War period on the island and Lisa soon found herself caught up in imagining life on Man during that turbulent time in history.

"I didn't realise there was a famine on the island during the Civil War," she remarked to Michael as she read one of the signs on display.

"Me either," Michael shrugged. "But then the only Manx history I know is whatever Mark has tried to cram into me when I visit."

Lisa laughed. "Do I take it you're not a history buff, then?"

"Not really," Michael frowned and glanced around. "Look, Lisa, I'm sure you're wonderful, but I have a girlfriend back in London. I just don't want to give you the wrong idea, you know?"

Lisa laughed again. "No worries," she assured the red-faced man. "I'm very happily single."

Michael nodded. "I'm sorry, I probably shouldn't have said anything, but I didn't want you to get the wrong idea."

"I'm glad you spoke up," Lisa told him. "This way we both know where we stand."

"I think Mark is getting in over his head," Michael remarked, glancing over at his brother. "Your friend Darcy is, well, not his usual type."

Lisa grinned. "I've known Darcy since we were both six, and since she hit puberty she's yet to find a man whose type she isn't." She frowned. "Did that make sense? What I mean is, every man she meets falls for her."

"I didn't fall for her," Michael argued.

"You're attached," Lisa told him. "Darcy doesn't go after men who are otherwise involved. I suppose I should have said, any man she wants, she gets."

Michael shrugged. "She just doesn't seem like the kind of girl Mark usually goes for, that's all. I'm sure he's flattered by the attention, though. She is gorgeous."

"Yes, she is," Lisa said with a sigh.

Michael laughed. "Should I tell you how happy I was when my better-looking and smarter big brother moved away?" he asked Lisa. "We're only eighteen months apart and we often went out together. Just about every girl I met found Mark smarter, cuter, and more fun. I was lucky my current girlfriend didn't meet him until we'd been together for six months. By that time we'd been together too long for her to dump me in favour of Mark."

Lisa laughed. "I think you're exaggerating," she said.

"Maybe just a little," Michael conceded. "But you know what I mean."

"I do," Lisa agreed. "But Darcy is sweet and kind and caring and she would never try to steal a man from me, even if just about every guy I've ever met has dumped me and gone after her once they've met her."

"How'd that work out for them?"

Lisa laughed. "Darcy wouldn't even give a man the time of day if he'd treated me like that."

Michael glanced back over at Darcy and Mark. Darcy was listening to something Mark was saying and she appeared to be hanging on his every word. "I just don't want to see my brother get his heart broken," he told Lisa.

Lisa nodded. "I get that," she replied. "Darcy is just coming out of an on-again, off-again relationship with her boss. I think what she really needs is a nice guy with whom she can have some casual fun. Darcy isn't looking to settle down at this point."

"I'll make sure Mark understands that," Michael said. "Thanks."

Lisa smiled. She'd talk to Darcy later, and let her know what she'd told Michael. If Darcy didn't agree with Lisa's assessment of the situation, she could work things out with Mark herself.

Moments later, Darcy and Mark joined Lisa and Michael.

"Are you enjoying the display?" Mark asked Lisa.

"It's wonderful," she assured him, grinning at how worried he seemed. "I'm ashamed to admit I don't remember a lot of the island's history we were taught in school, so I'm finding it all fascinating."

"My target audience, when I'm building displays, is always people who know nothing about the island," Mark told her. "A great many of our visitors come over to enjoy the beaches or the TT without ever thinking about the island's heritage. I hope, with everything I design, to share history and culture in a way that's interesting and thought provoking."

"Well, I think you've done a great job here at least," Lisa told him. "I've never actually been around this particular museum, but I've heard good things about it."

"We could go around now," Mark said. "I have a set of keys."

Darcy laughed and put a hand on his arm. "Your enthusiasm is adorable," she told him. "But it's Friday night and we're all dressed up for a party. You'll have to show us around your museum some other time. For tonight, I'm thinking we should go dancing."

Mark opened his mouth and then snapped it shut as Darcy snuggled up closer to him. "There's a great new club that just opened up in Douglas," Darcy said, fluttering her lashes at him. "We should go there."

"Well, well, well, look who's here." The deep voice sounded amused.

Lisa looked up and just barely held back a sigh. She'd been hoping Finlo would stay away from Darcy.

"Finlo, you're looking very handsome tonight," Darcy said, grinning at the new arrival while sticking close to Mark. "Do you know Mark Blake?"

Finlo smiled. "Of course I know Mark," he said easily. "Thanks to William, I think I know just about everyone associated with Manx National Heritage."

William Corlett, Finlo's cousin, was the director of the Manx History Institute, an organisation affiliated with MNH that, among other things, provided support for people interested in doing research on the island.

"I wasn't sure you'd be here tonight," Mark told Finlo. "William said you had a last-minute charter to Tenerife."

Finlo shrugged. "I let one of the other guys have it," he said. "I can't snap up every beautiful beach holiday destination and leave the others with the boring business trips to London and Manchester. Sometimes I have to let someone else have a long weekend in Tenerife."

"You poor thing," Lisa couldn't stop herself from saying sarcastically. Finlo owned the island's only charter airline service. By all accounts, it was very successful and Finlo not only made good money, he was able to enjoy being paid to travel all around Europe.

Finlo laughed. "Yeah, it's a tough life," he said. "Anyway, I didn't want to have to call in my air crew. I assumed Darcy had other plans for the weekend."

Darcy flushed at Finlo's words. "I'm busy making new friends," she replied. "But I'm sure Cindi would have gone with you."

Finlo laughed again. "I've sent Cindi with Doug," he told Darcy. "I'm hoping she decides to chase him for a while."

Lisa bit her lip before she could say something she might regret later. The Cindi they were discussing was a young air hostess who'd developed a huge crush on her boss. Even Finlo realised that she was too young for him, although Darcy had commented more than once that he was having difficulty persuading Cindi of that fact.

"Anyway, it's my weekend off, and we're all off to *Disco-Mann* to drink too much and dance the night away," Darcy told Finlo, tossing her hair.

"Really?" Finlo asked. "I never thought of Mark as much of a dancer."

Mark grinned. "I'm not, but I'm a great spectator," he said.

Lisa shook her head. She couldn't imagine what Mark and Michael must be thinking. "I just have one or two more panels to read," she said suddenly. She took a few steps away from the group, gesturing towards the display boards that she had been studying a short time earlier. Michael followed after her, and Mark was quick to join them a few paces away from Darcy and Finlo.

"I love this portrait of Charlotte de la Tremouille," Mark told Lisa.

"Oh, I think I remember her," Lisa said. "She was married to the Great Stanley, right? The one who came to the island during the Civil War and then went back across and got executed."

"That's right, more or less," Mark said with a smile.

Lisa read the brief biography of the woman that was displayed next to her portrait. She glanced back at Darcy and frowned. Darcy appeared to be having a heated exchange with Finlo.

"Should I break that up?" Mark asked Lisa.

Lisa shrugged. "I never know what to do with those two," she admitted. "Darcy deserves someone better than that, but she doesn't seem to see it."

Lisa and the guys moved a few feet further away from Darcy and Finlo, with Lisa still eagerly reading the information on the display. After another minute, Darcy joined them. Lisa studied her friend's flushed face, trying to work out what had happened.

"It's getting late," Darcy said as a greeting. "Maybe we should skip dancing and just go somewhere quiet for a cuppa."

"They're just putting out the puddings," Lisa told her. "Maybe we should just stay a little bit longer."

Darcy laughed, but it sounded forced. "By all means, let's stay for pudding."

Lisa narrowed her eyes and stared at her friend. "Are you okay?" she asked, ignoring the two men who were busy pretending they weren't listening.

"I'm fine," Darcy said softly.

"Let's attack the puddings, then," Mark said heartily, taking Darcy's arm. "I'm dying to try to the chocolate mousse cups. I've heard good things about them."

The foursome filled plates with a sampling from the huge array of delicious goodies and then found a quiet corner with a few tables and chairs in it.

"This is amazing," Lisa said around a mouthful of shortbread with caramel sauce.

"I don't usually eat sweets," Darcy said. "But I'm in love with these mini apple tarts."

"And they're full of fruit," Mark replied. "So they're practically health food."

Half an hour later, with the group still ensconced in their quiet corner, Henry Costain wandered over.

"Sorry to interrupt," he began, "but I'm just checking to make sure everything's going okay."

Mark introduced the man to the others. Henry had been working for MNH for pretty much all of his adult life and he was now getting close to retirement age. Everyone who worked with him appreciated his hard work and dedication. He would be a hard person to replace, when he did decide to retire.

"Everything's fine, thanks," Mark assured him. "I think they'll start packing away the puddings in another twenty minutes or so and that should be everyone's cue to start leaving."

"Sounds good," Henry nodded. "I'll just stay out of the way until they start packing up then."

"So what are we going to do once the party is over?" Darcy asked Mark as Henry strolled away.

"I thought I'd go home," Mark told her. "I have to work tomorrow."

"But tomorrow's Saturday," Darcy replied.

"I have to give a tour of the Manx Museum to a group of academics from a university in Norway," Mark explained. "And I have to be there at nine because they have an early flight home. By the time this wraps up, I'll be ready to call it a night."

Darcy frowned. "In that case, I'll have to let you buy me dinner tomorrow night," she told him. "You can pick me up at seven." Darcy dug around in her handbag and pulled out a small notebook. She scribbled something on a piece of paper and handed it to Mark. "There's my address. I'll see you tomorrow."

Mark took the paper and looked at it for a moment. "Yeah, okay," he finally muttered. "Seven, tomorrow."

"Exactly," Darcy smiled at him. "Are you ready to go?" Darcy asked Lisa.

"Um, sure," Lisa said, getting to her feet. "It was nice meeting you both," she said, smiling at the two men.

Michael stood up and offered his hand. "It was nice meeting you as well," he told her as they shook hands. When he extended his hand towards Darcy, she laughed.

"Shaking hands is way too formal," she said, giving the man a quick hug and a kiss on the cheek. Mark was now on his feet as well and Darcy gave him the same treatment.

Both men looked a bit dazed by Darcy's affectionate goodbye, so Lisa didn't bother trying to shake hands with Mark. Instead, she simply followed her friend out of the room. Outside, Darcy quickly hailed a waiting taxi.

"Well, that was fun," Darcy drawled after she gave the taxi driver Lisa's address.

"It was okay," Lisa replied.

"It's a shame Michael is heading back across on Sunday. He seemed like your type," Darcy said.

"He has a girlfriend," Lisa told her.

"Ah, well, that's too bad, as well," Darcy laughed. "I was going to suggest you try to persuade him to come back and go with you to Joney's wedding."

"I can go to Joney's wedding on my own," Lisa replied. "So that's that taken care of."

"You don't want to go on your own," Darcy insisted. "Weddings are no place to be on your own."

Lisa shrugged. "I'd rather be on my own than spend the day with someone I don't like."

Darcy shook her head. "I'd rather spend the day with a man I dislike than sit all by myself watching someone I know promise to love someone else forever. Weddings are sad and strange places, and I'm terrified by the idea of being alone at one."

"You'll have me," Lisa said with a grin.

Darcy laughed. "It'd be just my luck you'll find a date and I won't," she said with a dramatic sigh.

"The wedding is months away," Lisa pointed out. "I'm sure you'll go through a dozen men between now and then."

Darcy laughed. "Mark seems nice," she said. "He's probably way too nice for me, but if he's half as kind as he seems, he'll make a nice change from Finlo."

"Michael is worried that you're going to break his brother's heart," Lisa told her.

Darcy shook her head. "I'm just looking for a friend, really. If Mark looks like he's getting serious, I'll let him down nicely."

"Just a friend?" Lisa queried.

"Well, a male friend who's good-looking enough to make Finlo jealous," Darcy clarified. "Not that I have any intention of ever getting back together with Finlo, but I love the thought of him being jealous."

"That's childish," Lisa said.

"I know," Darcy sighed. "Maybe I'm not quite entirely over Finlo," she admitted. "But that doesn't mean I want him back. Not that I ever had him," she added with yet another sigh.

"Maybe you should give Mark a proper chance?"

Darcy shrugged. "We'll see."

The taxi pulled up in front of Lisa's bungalow. "Are you coming in?" Lisa asked.

"Can I?"

"Of course. You don't have to ask!" Lisa told her friend.

Inside the house, she switched on a few lamps. "Shall I open a bottle of wine?" she asked Darcy, pretty sure she'd read her friend's mood correctly.

"Yes, please," Darcy replied softly.

"No tears," Lisa said sternly.

"No tears," Darcy repeated.

"Go get into your pyjamas and wash your face," Lisa told her friend. "I'll open the wine and find some munchies."

Wordlessly, Darcy gave her a hug and then headed to the spare bedroom where the wardrobe held everything Darcy could possibly want for a short stay.

Lisa headed into the kitchen and dug a bottle of white wine out from the back of the fridge. She opened her cupboards, wondering if pretzels or crisps went better with white wine. As she was unsure, she poured both into bowls.

From a shelf she selected two of her fanciest wine glasses, deciding that a night with her dearest friend was definitely a special occasion. The Darcy who joined her a few minutes later was almost unrecognisable as the same woman who'd dazzled at the House of Manannan.

Darcy was wearing plaid flannel pyjamas with a fuzzy pink bathrobe over the top. Matching fuzzy slippers had replaced the stilettos. With her face scrubbed clean and her hair in a simple ponytail, Darcy looked no more than fifteen.

Lisa pulled her into a quick hug, before pouring her a glass of wine. "You start on this while I go change," she told her friend. "And feel free to root around for something better than crisps and pretzels."

Darcy took a long drink and then grinned at her friend. "Go change. I'll make us a snack."

Lisa kicked off the heels with a small squeal of delight. There was nothing like the feeling of peeling off tights and fancy clothes and pulling on warm fluffy pyjamas, she thought as she changed. In the small master bathroom she happily washed off the makeup that Darcy had applied earlier and then took her hair down. She brushed it into place, smiling at herself in the mirror.

Five minutes later she found Darcy mixing up a bowl of something in the kitchen.

"What are we having?" she asked curiously.

"Salad," Darcy grinned as Lisa's face fell. "Don't frown," she chided. "I'm mixing up a dressing you'll love and I've thrown together some garlic and parsley butter. Now that you're here, I'll smother it on a baguette and stick it under the broiler while we make our salads."

"I didn't even know I had lettuce," Lisa said with a laugh.

"Well, you did, but you won't after tonight."

"I need to go grocery shopping tomorrow," Lisa said with a sigh. "I don't have a handsome historian taking me to dinner tomorrow night."

Darcy grinned. "So tonight we start Operation Find Lisa a Man," she said.

"No, nope, no way, not interested," Lisa replied.

Darcy took the day-old baguette from Lisa's breadbox and sliced it open. She slathered a thick layer of the garlic butter she'd mixed up over it and then slid it into the oven. "If you want garlic bread, you have to play along," Darcy said to her friend.

"No fair, how can I resist that?" Lisa demanded.

"I'll let you have some, but you have to promise to work with me on this."

"I'm not looking for a man," Lisa said, knowing she was repeating herself.

"But you'll go along to indulge me," Darcy replied as she piled lettuce onto plates. "Have some wine."

Lisa laughed. Darcy knew her too well. She'd go along to make Darcy happy and to make sure she got her share of the bread that smelled so good. Darcy was an incredible cook.

"You were right," Lisa told Darcy between bites a few minutes later. "This dressing is wonderful."

Darcy shrugged. "It's only a few ingredients," she replied.

"Which you needn't bother to tell me because I'll never remember," Lisa said. "Especially if we finish the wine."

"We are totally finishing the wine," Darcy told her, getting up to check on the bread. "Finish your salad," she instructed Lisa. "The bread is almost ready."

"I ate a lot at the party," Lisa said as she forked up the last bite of salad. "I can't believe how hungry I still am."

"You ate a bunch of little stuff," Darcy replied. "None of it was properly filling."

"I probably ate a thousand calories worth of mini puddings," Lisa said with a sigh.

"So you don't want any of this?" Darcy asked, pulling the now golden-brown bread from the oven. It was dripping with melted butter and Lisa could see big chunks of garlic dotted across its surface.

"I'll just have half," she told Darcy.

"Fair enough," Darcy said with a grin. She cut the bread in half and served it on Lisa's mismatched plates. Before she sat back down, she topped up both women's wine glasses as well.

"Okay," Darcy said after her first bite of bread. "Tell me everything you're looking for in a man."

Lisa thought about arguing, but she loved her friend too much. If this could distract Darcy from thinking about Finlo, it was worth it.

"He needs to be taller than me," she began.

"You're five feet seven, right?" Darcy checked.

"Yep, two inches shorter than you, same as we've been since we were fifteen."

Darcy laughed. "So anyone my height or taller will work. That'll be easy for me to check."

"He has to be good-looking enough to not frighten children," Lisa said.

Darcy shook her head. "He needs to be handsome," she argued. "You're very pretty and he needs to look at least as good."

"I'm very ordinary," Lisa countered. "Ordinary will do."

"It's a good thing I'm finding the man, not you," Darcy told her. "He'll be attractive for sure. What about brains or education?"

"Brains would be good," Lisa agreed, downing more wine. "I'd like a guy who's smarter than me."

"Really?" Darcy laughed. "You're the smartest person I know. I'm not sure I can manage that."

"I'm not that smart," Lisa argued. "You just think I'm smart because I'm good with computers."

"I know you're smart because you're good with computers," Darcy replied. "All that technical stuff is like Greek to me."

"You could learn it if you wanted to," Lisa told her. "You're a lot smarter than you act."

Darcy laughed. "I'm using my looks while I've got them," she told her friend. "When I'm middle-aged and invisible to men, then I'll use my brains."

"Which is pretty smart of you," Lisa said.

"Anyway, we aren't talking about me, we're talking about you," Darcy reminded her. "So I'm looking for a man who is smart, tall and gorgeous. What else?"

Lisa shook her head. "I don't know, what else is there?"

Darcy sighed. "You aren't very good at this game," she complained. "Hair colour, eye colour, preferred occupation, do you want someone athletic or a computer gamer? Would you prefer someone Manx or British or would you like to be a bit more exotic and have me find a stray American or, perhaps, a Frenchman or something? The categories are limitless and the more I know, the better my chances of finding you the perfect man."

Lisa laughed. "There is no such thing as a perfect man."

"But there is a man who is perfect for you," Darcy shot back. "We just have to find him."

Lisa shook her head. "Why don't you believe me when I say I'm happy single?" she asked.

"Because I knew you when you were dating George," Darcy replied.

Lisa flushed. "And look how well that turned out," she said sourly before gulping down the last of her glass of wine.

"I know he broke your heart," Darcy told her. "But I also know how happy you were for those seven months. I've not seen you as happy since."

"I had a lot of fun with George," Lisa admitted. "But I have a lot of fun on my own, as well."

"Just play along," Darcy told her friend sternly. "You should know better than to argue with me."

Lisa laughed. She did know better than to argue with Darcy when she was in this sort of mood. "Brown and blue," she said with a small sigh.

"I'm guessing that's brown hair and blue eyes, although if you really prefer, I'll try to find you a man with blue hair and brown eyes."

Lisa laughed again. "No, definitely not blue hair," she replied. "And I'm flexible on the brown as well, just no blond men."

Darcy grinned. "George was blond," she pointed out.

"Exactly," Lisa said. "I don't trust blond men."

"Are you flexible on eye colour?"

"Sure, anything other than brown, really."

"What's wrong with brown eyes?" Darcy asked.

"Nothing really, they're just dull, like mine."

"Your eyes are gorgeous," Darcy told her. "They're huge, and if you spent a few minutes every morning putting a bit of makeup on them, they'd be amazing."

Lisa rolled her eyes. "I do wear makeup, just not as much as you do."

"Okay, what else?" Darcy asked. "We flew a bunch of guys from Belgium over last week. They're meant to be here for a few months working on some project for one of the banks. I'm sure I can fix you up with one or two of them."

Lisa shook her head. "I love the island too much. I need a Manxman or at least someone who is here to stay."

Darcy nodded. "Okay, that makes sense." She glanced down at her empty glass and sighed. "I suppose I ought to get some sleep now that we've finished the bottle. Tomorrow is going to be an exciting day. I'm going to find you a man."

Lisa sighed. "Oh, goody," she said as she put the empty wine glasses in the sink. "Do the words 'fish' and 'bicycle' mean anything to you?"

Darcy shook her head. "Should they?"

"Irina Dunn said: 'A woman needs a man like a fish needs a bicycle,'" Lisa told her. "I think she's right."

Darcy just laughed.

3

Lisa was more than a little relieved when Darcy got called to work for the rest of the weekend. By the time the pair finished the quick breakfast that Lisa threw together, Darcy needed to head to the airport to catch a flight to Rome.

"I'll be back on Monday afternoon," she told Lisa. "And I'll start working on your perfect man the second I get back."

Lisa had simply sighed and nodded. Whenever Darcy was between men she turned Lisa's love life into her pet project. Now that she'd met Mark, though, there was a very good chance she'd quickly forget all about finding a man for Lisa. At least that was what Lisa was counting on.

Lisa had another long and busy week at work, and when Friday night finally rolled around again, Lisa was ready to try that long relaxing bath again. It wasn't meant to be, however. Darcy was already at her house, waiting for her when she got home.

"Grab a shower and put on your party clothes," Darcy told Lisa after she'd greeted her friend. "You have a very hot date."

Lisa frowned. "I don't want a hot date. I want a hot bath," she told Darcy. "Go away and leave me alone."

"Nope, can't do it," Darcy laughed. "Come on, I spent hours every day this week talking to every single male passenger we flew anywhere. This guy is just about perfect for you."

"Really?" Lisa said sceptically. "What makes him so perfect?"

"He's got brown hair and green eyes, he's taller than you and he's really, really smart," she answered smugly. "He couldn't be more perfect."

"What does he do?" Lisa asked.

"He works in IT for one of the banks," Darcy told her. "He's like head of the whole IT department and he knows more about computers than I know about anything at all."

Lisa laughed. "So he's a geek?"

Darcy shrugged. "Maybe he's a little geeky," she admitted. "But he's not unattractive and he meets all your other criteria. Let's face it, if you want someone smarter than you, chances are he's going to be something of a geek."

"Oh, thanks," Lisa replied. "But I really don't want to go out tonight. I was really hoping to just take it easy."

"Well, he's going to be here in about half an hour, so you don't have time to soak," Darcy told her. She narrowed her eyes. "Did you buy truffles for your bath?" she demanded.

Lisa flushed. "Maybe," she said, looking at the ground.

"Yay," Darcy giggled. "We can share them while you get ready."

Lisa opened her mouth to protest and then shook her head. It was probably easier to just go out with the guy than to try to convince Darcy to cancel the date. How bad could the man be?

Conscious of the time, she and Darcy munched their way through half a dozen truffles while Darcy helped her pick out a pair of trousers and a light jumper that were casually dressy. Darcy did her makeup and fixed her hair while Lisa sipped from a necessary glass of wine.

"I hate blind dates," she muttered under her breath as Darcy rummaged through Lisa's wardrobe for shoes.

"Don't think of it as a blind date," Darcy told her. "Think of it as a wonderful opportunity to make a new friend who could turn out to be something more."

Lisa laughed. "I think I'll just think of it as a blind date," she replied.

When the doorbell rang, Lisa downed the rest of her wine and then followed Darcy to the door.

Darcy pulled open the door and Lisa bit back a slightly hysterical laugh. The man blinking back at her was not exactly what she'd been hoping for.

"Norman, I'm so glad you made it," Darcy gushed, pushing Lisa out of the way and dragging the man into the house.

"Yes, well, um," the man muttered. He looked at Lisa and then frowned. "I thought you said your friend was blonde," he said to Darcy.

Lisa felt her face turning red. "Clearly I'm not what you expected," she said in response. "Let's just call it all off, shall we?"

The man shook his head. "No, no, it's fine," he said quickly. "I was just surprised, that's all."

Lisa frowned and gave Darcy a nasty look. "That's a shame," she said through gritted teeth, too polite to tell him how she really felt.

"Sorry, I'm forgetting my manners," Darcy laughed lightly. "Norman Clucas, this is Lisa Mylchreest. Lisa, this is Norman."

Lisa reluctantly gave him a small smile and held out her hand. Norman took it and pumped it enthusiastically. He was only just a tiny fraction taller than Lisa and Lisa suddenly realised why Darcy had dug out flat shoes for her to wear tonight. Lisa supposed that he did have brown hair, but it was hard to be certain, as he didn't have much of it. His thick glasses hid his eyes and left her wondering if they were really green or not.

"I've made a booking at my favourite Chinese restaurant," he told Lisa excitedly. "They have the best food in Douglas."

Lisa hid her dismay. She wasn't a big fan of Chinese food.

"I thought I suggested *La Terrazza*," Darcy said.

"You did," Norman nodded. "But then I thought that since I was paying for dinner, I ought to get to choose the restaurant. That just seems more fair."

Darcy opened her mouth, but Lisa held up a hand. "I'm sure you're right," she told the man. "Let's get going then, shall we?"

Darcy looked at her with a surprised expression. "You're going?" she asked.

"Oh, yes. I'm sure we're going to have a wonderful time," Lisa replied grimly. And after I tell you all about it, you're never going to set me up on another blind date, she added in her head.

"Great, well, have a lovely time," Darcy told her. "I can't wait to hear all about it when you get home."

"You will," Lisa grinned. "You definitely will."

Norman led Lisa down the short walk to the street in front of her house. "I thought maybe we could walk to the restaurant," he said hopefully. "Taxis are awfully expensive and it's only a short distance."

"Sure, it isn't too cold," Lisa agreed, pulling her jacket more tightly around herself. It was actually quite chilly for mid-September.

"I never learned to drive, you see," Norman said confidingly as they strolled along towards downtown Douglas. "I took the test seven times but I never passed."

Lisa nodded. She had no idea how to respond to that information.

"I suppose you can drive?" Norman asked.

"Yes," Lisa replied. "I got my license when I was seventeen."

Norman sighed. "I should try again," he told her. "Only the last time I took the test I sort of hit a parked car and they told me that maybe I shouldn't keep trying."

Lisa tried to smile encouragingly. "Well, it's something to consider," she said.

"Yeah," he shrugged. "At least I can walk almost everywhere from my flat."

"Where do you live?"

"Seaside Towers," Norman told her, naming a fairly recently constructed building that housed very expensive luxury flats.

"Wow," Lisa was impressed in spite of herself. "Those are supposed to be really lovely flats."

"Mine's nice," Norman told her. "I'm on the third floor and I have great views of the sea."

They'd reached the promenade now and Norman stopped and pointed down the long stretch of road. "I'm right there," he told Lisa. "In the corner unit, three floors up from the bottom."

Lisa nodded, glancing at the building, but it was really too far away for her to see anything.

"Maybe after dinner you can come over and check out the view," Norman told her.

Lisa looked at him curiously. Was that a proposition, or was he seriously just inviting her to enjoy his view? Norman blinked back at her from behind his thick glasses. Not a proposition, she decided.

A few minutes later they'd made their way to the restaurant Norman had chosen.

"I suppose you didn't really need to make that booking," Lisa commented as she looked around the mostly empty dining room.

"Always better safe than sorry," Norman told her.

The young blonde hostess looked up from her phone and sighed. "Table for two?" she asked, snapping her gum.

"I made a booking," Norman told her.

The girl behind the hostess stand raised an eyebrow. She turned and looked slowly around the room. There were around twenty tables in the space and only two of them were occupied.

"Good thing," the girl said with a smirk. "Follow me." She led Lisa and Norman to a small table in a dark corner. "This okay?" she asked. Without waiting for a reply, she dropped two menus on the table and returned to her spot by the door.

Norman frowned after her as Lisa slid into a chair. Lisa picked up one of the plastic-coated menus as Norman dropped into the seat opposite.

"So what's the best thing on the menu?" Lisa asked as she tried to read it in the very dimly lit room.

"I'm sure everything is delicious," Norman told her unhelpfully.

Lisa pulled out her phone and turned on the flashlight function. The illumination revealed so many strange and sticky-looking patches on the menu that Lisa immediately switched it back off.

"Did you guys want drinks?" The waitress was a younger and blonder version of the hostess, and she too seemed less than interested in her job.

"I thought maybe a bottle of wine," Norman said hesitantly.

"Certainly can't hurt," Lisa said with a sigh.

"Red or white?" the waitress asked.

"You don't have a wine list?" Norman asked.

The girl sighed deeply. "I'll go ask," she said grumpily.

"I thought you said you ate here a lot," Lisa said to Norman after the girl had stomped away.

"What I meant was, it's somewhere I've always wanted to try," Norman replied. "It always smells good when I walk past."

Lisa looked around at their fellow patrons. A lone man sat at a table that was at least half covered in presumably empty beer cans. He was picking listlessly at the plate of food in front of him. The only other occupied table had an older couple sitting at it. They were both significantly overweight and both were busily shoveling food into their mouths from the dozen or more plates that filled their large table.

"I'm sure it will be good," Norman muttered unconvincingly.

"Here." The waitress dropped the wine list on the table and then wandered away. Lisa noticed that she was glued to her phone screen as she went.

Norman held up the paper. "Not exactly what I was expecting," he said with a sigh.

Lisa took the sheet from him. The handwritten list read:

White wine

Red wine

Pink wine

Beer

Lisa stared at it for a moment and then burst out laughing. After a moment Norman joined in.

"Let's get out of here," he whispered as the waitress headed back towards them.

"I'm sorry, but I'm not feeling very well," he told the woman as he and Lisa got to their feet.

"Whatevs," the girl said with a shrug.

Outside, Lisa drew a deep breath and then started laughing again. "That was horrible," she gasped out when she'd finally stopped.

Norman grinned at her. "On the plus side, you'll have a terrific story to tell your friend Darcy, won't you? My date from hell, right?"

Lisa shook her head. "The restaurant from hell maybe," she said. "That wasn't your fault."

"I picked it," Norman said. "I feel responsible."

"I feel hungry," Lisa told him.

Norman laughed. "We'll never get a table anywhere fancy now. How about pizza?"

"Pizza sounds perfect," Lisa replied.

There was a little pizza place right around the corner and while it was busy, they still had a few tables available. Lisa was perfectly happy with the small table near the kitchen door, as long she knew food was on the way.

Norman insisted on choosing a bottle of wine. Lisa knew very little about wine, and didn't really care. "Whatever goes best with pizza," she told him when he asked for her preference, "and garlic bread."

The wine was delivered quickly, along with their plate of garlic bread, and after several mouthfuls of each, Lisa felt herself relax. "That's better," she said with a sigh as she sat back in her seat. She'd finished one slice of bread and had just added a second to the small plate in front of her. After another sip of wine, she smiled at Norman.

"So, tell me all about yourself," she suggested politely.

Norman flushed. "There isn't much to tell, really," he said, taking a big drink of wine. "I grew up in London and went to university in Edinburgh. I worked there for a couple of years, and then I was offered a job over here and I took it. I've been here ever since."

"Darcy told me you work in IT," Lisa said.

"Yeah, in banking. I also have my own little company that designs computer games. That's where I make a lot of my money."

"Wow, that's really great. Any plans to give up the day job?"

Norman shrugged. "I tried that about a year ago, but I got bored and went back to work. I don't actually need the day job, financially, but the games company mostly takes care of itself, and I got tired of sitting around all day."

Lisa shook her head. "I can't imagine not having to work," she told him. "I'd read books all day. I'd finally get around to reading all of the classics everyone is supposed to read but no one ever does. Then I'd read a little bit of everything else."

"I'm not a huge fan of fiction," Norman replied. "I like to read about battle strategies and military history, but that's about it."

Lisa chewed her bread thoughtfully. "I'd learn to cook," she announced. "I'd read a dozen cookbooks and then I'd try cooking everything in all of them. I'm sure I could get quite good at cooking if I tried hard enough."

"I don't cook," Norman told her. "I eat out for every meal, except breakfast. I have toast and an orange every day for breakfast."

"Every day?" Lisa asked.

"Every single day."

"Surely you have an apple once in a while for a change?"

"Nope, I like oranges."

Lisa grinned. "What sort of bread?"

"I like the sliced white stuff that's made locally," Norman replied. "I put a thin layer of butter and a teaspoon full of orange marmalade on each slice and I have three slices every morning."

"Do you have a three-slice toaster?" Lisa asked.

Norman shook his head. "I toast two slices and then butter them. Once the butter has melted in slightly, I add the marmalade. When I'm ready to eat them, I start the third slice toasting."

Lisa forced a smile onto her lips. Maybe he was joking, at least slightly? "What do you drink?"

"I have a cup of tea, with one teaspoon of sugar in it, most mornings. If I had a late night the previous evening, I might make a cup of instant coffee instead."

Finally, a bit of variety, Lisa thought. "I try to have something different nearly every day," she told the man. "Today I had cereal and milk."

"I don't like cereal," Norman told her.

Lisa bit her tongue. For her, cereal was something like its own food group. There were many nights when she would get home from work and be too tired to bother cooking for just herself. A bowl of sugary cereal, drowning in milk, made a perfect evening meal. The pizza's arrival interrupted the conversation.

Lisa tore into it eagerly and took a huge bite. The delicious blend of tangy tomato sauce, cheese and ham delighted her. "Oh, this wonderful," she said in between bites.

"It's very good," Norman answered politely as he nibbled on his slice.

"You don't really like pizza, do you?" Lisa asked.

"Not much," Norman admitted.

"But you suggested this place," Lisa pointed out.

"I thought you would like it," he replied. "After the first disaster, it seemed like a good, safe bet."

"I do like it," Lisa told him. "But I feel bad that you don't."

"It's fine," he insisted. Lisa watched as he took a large bite of pizza. He tried to grin at her as he chewed. Lisa had to look away after a moment. He so obviously didn't like the food that it was destroying her enjoyment of it.

"So what do you like to eat?" Lisa asked curiously. "Besides toast and oranges."

Norman shrugged and pushed his plate aside. "Mostly I like plain things. I don't really like it when all the flavours are mixed up in a dish. I like grilled chicken and mashed potatoes or maybe a lamb chop or a pork chop, just plain with some roast potatoes, something like that."

"I see," Lisa replied. "What about puddings?"

"Oh, I never eat pudding," Norman told her. "All those empty calories? No way."

Lisa held back a sigh. Norman seemed like a really nice guy, actually, but there was no way this relationship was going anywhere. A man that didn't like puddings or pizza? It would never work.

Lisa decided to make the best of it and eat as much of the pizza as she wanted. Normally, on a date, she'd only eat a few slices so that her date wouldn't think she was greedy. At this point, she didn't much care what Norman thought of her, though.

With the pizza mostly eaten and the bottle of wine empty, the pair made their way out of the restaurant. Lisa had grudgingly pretended that she didn't want any pudding. At least she had plenty of chocolate biscuits at home. And home was the only place she was interested in going right now.

"It's a lovely night," Norman remarked as they emerged onto the promenade.

"It really is," Lisa agreed. It was cool, but not cold, and the clear skies showcased a nearly full moon.

"Maybe you'd like to walk along the promenade for a bit?" Norman asked.

"We could," Lisa said. Aware of how reluctant she sounded, she continued. "That is, sure, why not?"

The street was full of happy couples, giggling teenagers and family groups. Everyone was out enjoying the nice weather. Autumn and winter would soon bring heavy rains and colder temperatures, which made tonight a night to enjoy.

As they walked along, Lisa glanced in the windows of the various shops. Everything was shut for the night, of course, but she spotted a couple of things that looked interesting. She'd have to have a shopping spree one day soon, she decided.

Norman stopped suddenly and Lisa very nearly just kept walking. After a few steps, however, she politely turned back. "Is something wrong?" she asked.

"I just thought you might like to go in here," Norman told her.

Lisa looked over at the amusement arcade. Dozens of pinball machines and video games competed for attention with their flashing lights and cacophonous noises. Lisa bit back a sigh and smiled at Norman. "Sure, why not?" she muttered, wishing she'd taken a few headache tablets with the meal.

Inside the door, Norman purchased a handful of tokens, carefully counting half of them into Lisa's hand. "This is where I spent most of my time when I wasn't working," he told Lisa, leaning in close to her ear so that he could be heard over all the noise that surrounded them.

"Surprise, surprise," Lisa muttered as she looked around the room. There were about half a dozen teenaged boys playing on complicated-looking machines that Lisa had never seen before. The rest of the space was taken up with what Lisa considered "vintage" games from the nineteen-eighties and nineties. About twenty-five men, seemingly ranging in age from around thirty to perhaps seventy, were scattered in front of the fifty or so arcade games.

"I'm just going to check out *Hungry Monsters*," Norman told her.

Lisa nodded. That particular classic game had once been one of her favourites, but if Norman wanted to play it, she could find something else to amuse her. An hour later, she'd had a go at several games that she'd enjoyed during her university years. The arcade at the university had been a much friendlier place, though. Here it seemed like everyone was going out of their way to avoid interacting with anyone else. Lisa had smiled and even said hello to a few people, but had only received nervous looks in return.

Now, with only a single token left, she decided she had better find Norman. He was still where he'd said he'd be, stationary in front of *Hungry Monsters*. Lisa watched as his character raced around the tiny electronic maze, trying to collect the objects in the correct order before the monsters got to him. After a few minutes Norman's electronic self was gobbled up.

"Yes!" he said excitedly. "That's my best score ever. Let's see someone beat that."

Lisa glanced at the screen as Norman put his initials in. "I used to play this one all the time at university," she told him.

"Really? I bet you never did as well as I just did." Norman glanced over at her, his eyes slightly feverish looking. "That was just amazing. I can't even believe it."

Lisa shrugged. "I only have one token left. Maybe I should have a go."

"By all means," Norman laughed and took a step backwards. "When did you play last?"

"Oh, it's been a few years," Lisa told him. "I'm seriously out of practise."

"Never mind," he told her. "I'm sure you'll do quite well, under the circumstances."

Lisa bit her tongue and dropped her last token into the slot. She rubbed her hands together and then grabbed the familiar joystick. "Like riding a bike," she muttered to herself as her little pixelated self appeared on the screen.

Half an hour later, much to her dismay, her character was gobbled up. She looked at her score. It was several thousand below her personal best. "Darn, didn't get my best ever," she said. "I suppose I should play more often."

She glanced over at Norman and then looked away to hide her smile. He was staring open-mouthed at the screen. Lisa tapped in her initials on the top of the leader board and then turned around to find at least a dozen men had wandered over to watch her performance.

"Way to show us how it's done," one of the men shouted, raising his hand in the air. Lisa exchanged a high-five with him and then did the same with dozens of members of the suddenly animated crowd.

"First score on that machine over one million points," a man in a T-shirt with the logo of the arcade on it said. "That's earned you a prize."

Lisa flushed. She hadn't been expecting all of this attention. A glance at Norman showed her that he wasn't all that excited about it, either.

"Prize, prize, prize, prize...."

Really? Lisa thought as the crowd began to chant excitedly. *I wonder what I've won.*

At the desk in the darkest corner of the space, the man in the arcade T-shirt laid out her choices. "You can have a T-shirt with the arcade logo on it, a giant cuddly toy or a coupon for two hundred and fifty free tokens."

Lisa looked at the misshapen cuddly toy. When she couldn't work out what sort of animal it was meant to be, she eliminated it from consideration. The T-shirt was an ugly, almost fluorescent green, but at least it would be useful for when she next wanted to paint or decorate. She couldn't possibly imagine ever using the free tokens. After tonight she didn't plan on visiting the arcade again.

"The T-shirt is a collector's item," the man behind the desk told her. "The only way to get one is to score big on one of the games."

"Or work here," Lisa suggested.

"Oh no," he told her. "I had to earn mine fair and square. Employees who haven't hit a big score only get hats." He gestured towards a spotty teenaged boy who was standing on the edge of the crowd. Sure enough, he was wearing an ugly green hat that said "STAFF" across it in big letters. The boy gave Lisa a vague smile.

Lisa sighed. "I think I'll take the T-shirt," she told the man. Everyone in the crowd cheered as the man dug keys out of his pocket and opened a locked case behind the desk. After checking on her size, he pulled out a shirt.

"You can change in the loo if you want to," he suggested as he handed her the shirt.

"Oh, I wouldn't want to do that," Lisa replied. "I would be afraid I might spill something on it or something. I want to keep it clean." Right up until I start painting in it, she added silently.

The crowd cheered again. Lisa grinned at Norman. "I think that's enough excitement for tonight, don't you?" she asked.

"Sure," Norman snapped back at her. "Let's go."

He headed for the front of the arcade at a rapid pace that had Lisa struggling to keep up. She could have gone faster if she hadn't needed to stop to high-five nearly everyone on her way out. When she finally got outside, Norman was standing in front of a shop a few doors away.

"I think I should head home," she told him when she joined him.

"That would probably be best," he answered shortly.

The pair made their way back down the promenade, heading towards Lisa's house. After several minutes where Lisa struggled to keep up with the accelerated pace that Norman was setting, she'd had enough.

"I gather I've upset you in some way," she said, causing him to stop walking.

"No, not at all," he muttered, not meeting her eyes. "I'm just really tired, that's all."

"I am as well," Lisa told him. "Why don't you just head for home and I'll walk myself the rest of the way? It isn't far and Douglas is very safe."

"No," Norman told her. "I'll walk you to your door."

Lisa could only hope that he wasn't going to try to get a kiss from her at her door, but it turned out she had worried unnecessarily. When they reached the short path from the street to her door, Norman stopped.

"Thank you for an interesting evening," he said stiffly. "I hope you have a wonderful life."

Without waiting for a reply, he turned on his heel and strode purposefully away. Lisa stared after him for a moment, feeling stunned, then she turned and made her way to her door.

"He dumped me," she told Darcy as the other woman came rushing up as soon as Lisa let herself in. "He totally and completely kicked me to the curb, right out there on my doorstep."

Darcy grinned at her. "He was too short for you anyway," she laughed.

Lisa shook her head. "Wait until I tell you the rest."

"I'll open the wine," Darcy replied.

In Lisa's kitchen, Darcy opened a bottle of wine while Lisa dug out a box of her favourite, highly indulgent, chocolate-covered biscuits.

"Where do I start?" she asked as she plopped down at the kitchen table.

"What was the food like at the Chinese restaurant?" Darcy asked.

"Italian," Lisa laughed.

Darcy laughed until she cried as Lisa told her the story of her evening. "Hang on, let's see this T-shirt," she demanded as Lisa finished.

"I left it in the other room," Lisa told her.

Darcy raced off and came back wearing the shirt over her clothes. "It's lovely," she cooed. "Neon green is such a flattering colour, isn't it?"

Lisa laughed and drank more wine. "I can't believe it, but it actually suits you. Sometimes I hate you, you know that?"

"I hope you are hating me because I look good in this hideous shirt and not because I fixed you up with a loser," Darcy told her as she pulled the shirt off over her head.

"Oh, I don't mind about Norman," Lisa said with shrug. "He was okay, really, at least until I beat his high score."

Darcy giggled. "I've never even tried any video games."

"I used to play at university when my flatmate had guests," Lisa told her with a wry smile.

Darcy flushed. "I think I can see how you got so good," she said.

As Darcy was the flatmate in question, Lisa knew she understood perfectly.

"Anyway," Lisa said suddenly. "Why didn't you have a date tonight?"

"Oh, I got back later than expected from Paris. Mark and I didn't have firm plans for tonight anyway. We're going to have dinner together tomorrow night, instead."

Lisa frowned at her friend. "It isn't like you to stay in on a Friday night," she said slowly. "Are you okay?"

"I'm fine," Darcy insisted. "I just didn't feel like sorting something out at the last minute. The Paris flight was late because Finlo was waiting for some dumb blonde to turn up and then we couldn't get a take-off slot for ages. By the time we'd landed, Mark had made other plans with some of the people he works with, that's all."

"Have you been seeing a lot of Mark, then?" Lisa asked.

"I haven't seen him since the night we met," Darcy replied. "I've been too busy with work and so has he. Like I said, we're having dinner together tomorrow night."

"And Finlo has a new playmate?"

Darcy shrugged. "I'm not sure what the story is with that," she said.

Lisa could hear the unhappiness in her voice. "Go on," she suggested.

"I don't know anything," Darcy told her. "Apparently, Finlo took that blonde woman I just mentioned to Paris on Monday for her work and he was meant to be flying her home today. She got held up in traffic, we were told, and we had to wait for a couple of hours for her to get to the airport. By the time she got to the plane, she was all out of sorts and she spent the entire flight snapping at me and being rude."

Lisa jumped up and pulled Darcy to her feet. She gave her friend a big hug. "You shouldn't have to put up with that sort of behaviour," she told Darcy.

"Of course I have to put up with it," Darcy replied. "It's my job."

"You need a new job," Lisa told her.

"Yeah, among other things," Darcy said with a sigh. The pair sat back down and both finished off their glasses of wine. Lisa grabbed the bottle and poured the last of it as evenly as possible into the glasses.

"Anyway, once we landed, Finlo whisked his new friend away in his fancy sports car and left Jack and me to sort out the plane and the paperwork."

"And you decided that you didn't feel up to a night out," Lisa added.

"Yeah, I assumed I could crash here again, if you don't mind."

"You should just move into my spare room," Lisa told her.

"Don't tempt me," Darcy laughed. "My flat is nice and close to the airport, but other than that, it has nothing going for it."

"Well, you know my spare room is as good as yours," Lisa said. "And hopefully tonight's little escapade has put you off the idea of setting me up on any more blind dates."

Darcy shook her head. "No way, I'm only just getting started," she replied.

Lisa's heart sank.

4

Darcy was up and away early, leaving Lisa with the rest of her weekend free. She caught up on laundry and gave the house a fairly superficial cleaning. In the grocery store, Lisa stocked up on cereal and milk as well as the few things she needed for quick meals after work each day. She nearly bought herself a bag of oranges, but decided against it. For a moment she was tempted to buy every bag of oranges in the shop, hoping that they would then be sold out the next time Norman came shopping, but as she wasn't even sure where he did his grocery shopping, it seemed like a silly idea.

The week ahead was scheduled to be another busy one, as Lisa put the finishing touches on the project she'd been managing for the last several months. By midday on Wednesday, she'd finally completed every last task and she gave herself a small round of applause as she sent the email to her boss informing him of that fact. She leaned back in her chair and stared at her ceiling for a moment.

As far as she knew, the small consultancy firm that she worked for had nothing in the pipeline. The project she'd just completed had offered a fairly large bonus if she'd met all of the required deadlines, and she'd beaten them all. She was just mentally planning an exotic holiday with the extra money when her internal line buzzed.

"Ah, Lisa, congratulations on finishing the Westlake Project," Lisa's boss, Dan Green, told her. "Can I see you in my office, please?"

"Now?" Lisa asked in surprise. She'd been expecting him to offer her the afternoon off as a bonus for getting the project done early.

"Now would be good," Dan replied. "I've a nice new project for you to dig into."

Lisa put down the phone and grinned. She didn't really feel like a holiday anyway. She loved new projects.

Dan stood up to greet her when she entered his office. He was somewhere in his fifties, with greying hair and brown eyes. He was something of a keep-fit fanatic and every time Lisa visited his office, Dan seemed to have added another photo of himself crossing the finish line at some marathon or race.

The first thing he did was offer his congratulations to her. "You did a wonderful job on the Westlake project," he said again. "You're becoming something of an expert on out-of-house projects."

The small company that Lisa worked for specialised in providing bespoke payroll software to businesses across the island. The company was becoming increasingly well known, however, for supplying local project management consultants for island firms looking to install new systems in other areas.

The project Lisa had just finished fell into the latter category. A local estate agency had purchased an expensive listings management programme from a company in the UK. When the technical requirement of the installation and conversion proved beyond the capabilities of their regular staff, the company hired Lisa's firm to deal with it. She'd been given a two-week crash course in the software at the company's headquarters across and then successfully managed the installation and staff training.

"I have another project like the last one," Dan told her. "Another local group has bought software that they are struggling to install."

Lisa grinned. "Bad for them, but good for us."

"Exactly," Dan smiled.

"So who is it this time?"

"Manx National Heritage," Dan told her. "They've purchased an expensive Point of Sale system for all of their sites. It's meant to provide data in real time to the various departments that are interested in what's going on around the island. The system has a bunch of very sophisticated reporting capabilities that will help them with things like anticipating staffing demands and fine-tuning opening and closing dates for sites on an individual basis."

"It sounds good," Lisa said.

"It is good, and once they get it working, it will give them a lot of valuable information, but first they have to get it all installed and get their staff trained on how to use it."

"And that's where I come in?"

"Exactly," Dan nodded. "The company they've purchased the software from, SDDC, is fairly new and they've given MNH a terrific deal on the system because it's only barely out of beta. Apparently, SDDC think having MNH install it at all of their sites will give them some great publicity and give them a chance to work out all sorts of niggling bugs before they start trying to sell it to any of the big UK heritage organisations."

"Makes sense."

"Unfortunately for MNH, their IT department is too small for them to be able to provide a full-time person to deal with the installation. There are conversion issues as well, as each site currently uses one of four different POS systems and none of them talk to the others."

Lisa sighed. "So nothing challenging, then," she said dryly.

"I'm sure you can handle it," Dan told her. "If you do as well with this as you did with the Westlake project, we stand to get some very positive publicity out of it as well."

"I'll do my best," Lisa assured him.

"I'm sure you will," Dan grinned. "For today, I want you to go home and celebrate getting done with Westlake. Tomorrow morning you need to report to the Manx Museum at nine o'clock. Mark Blake, their head of special projects, will meet you there. He's going to start taking you around the various sites so that you can see what's currently being used at each location and poke around for any possible problems."

"I've met Mark," Lisa told him. "He's actually dating my best friend."

"The lovely Darcy?" Dan asked. "He didn't seem to be her type when I met him."

Not sure how to reply, Lisa ignored the remark. "But why am I working with him? Surely it would make more sense to have me work with someone from the IT department?"

"He's who MNH can spare," Dan shrugged. "He's pretty familiar with the various systems and their idiosyncrasies and he's just finished setting up a new exhibit and was able to clear his calendar to work on this. You know as well as I do that sometimes it's better to work with someone outside of IT on new installs, anyway."

Lisa nodded. "They can sometimes be more flexible in their approach, certainly, but I hope I don't have to spend too much time explaining technical things to him."

"He struck me as a pretty bright guy," Dan assured her. "I think you two will get along well."

"So tomorrow is all about visiting sites, then what?"

"Friday will be more site visits," Dan told her. "There are quite a few places you need to visit and they're scattered all over the island. I have Helen booking your flights for Sunday night now. She'll give you the details once we're done here. Unfortunately, the company in question is located in Morecombe, so I'm not sure what you'll do with your free time, but we'll provide a hire car in case you want to try to find some shops or something."

Lisa laughed. "I doubt I'll go anywhere other than back and forth to work. How long will I be away?"

"The training is only one week this time," Dan told her. "I got the feeling that you'll be getting one-on-one tuition with one of SDDC's senior programmers."

"So it is a really small company, and MNH is their first real customer," Lisa guessed.

"Probably," Dan grinned. "If it all goes pear-shaped, maybe we can get hired to install whatever MNH ends up having to buy to replace this system with."

Lisa shook her head. "If it all goes pear-shaped, MNH is going to blame me."

"Probably," Dan shrugged. "That's why I know you'll do such a good job."

Lisa grinned. "I'm sure I appreciate your confidence in me."

"I think that's all I need to tell you," Dan said, flipping through some notes on his desk. "Do you have any questions?"

Lisa shook her head. "I'll get my travel itinerary from Helen and then go home and put my feet up for the afternoon so I have lots of energy for tramping around historical sites tomorrow. I'm sure I'll have lots of questions after I've talked to Mark and seen what I'm dealing with, so I might be ringing you at home Friday night."

"Never a problem," Dan assured her.

The company was Dan's baby. He'd built it up slowly and carefully, hiring the best people he could find to fill positions as they developed. He was very hands-off, because he trusted his staff, but he was more than willing to jump in and do anything and everything that was necessary to ensure their success as well. Lisa knew she was more than welcome to ring him any time if she had any questions or concerns about her work.

Dan's administrative assistant, Helen, had started with the company in its earliest days. She was of a similar age to Dan, and Lisa always wondered if the pair had ever considered a romantic relationship. As far as Lisa knew, they were both single.

"Hi, Lisa, congratulations on the Westlake project," Helen greeted her as she left Dan's office.

"Thanks, Helen," Lisa grinned. "I love your hair."

"Thanks," Helen twisted a lock thoughtfully. "I wasn't sure about going this short, but my sister talked me into it and now I love it."

"It really suits you," Lisa told her.

"I'm not sure about that, but I do know for sure that it is a lot easier to look after. I can sleep in for an extra ten minutes every morning now."

Lisa laughed. "It doesn't sound like much, but there are plenty of days when I would give just about anything for ten more minutes of sleep."

Helen laughed. "Exactly. Anyway, I've just finished up with your travel arrangements. You'll fly out of Ronaldsway on Sunday afternoon.

You're flying with Quayle Airways so you can fly into Blackpool. None of the local commercial carriers are flying to Blackpool at this time of year."

Lisa made a face that stopped Helen in her tracks. "Is there something wrong?" Helen asked.

"Darcy works for Finlo, but they also dated for a while, that's all," Lisa told her. "I'd just rather not give him any business."

Helen frowned. "MNH actually made the flight arrangements. I understand they have some sort of agreement with Mr. Quayle for special rates. I was pleasantly surprised when they told me the cost for the flight."

"Finlo's cousin runs the Manx History Institute. That's probably the connection," Lisa told her.

"Well, I can try to get you booked on something commercial, but you'd have to fly into Manchester, probably, and then hire a car from there. Blackpool is the closest airport. I hate to think of you having to drive all over the UK."

Lisa grinned. "I think I could manage, but don't change anything. It's fine, really. I'll just make sure I eat all of the snacks on the flight so that Finlo loses money on me."

Helen laughed. "I've heard he has fancy snacks onboard," she said. "I've never flown charter."

"You need to make Dan send you somewhere nice," Lisa told her.

Helen shrugged. "I don't actually like to travel," she confided. "I'm quite happy right here."

"Maybe you should book one of Finlo's flights around the island," Lisa suggested. "You just fly along the coast, all the way around. The scenery must be amazing and he does wine and snacks, or so I've been told."

"That's a thought," Helen replied. "But anyway, I've booked you into the nicest hotel I could find. I've requested that you and Mark be given rooms next to one another, but I can't promise that they'll actually do that."

"Mark is coming to Morecombe as well?" Lisa asked. "Why?"

"Apparently they have a special training programme for end users as well," Helen told her. "He's the only one being sent and he will be responsible for training all of the rest of the MNH staff."

"Good," Lisa said. "That's one less job for me. Training end users isn't my favourite thing."

Helen laughed. "Dan told me you complained a lot about training the various estate agents on the Westlake project."

Lisa shook her head. "I was very patient with them, but some of them were hugely resistant to change. I had one lovely older woman who told me that she'd been typing her listings on her typewriter for thirty years and she wasn't about to change now."

"What did you do?" Helen asked curiously.

"I persuaded her office manager that it would be easier if he just put her listing in himself, rather than push the issue. She was only a part-time employee and had only listed four houses in the previous six months, so it wasn't a huge burden for the office manager. That was far easier than trying to force the woman to learn to use a computer."

Helen grinned. "Well done," she told Lisa. "And very sensible."

"I wonder what the MNH staff will be like," Lisa replied. "I hope they're rather more adaptable than she was."

"I suppose you'll start finding out tomorrow," Helen said.

"I suppose I will."

Lisa took the printed itinerary that Helen gave her and headed back to her office. She cleared off her desk and shut her computer down. Grabbing her laptop, she headed for home. She was ready to curl up with a good book and a box of chocolates as a celebration of the successful completion of her project.

Before bed that night, she tried ringing Darcy to tell her about her new assignment. No one answered at Darcy's flat, and when Lisa tried her mobile, she was told that the phone was switched off. Presumably, Darcy was working.

When Darcy had first taken the job with Quayle Airways, Lisa had kept track of where and when Darcy was flying, but over the years she had stopped doing so. These days she rarely rang Darcy, relying on her friend to get in touch with her whenever she was available. Now she was sorry she didn't know where her friend was, but perhaps Mark would know more tomorrow.

At precisely nine o'clock the next morning, Lisa pulled on one of the big glass doors that marked the entrance to the Manx Museum. It didn't open. She flushed and tried the other door, but it didn't open, either. She took a step back and looked at the sign near the door that gave the museum's hours. They didn't open until ten, she discovered. A small hand-lettered sign underneath the list of opening hours read: "Deliveries outside of regular museum hours can be made at the back doors. Please ring the buzzer."

Lisa wasn't sure she qualified as a delivery, but she headed for the back doors anyway. Those doors were also locked up tightly, but Lisa found the small buzzer and pressed it. She couldn't hear anything when she did so, but after a moment she could hear someone unlocking the door.

Mark Blake stuck his head out through the wooden double doors and grinned at Lisa. "Good morning," he said. "What can I do for you?"

"I was told to meet you here at nine," Lisa replied. "I'm from Manx Consulting Solutions."

Mark looked confused. "You are?" he said. "But you're Darcy's friend, right?"

"The two aren't mutually exclusive," Lisa said with a grin.

Mark flushed. "I'm sorry, I just thought, that is, I suppose I just assumed that you and Darcy worked together."

"Your brother and I discussed my job," she told him. "Clearly it just wasn't interesting enough for him to mention to you."

Mark shook his head. "I'm sure that's not it," he said. He took a deep breath. "I'm sorry, can we just start over?"

Lisa grinned. "I think I can manage that," she told him. "Good morning, I'm Lisa Mylchreest, and I'm here from Manx Consulting Solutions."

"Hi, Lisa, it's great to see you again," Mark said, offering his hand.

Lisa took it and gave it a quick shake. "It's great to see you again, too," she replied. "I tried to ring Darcy last night to tell her that I was going to be working with you, but I couldn't reach her."

"When we had dinner on Saturday, she said something about a series of short hops all across Europe this week," Mark told her. "She isn't going to be back until this Saturday. But anyway, come in," he flushed again. "Sorry, I'm totally flustered today."

"It's fine," Lisa told him as she crossed into the museum. "I didn't mean to surprise you like that."

"Let's go down to my office and we can get started," Mark suggested.

"That sounds like a plan." Lisa followed him through a handful of exhibits until they reached a door that said "Staff Only." Mark waved a card in front of a wall-mounted reader and then pushed the door open.

"We'll have to get you a card for access," he muttered.

"I'm sure that would be useful," Lisa answered.

A number of offices opened off the short corridor that was on the other side of the door. Mark walked all the way to the end of the hall and then motioned Lisa into the last office.

"I'm sorry, it's a bit of a mess," he told her as she stepped inside.

Lisa looked around slowly. The nicest thing she could say was that it appeared to be a fairly organised mess.

Mark grabbed a pile of papers off the lone visitor's chair and motioned Lisa into it. "Please, have a seat," he told her as he looked around the room, presumably trying to work out where to drop the papers in his arms. Lisa sank into the uncomfortable seat and grinned at his confusion. After a minute, Mark shrugged and dropped the pile on top of one of the many stacks of similar looking papers on his desk.

"I was hoping to get more time to get organised before we got started," he told Lisa. "I was originally told we were going to start on Monday."

Lisa bit back an almost instinctive apology. The schedule wasn't her fault, after all. "I don't expect we'll need to spend much time in your office, anyway," Lisa told him. "I need to get out to the sites and see what's going on there."

"I thought you might like a peek at the new system first," Mark suggested. He clicked an icon on his desktop computer and a login screen appeared. Moments later, he was showing her a list of all of the island's heritage sites.

"In theory, once the system is live, I'll be able to click on any site and see exactly how many tickets in each category have been sold on any given day. We should be able to track customers who purchase multi-site passes as well, seeing how many of the sites they actually manage to visit and how long they spend at each one."

Lisa nodded. "May I have a go?" she asked. Mark stepped aside and Lisa slid into his chair. She clicked through a few different options on each site. "Is this dummy data, then?"

"Yes, the man who came across and installed the system in here filled the database with some dummy records to show me how the various reports work."

Lisa took out a notebook and began scribbling notes to herself as she worked through each of the different reporting options. "Are there other reports you'd like to see?" she asked after a while.

"Can you do that?" Mark asked.

"I can do anything you want with the data," Lisa told him with a grin. "Tell me what you'd most like to see."

Mark went to his file cabinet and pulled out a folder. "Here's the spec sheet for what we requested when we asked for bids on the system," he told Lisa, handing her a thick document. "I think these guys fulfilled about ninety per cent of our requests, but there are a few other reports we requested that they don't offer and that I'd love to get."

Lisa glanced through the document quickly. It was much more professionally done than she'd expected. "This is great," she told Mark. "Can I take this home and read through it? That way I can start a list of things to discuss with them next week."

"Of course you can," Mark told her. "It's an extra copy."

"Right, well, it does look like quite a useful system," she replied. "I can see why you guys are excited about it and I'm looking forward to working with it. Maybe we'd better get started on site visits, though. We only have a few days."

"The best place to start, therefore, is right here," Mark told her. "I'll show you the system we have at the entrance doors here. If we're quick, we can finish before the museum opens."

Lisa followed Mark back down the corridor and into the museum. They walked past several displays that Lisa would have liked more time to study.

"I haven't been here since I was kid," she remarked. "A lot has changed."

"I hope for the better," Mark replied with a grin.

"I'm sure," she said. "Although it's hard to tell in the dark."

"I'll have to give you a tour one of these days," Mark said as they reached the front of the building.

Behind the desk, just inside the door, Henry Costain was sorting out piles of site brochures.

"I've fired everything up early, like you asked," he told Mark when they arrived.

"Terrific," Mark smiled at him. "Lisa, I think you met Henry at the House of Manannan? He's been a fixture with MNH for more years than I've been alive and he knows more about the sites than anyone else around."

"It's a pleasure to see you again," Lisa told the man who'd flushed bright red at Mark's introduction. She extended her hand and gave Henry's a small squeeze. "I hope you're looking forward to the new computer system."

"Oh, yes," Henry said enthusiastically. "The current system is a dinosaur. People come here because we're the most logical first stop, but then we sell them tickets to other sites that then have to be reprinted when they get to those other sites, because our tickets won't talk to their computers. It's all very frustrating. Mark showed me some of the other things the new system can do as well, and I'm all for it."

Lisa smiled. "I hope everyone shares your enthusiasm," she told the man.

Mark spent the next several minutes walking Lisa through the capabilities and limitations of the current POS system that the museum used. She took copious notes and then grinned at him.

"I think I've seen enough here," she told him. "This will be an easy one to revisit as well. Maybe we should get out in the field before it starts to rain."

Mark glanced out the large windows that flanked the building's entrance. "It does look like rain," he frowned. "At least all the systems are indoors, but it won't be a very pleasant day for travelling all over the island if it rains."

"I suppose it can't be helped," Henry said. "Autumn is all about rain, isn't it?"

Lisa and Mark laughed and then headed back to Mark's office to grab their jackets and Lisa's bag.

Mark drove a large car, and it was at least as cluttered as his office. He flushed as he shoved piles of papers from the passenger seat onto the floor in the back. "Sorry, I wasn't thinking," he told Lisa as he emptied the passenger foot well. "I should have done this last night."

"We can take my car," Lisa told him. "But it's at my house. I walked over, as I don't live far away."

"No, this is fine," Mark assured her. "I'm just not quite as organised as I should be at the moment. The exhibit that went live a few weeks ago has had a few teething issues and I've been back and forth to Peel nearly every day since. I promise you my office and my car are both usually much tidier."

Lisa wasn't going to argue. She climbed into the car and fastened her seatbelt, putting her bag on the floor near her feet. Mark climbed in quickly and, seatbelt fastened, pulled carefully out of the car park.

"I thought we'd try to get to Peel Castle and the House of Manannan this morning and then drive north to the Laxey Wheel and the Grove Museum this afternoon. A lot will depend on how much time you need at each site, though."

"I don't expect I'll need a lot of time," Lisa answered thoughtfully. "I need to see what the current systems are like and maybe have a play with them a little bit, as I did with the system here. I don't want to spend too much time on the old systems before I've been properly trained on the new one, though. This is more about figuring out the size and scale of the work than actually making any progress."

"Right, well, here we go," Mark grinned at her.

Lisa worked on her notes as they made the trip across the island. She was already getting excited about the challenges that were ahead of her. Working with Mark promised to be enjoyable as well.

"I think we'll start at the castle," Mark told her as they turned down the narrow and twisty roads in Peel. Lisa could see a tour bus that had just pulled up in front of the House of Manannan.

"I'm sure we'd rather miss all those tourists," she agreed.

"Exactly what I was thinking."

At the castle, Mark introduced Lisa to the two MNH staff members who were working at the castle that day.

"We try to rotate most of our staff so no one gets bored and everyone gets to learn about all the different sites," he told Lisa. " We have to balance that, of course, with allowing staff an opportunity to learn as much as they can about a site before they get sent elsewhere. And, of course, some of them ask to be permanently stationed somewhere and we try to honour those requests when we can, as well."

"Are there ways to track staff in the new system?" Lisa asked. She hadn't specifically noticed any.

"Yes, but I haven't the first idea how to access them," Mark laughed. "We already have an excellent payroll system, thanks to you guys, but there is meant to be something in the new system that will let us track which sites each person can cover and how much training they've each had and that sort of thing."

"Brilliant," Lisa grinned.

The two members of staff working at the castle were both young and very computer literate. One of them walked Lisa through the entire system that they were currently using and discussed its shortcomings with her while the other dealt with the handful of visitors that arrived while Lisa was there.

"It all seems pretty straightforward," she told Mark after less than an hour. "I have everything I need."

"Before you go," the member of staff that had been dealing with customers said, "there's a pod of seals splashing about on the rocks if you're interested."

Lisa grinned. "Where?" she asked excitedly. Mark led her through the site, past the many ruined buildings that were once part of a large castle system, to the sea wall. The seals that were diving under the water and sunning themselves on the rocks below enchanted Lisa.

"I'm so glad the sun came out," she said to Mark. "This is amazing."

Mark smiled at her. "I see them fairly often, but I'm always delighted to see them again."

"The castle bits are interesting as well," Lisa told him as she turned back towards the castle entrance. "I vaguely remember coming here in primary school, but mostly we just rolled down the hills and dared each other to go down into the crypt."

Mark shook his head. "I wonder if I'd have been any different," he commented. "I loved history, even as a small child, but rolling down the hills sounds like fun."

"You didn't grow up on the island, then?" Lisa asked.

"No, I'm from London, originally," he replied. "But, I got the job here right after university and I've been here ever since. I can't imagine living anywhere else now."

Back at the entrance, Lisa thanked the staff for their time, and for telling her about the seals. The drive to the House of Manannan took only a few minutes.

Inside Mark showed Lisa the unique ticketing system that they used there. "Because of the timed nature of each section of the museum, we need to track people more efficiently here than anywhere else," Mark told her.

Lisa spent a few minutes poking around the system under the watchful eye of yet another young and enthusiastic MNH staff member.

"I hope the new system is half as good as they say it is," the young girl told Lisa. "It should make my job a lot easier."

"What are you most looking forward to with the new system?" Lisa asked her.

"Being able to track where people are in the museum," she told Lisa. "People sometimes get frustrated when they have to wait in between sections. This new system is supposed to help us cut down on the waiting time."

Lisa nodded and took more notes. "Maybe you could show me, just briefly, exactly what she means?" Lisa asked Mark.

"You did say you've never been around the House of Manannan, didn't you?" Mark replied, shaking his head.

Lisa flushed and looked at the floor. "I'm sorry to say I haven't," she admitted.

"We don't have time to see it properly," Mark told her. "But we can have a quick walk-through and I can show you exactly what Lynne is talking about."

The walk-through fascinated Lisa. Each separate section of the museum had its own short presentation that gave a snapshot view of a point in the island's history. They didn't take the time to watch the presentations, but what Lisa saw was intriguing.

"I'm definitely coming back and having a better look at all of this," Lisa said when they reached the end. "It looks to be a wonderful museum."

"I think it's exceptionally well done," Mark said. "But I may be not entirely impartial."

Lisa laughed. "I think you're right, anyway," she told him.

"Actually, I think I'm starving," Mark told Lisa with a smile. "How about we stop for lunch on the way back across the island?"

"That sounds perfect," Lisa replied. "I'm starving as well."

5

There was a small pub on the road back from Peel towards Douglas. Lisa wasn't even sure what the pub was called, but she knew the food was excellent. Mark squeezed his car in the last parking space in the tiny car park and they headed inside eagerly.

There was a fire burning in the fireplace and Lisa was delighted to find a small table near it.

"I love wood-burning fireplaces," Lisa told Mark. "I have a gas fire in my house, but it isn't quite the same."

"You're right," Mark agreed with her. "I have a gas fire in my flat as well, but it never feels quite as cosy as a real fire."

Lisa spent a few minutes looking over the menu, with her mouth watering. "I haven't actually eaten here in years," she told Mark. "Their fish and chips used to be my favourite. Is it still good?"

"Well, it's my favourite," Mark told her.

Food ordered, they settled in with cold drinks to wait for its arrival.

"I think I should tell you something up front," Lisa told Mark. "I really don't feel comfortable talking about Darcy with you. Your relationship is your private business and I don't like to mix business with pleasure."

Mark flushed. "I was thinking something very similar," he told her. "But I didn't know how to bring it up."

"Well, at least we cleared the air," Lisa told him. "What shall we talk about then?"

"Let's talk about you," Mark suggested. "I'm assuming you're single?"

"Oh, indeed," Lisa told him with a laugh. "Although Darcy's doing her best to find me a man."

"What sort of man are you looking for?" Mark asked. "Perhaps I can help you find someone. I know quite a few single men."

Lisa shook her head. "I'm not looking for any kind of man," she told him. "Darcy just thinks I should be."

"And Darcy can be a force to reckon with when she wants to be," Mark replied.

"Exactly!" Lisa told him. "But let me tell you about the last blind date that Darcy arranged for me."

Mark laughed until his eyes watered when she told him about the wine list at the Chinese restaurant. "Please tell me you're kidding," he begged her through his laughter.

"I wish," she replied with a grin.

"Tell me the date got better from there," he said in a hopeful tone.

"Well, I won a T-shirt," she replied.

When she told Mark the rest of the story, she could see new respect in his eyes.

"I don't spend a lot of time there now," he told her. "But when I first moved to the island I used to hang out at that arcade once in a while. I only ever saw one other person win a T-shirt from the place. It's actually quite an accomplishment."

Lisa shook her head. "It didn't feel like an accomplishment," she told him. "It felt silly."

"I was never good at *Hungry Monsters*," Mark told her. "What's your secret?"

Lisa grinned. "It's all about patterns," she told him. "The monsters follow specific patterns that are never truly random. Once you've worked them out at each level you just have to make sure you stay away from them."

Mark shook his head. "I'll take your word for it," he told her. "I don't plan on playing it again in a hurry."

"Neither do I," Lisa told him with a laugh.

The food arrived before the conversation could continue. For several minutes the pair crunched their way through the delicious fish and chips meal that was every bit as good as Lisa remembered.

"How about pudding?" Mark asked as Lisa finished off the last of her chips.

"I'm stuffed," Lisa groaned. "Do they still have sticky toffee pudding?"

"They do," Mark grinned her, "and I'm going to have it."

Lisa sighed. "You'd better order me the same," she told him. "Otherwise I'll just make sad faces at you while you eat yours."

Mark went back to the bar to place the order. "It'll only be a couple of minutes," he told her when he returned. The staff was true to their word. Only a short time later their puddings arrived, each covered with a generous helping of hot custard.

Lisa didn't say a word as she enjoyed the delicious treat. Once she was scraping her plate for the last of the custard, she glanced up at Mark. He'd finished his own pudding. Now he was grinning at her.

"That was really good," he said.

"It certainly was," Lisa replied. "But now I really don't feel like doing any work. I feel like taking a nap."

Mark laughed. "I know what you mean, but we have to do a couple more sites today. There isn't enough time tomorrow to hit them all."

Lisa nodded. "Where to next?" she asked.

"The Laxey Wheel," Mark told her.

Lisa insisted on paying for lunch on her company credit card. "It will go into the expenses for the project," she told Mark. "Flights, hotels and food in Morecombe all next week will make today's lunch seem cheap."

The day remained dry and at least partly sunny, and Lisa felt lucky that she wasn't in her office today. They made their way back across the island into Douglas and then turned up the coast road towards Laxey.

"You must have visited the Lady Isabella before," Mark told her, referring the Laxey Wheel by its given name. "It's been on the school trip list for every primary school on the island for many years. It's such an important part of the island's mining history in the nineteenth century and one small claim to fame for us as well. It is the largest working waterwheel in the world, after all."

Lisa nodded. "We visited just about everywhere in our school days," she told him. "I remember climbing up. One of my friends was afraid of heights and didn't want to do it, but the teacher made her."

Mark frowned. "I hope she was okay."

"She was fine," Lisa laughed as she remembered. "Her name was Kim and she had a huge crush on a guy called Max. Somehow she managed to get Max to hold her hand and that seemed to take care of her fear."

"And did they live happily ever after?" Mark asked.

"They did date for a while after that," Lisa said, struggling to remember events from years earlier. "I know Kim ended up marrying some guy she met at university, but I've no idea what happened to Max."

"Well, if heights don't bother you, we can have a quick climb up the wheel today if you'd like," Mark offered.

"Let's see how we're doing for time once I've poked around the ticketing system," Lisa suggested. "You wanted to get to Ramsey as well, right?"

Mark nodded as he pulled his car into the car park in central Laxey. "It's probably easier to walk from here than to try to get closer," he told Lisa.

"I don't mind a walk," Lisa assured him. "It's the perfect autumn day for it, and I ate an awful lot of lunch."

Now that Lisa had seen some of the systems, the visit to the wheel took even less time than the previous visits had taken. The ticket booth was tiny and felt cramped with Mark, Lisa and the two MNH staff members all crowded into it as well, so Lisa hurried as much as she could.

"I think we should climb the wheel," Mark told her as they exited the compact ticket booth.

"A bit of physical activity sounds good after being squashed in there," Lisa told him with a smile. She wasn't so sure a few minutes later as they climbed the spiral staircase.

"I didn't realise there were a million steps," she complained.

Mark laughed. He was several stairs in front of her and seemed to be climbing effortlessly. "There are actually less than a hundred," he replied.

"No way," Lisa muttered.

The reward was worth the effort, however. The pair spent several minutes enjoying the wonderful views of the surrounding countryside.

"If we had more time, I'd take you to the mine as well," Mark told her.

"We should have skipped pudding," Lisa suggested.

"The mine isn't going anywhere," Mark shrugged. "You'll need to do some work at each site with the installation. We'll have to plan your time while you're working so that you can take some proper tours as well."

"I'm not sure my boss would agree with that," Lisa replied. "But it sounds good to me."

They made their way carefully back down the steps and then headed back towards Mark's car.

"It's gone three o'clock," Lisa said in surprise once she'd settled into the passenger seat. "I've really lost track of time today."

"Only one more stop," Mark assured her. "We'll visit the Grove Museum and then call it a day."

"And that's one place I've never been," Lisa told him. "I feel as though I ought to apologise to you for that."

Mark laughed. "While I think everyone on the island should visit all of the heritage sites regularly, I do understand that very few people do. Still, it is a fascinating museum. A man named Duncan Gibbs originally built the house as a Victorian summer retreat for himself and his family. It eventually became the full-time home for his two daughters, Alice and Janet. Neither ever married and money was apparently something of a concern for them, so the house was never really modernised or updated. I've been told they took some persuading to add electricity when it became readily available in Ramsey, and that was about the only change that they ever made. When they both passed away, in the nineteen-seventies, they left the house to the nation as a museum and we're very fortunate to have it. It's almost like a house-sized time capsule."

"It sounds fascinating," Lisa said. "I'm not sure why I've never visited."

"It's on the school tour circuit now, but it probably wasn't when you were at school," Mark replied. "Perhaps we need to do a better job of marketing our sites as interesting places to visit even if you don't have small children."

The car park at the museum was nearly empty. They made their way past pens that housed native Manx Loaghtan sheep before reaching the house itself.

It only took Lisa a few minutes to make the notes she needed. "The ticket system here is very straightforward," she remarked. "This one should be an easy switch, once the staff is trained on the new software."

"I hope they're all easy," Mark told her. "And I hope all of the staff share my enthusiasm for the changes."

"Hrumph." The elderly woman in Victorian dress who was working at the ticket window frowned and turned to look out the window. Lisa remembered that she was called Norma.

"Are you unhappy about the changes, Norma?" Lisa asked her.

"Not my place to complain," Norma replied without turning around.

"But if you share your concerns with me, I can make sure we address them," Lisa told her.

"I just don't want to fuss with a new system," the woman replied. "It's too many changes. We just got the current system a few years ago and it took me over a year to learn how to use it. I'll be dead and buried before I learn another one."

Lisa wrote a few notes in her notebook and then touched the woman on the shoulder. She waited until the older woman had turned around to look at her before speaking.

"I'm going to do everything I can to make this new system as easy for you to learn as possible," she promised. "I've taken notes on what you need to do to produce tickets now and I think I might even be able to make the new system more user-friendly than what you're doing now."

The woman shrugged. "Might be time for me to think about retiring, anyway," she told Lisa. The woman glanced at Mark and then moved away towards the front door of the building. A couple of new arrivals meant that Lisa had to drop the conversation.

"Let's take a quick walk through the building," Mark suggested. "We'll have to find time for a proper tour another day."

Lisa was fascinated by the intimate glimpse into the Victorian and Edwardian eras that the museum gave her. "The furniture is incredible," she said as they moved through the building. The kitchen was so unlike her much more modern equivalent that she could only stare at it.

"I like to cook," Mark told her. "But I'm not sure I would feel that way if I had to use this kitchen."

"I don't like to cook," Lisa replied. "And I would hate it even more in a kitchen like this."

Upstairs Lisa stared with grim fascination at the various objects that were made from human hair. "Why would you make stuff out of hair?" she asked Mark.

"It was quite common in the Victorian era," he told her. "Often they used the hair of someone who had recently passed away. It was seen as a way of remembering and commemorating that person."

"A seriously creepy way," Lisa said.

Mark laughed and led Lisa through the rest of the building. The active beehive caught her attention as well.

"Bees? Are they making honey?"

"That's sort of what bees do," Mark replied.

Lisa watched for several minutes as bees made their way in and out of the short tubes in the wall. The hive was actually inside the museum, but the tubes let the bees travel outside to collect pollen.

"You can buy honey from the hive in the gift shop," Mark told her.

"That's our next stop, right?" Lisa asked.

In the end, Mark insisted on buying Lisa a small jar of honey. "I need to keep you sweet to make the system installation go smoothly," he teased.

"And we get to do this all again tomorrow," Lisa laughed.

Back in Douglas, Mark dropped Lisa off at her home. "I don't live far away," he told her. "I'll pick you up here in the morning if you like. We have a very full schedule for tomorrow."

After agreeing to another nine o'clock start, Lisa settled in for a quiet evening at home. Darcy finally rang her back around eight.

"How's Europe?" she asked Darcy.

"Boring," Darcy answered. "I'm working with Finlo and he's definitely taken up with that woman I was telling you about. He rings her every time we land and he doesn't want to go out and have a drink after a long day or anything. Honestly, I suggested we could just go out as friends tonight, you know, since neither of us knows anyone in Prague, but he didn't want to risk upsetting Brittany."

"Brittany? That's a dumb name," Lisa said firmly.

"I know, right? Anyway, she's a dumb woman, although I should say girl, since I don't think she's any more than twenty-two."

"You're better off with Mark," Lisa replied. "He's really nice."

"You said in your message that you were going to be working with him," Darcy said. "How's that going?"

Lisa filled her friend in on her day. "Anyway, Mark seems as if he's going to be really good to work with," she concluded. "I'm actually looking forward to tomorrow."

Darcy sighed. "Maybe I need a new job," she said. "I'm really not looking forward to tomorrow. We have a whole planeload of London bankers to fly from Prague to Paris. Then we have to wait for them to conduct some business there before we fly them back to London. They'll be demanding and obnoxious and at least half of them will try to chat me up," she sighed again. "I'm getting too old for this."

"You have a good degree in business management," Lisa reminded her. "Maybe you should start using it."

"Anyway, at least it's Friday tomorrow," Darcy said. "And I have the weekend off. I'll come see you tomorrow night."

"What about Mark? Are you seeing him this weekend?"

"Probably," Darcy replied vaguely before begging off to get some sleep.

Friday morning was overcast with light drizzle, so Lisa was happy that Mark was picking her up at home. She didn't feel like going out in the rain any earlier than she absolutely had to. Mark's car pulled up in front of her house at exactly nine o'clock.

Lisa rushed out, locking her door behind her, before Mark felt obliged to get out of the car.

"I hate rain," she announced as she slid into her seat.

"You live in the wrong place," Mark told her.

"I love it here, otherwise," Lisa said. "I just wish the rain could limit itself to falling when I'm asleep."

"I suspect a lot of people would agree with that sentiment."

"So what's on the schedule for today?" Lisa asked.

"Castletown mostly," Mark told her. "There are five sites in or around Castletown, and then we have to head down to Cregneash as well."

"I've been to Castle Rushen for sure," Lisa told him. "But I think that's the only one I've visited in the south."

"I don't know how much time we'll have for sightseeing today," he replied. "But even if we just spend a few minutes at each site, you should get a feel for them. One day I'll have to give you proper tours of all of them."

"As you said yesterday, I'll have to spend some time at each site as the system goes in. Maybe you can give me proper tours on our lunch hour or something."

"I might just hold you to that," Mark grinned at her.

They rode in companionable silence for a while. Lisa watched out her window as the light rain turned into something altogether heavier.

"It's not going to be a great day for this," Mark said as they pulled into the car park for Rushen Abbey. "Unfortunately, we have to walk from here."

Lisa reached into her bag and pulled out a small folding umbrella. "I brought this," she said. She glanced out the car window. "I'm not sure it's up to the job, though."

Mark grinned. "I think I can do better than that," he told her. He reached into the back of the car and pulled out a large and sturdy-looking umbrella. Pulling it awkwardly between the seats, he handed it to Lisa and then dug around in the back again. After a moment he frowned.

"I think I did too good a job tidying," he said with a sigh. "I must have left my other brollie at home."

Lisa glanced back and realised that Mark had cleared out most of the junk that had filled the back of the car. Apparently, he'd cleaned out more than just the junk, though.

"I suppose we'll have to share," Lisa told him.

Mark grinned. "On three, then?"

Lisa counted to three and then threw open the car door. She extended the umbrella and pushed it open. The huge canopy advertised Manx National Heritage, which made her smile as Mark rushed around and dove underneath its protective cover. Lisa climbed out of the car and grabbed her bag as Mark held the umbrella over her.

"Off we go," she muttered as they fell into an awkward shuffling gait, jockeying for space under the umbrella. They headed for the entrance to the museum.

Inside Lisa shook her head gently and grinned as rain scattered around her. Maybe dogs had the right idea, she thought.

"I'm not sure the umbrella did either of us much good," she told Mark, as she noticed how wet he'd become.

"The wind was blowing the rain sideways," Mark replied. "Can't really do much about that."

At the desk Lisa spent several minutes looking over the computer system.

"This one is completely different from everything I've seen so far," she remarked.

"This site is one of the newer ones and we tried out a new ticketing system here. No one likes it, so everyone will be happy when this one goes," Mark told her.

"I can see why no one likes it," Lisa replied as she clicked through the various screens. "It makes what should be a quick and simple job far more difficult than it needs to be."

"It's complicated because we wanted to be able to tie all the sites together," Mark tried to explain. "But every time we added a new site to this system it added a page that needs to be clicked past in order to move on. Our IT guys and girls spent the best part of a year trying to simplify things here, before we decided to go with a whole new system and they gave up."

"And since then it has taken what, two more years, to actually get a new system agreed upon," Jane, the middle-aged woman behind the desk, spoke up. "And in the meantime, I've had to fight with this stupid thing every day."

Lisa smiled sympathetically. "I'll try to make yours one of the first sites we convert to the new system," she promised. "If you can make this thing work, you'll be an excellent person to test the new software on. You must have endless patience with computers."

Jane flushed. "If you can get that new system in here tomorrow, that'd be just fine by me," she told Lisa.

"It won't be tomorrow," Lisa told her. "But I will do my best to get it to you quickly." She made several notes in her notebook and then smiled at Mark.

"Okay, I'm done here," she told him.

"Great. I was going to suggest a tour of the site before we left, but I don't think this is the weather for it," he replied.

He did insist on showing her around the main museum building with its exhibits and displays that gave a history of the abbey and the subsequent uses of the site. Lisa stared at the model of the abbey for a moment.

"It's fascinating," she said as Mark pointed out various things. "I never really thought that much about how Henry VIII's changes would have affected so many people, even people here on the island, rather far away from him."

She peeked out the doorway that led to the site itself. Rain was still pouring down as she tried to see as much as she could of the ruins that were all that remained of the once flourishing Cistercian abbey.

"Another day I will take you around properly," Mark told her.

"I'll look forward to it," Lisa said.

On their way out, Mark grabbed a second umbrella from the small gift shop. "Put this on my account," he told the young woman behind the counter as he pulled the price tag off of it.

The walk back to the car was slightly drier and much easier with each of them carrying their own umbrella.

Mark drove the rest of the way into Castletown now, parking in a small car park behind the Old House of Keys building. "I thought we'd start at the Old Grammar School," he told Lisa. "They have the same system as the castle and the Old House of Keys. The Nautical Museum has a different system, because otherwise things would be too easy for you."

Lisa laughed. "Off we go, then."

They made their way across the car park to the tiny Old Grammar School building. The rain was still falling, although it was lighter and the wind had died down somewhat. Both Mark and Lisa still used their umbrellas, though.

"If we're lucky, it'll clear up some before we head to the Nautical Museum," Mark told her. "I'd rather walk if we can. It isn't really far, unless it's pouring."

Inside the small building, Lisa looked around. "I'm sure I've been here before," she said, almost to herself. "But I don't remember any of it, really."

Mark grinned. "The building was built around 1200 as a church for the good people of Castletown. In the 1500s it was converted into a school for boys and, believe it or not, it remained a school until 1930."

Lisa looked around the snug interior and shook her head. "1930 doesn't seem that long ago," she said. "But I can't imagine taking classes in this tiny space."

Mark showed her the small computer that was used for printing tickets. "There is no charge for visiting this site," Mark told her. "But we provide our guests with a chance to purchase tickets for the other sites here, as well as multi-site tickets."

Lisa poked around the computer for just a few minutes. The system they were using, while different to the others, seemed straightforward enough. "I think I've seen everything I need to see," she told Mark.

"Is the new system going to be hard to learn?" the older woman who'd been standing nearby asked in a timid voice.

"I hope not," Lisa told her with a grin. "I need to learn it next week."

The woman smiled. "It's just that I've only just mastered this system, you see," she said. "And I'm not sure I'm up to learning a whole new thing."

"From what I've seen of the new system so far, I think you'll find it is very similar to what you already have," Lisa told her. "I'm hoping we can customise the interfaces at each site to make everyone as comfortable as possible with any changes. The biggest differences, however, will be with the reporting capabilities, and that isn't your problem at all. Mark has to worry about that."

"Lucky him," the woman laughed.

"I'll be handing each installation personally," Lisa continued. "Please feel free to ask as many questions as you need to as we go along. I plan to write a basic instruction manual for each site as well, so hopefully after we've finished you will always have an easy reference guide."

"That all sounds wonderful," the woman told her. "I'll be keeping my fingers crossed it all works out."

"Me too," Lisa told her with a grin.

"I think the House of Keys is probably next," Mark told her. "And then we can try to squeeze the castle in as well before lunch."

Lisa nodded, still adding notes to her notebook as they walked the short distance from the school to the Old House of Keys building. Luckily the rain had stopped, although the air still felt quite damp.

"You probably haven't been here," Mark said as they stepped into the foyer of the building. "It opened in 2001, but we don't get regular school groups through, at least not yet."

Lisa nodded. "I vaguely remember reading about it opening, but visiting was never something that appealed to me."

Mark shook his head. "Some day, when we have some extra time, I want you to tell me what we could do to make our sites more appealing to people just like you," he told her.

The House of Keys computer system was the same as the one Lisa had just seen at the Old Grammar School.

"Tickets here are timed," the man behind the ticket desk told her solemnly. "We only admit a set number of people at each time and the presentation takes forty-five minutes. I'd love it if the new system would stop letting other sites sell tickets for here. Do you have any idea how many people buy tickets elsewhere and then never show up here? Or how many turn up late and expect us to let them in anyway? It's very disturbing."

Lisa made a note of his concerns. "We'll have to see if we can find a way to make things easier for you here, while still providing visitors with a chance to purchase their tickets wherever it is most convenient for them," she told him.

"Will you be staying for the next presentation?" he asked her.

"I wish I could," she replied, mostly truthfully. "But we have several more sites to visit before heading across on Sunday. I'll have to make a point of seeing it once I'm down here working."

"I hope a somewhat late lunch is okay?" Mark asked as they left the building. "I'd like to tick the castle off our list before we get lunch, and I know a great little restaurant almost next door to the Nautical Museum."

"I'll see if I can hurry even faster at the castle," Lisa told him with a grin. "I'm starving."

She didn't need long at Castle Rushen. The system, as promised, was identical to the one she'd already seen twice. "The only thing I can remember about this place is the peacock on a tray," she told Mark as she clicked through the computer screens.

Mark laughed. "There is a lot more to it than just that one display," he told her. "But there certainly isn't time to go around here today."

The rain held off as they left the castle and headed for the Nautical Museum. Just a few doors down from their goal was the restaurant Mark had mentioned.

"I hope you like Italian food," Mark said as he held open the restaurant door for her.

"I love it," she assured him. And she loved every bite of the garlic bread, salad and spaghetti Bolognese that she ordered.

At the Nautical Museum she quickly investigated the computer system. "It's very basic," she commented.

"It is indeed," Mark told her. "It was one of the first sites to get a computerised ticketing system and we've never upgraded it. At the moment, you can't buy tickets here for other sites, which is one reason why we're eager to get this place converted."

The museum itself was fairly compact, so Mark took the time to give Lisa a quick tour. "You need to see the Peggy," he told her.

The ship that had been built around 1790 had later been left for a hundred years, walled up within her boathouse. Lisa was impressed by its story and by the trapdoors and hidden panels in the house that was now the museum.

"The island certainly has had its fair share of characters," she said to Mark as they emerged from the museum.

"And it still does," he replied. "Or don't you follow Manx politics?"

Lisa laughed. The pair made their way back to the car park as a light rain fell again. Neither bothered with their umbrellas, as the rain felt more like a mist that surrounded them than something falling from the sky.

"I'm rather soaked," Lisa said as an apology as she climbed into the car.

"As am I," Mark said with a shrug. "It's not the first time this car has been full of damp passengers. I've often brought full carloads of people from digs at the abbey back into Douglas after a sudden rainstorm. Then everyone is wet and also muddy. I suppose that's another reason why I don't have a fancy car."

Lisa watched out the window as he drove carefully south, heading for Cregneash Village. They drove around the outskirts of Port St. Mary.

"I've always thought it would be nice to live down here," Lisa remarked.

"It has a very different feel to the north of the island," Mark said. "I stayed down here for a few months when I first arrived, but never really felt settled for some reason. The people who do live down here seem to love it, though."

"I went out with a guy from Port Erin when I was in school," Lisa told him. "We met in a bar in Douglas and he used to drive up every weekend to see me. In the end, the distance was too much for us, though."

Mark laughed. "And yet they are only what, twenty or twenty-five minutes apart? The Manx have their own strange sense of distance."

Lisa grinned. "My parents looked at retiring to Ramsey when they started building some nice communities up there, but they decided they didn't want to be that far away from everything."

Cregneash Village felt like falling backwards through time to Lisa. It was too late in the day for them to tour the whole site, but Lisa felt like she had a good feel for it from just the ticket and information building.

After she'd poked around the computer system for a bit, she followed Mark back outside. "Yet another site I want to see more of," she sighed. "When will I find time to do all my work?"

Mark laughed. "We'll have to plan your days very carefully," he told her. "If we're quick, we can probably tour a site on your lunch hour every day."

"You're going to have enough to do without spending your free time dragging me around the sites," Lisa argued.

"I'll enjoy it," he told her. "You seem like you'll be an appreciative audience."

"I'll certainly try," she laughed.

"Let's just walk over to Harry Kelly's cottage," Mark suggested. "You can see how the Manx really lived a hundred years or so ago."

Inside the small cottage, Lisa shook her head. "I can't imagine living in such a small space, especially with a family," she said. "My house feels small to me, and I live alone."

The pair made their way back to Mark's car and headed back towards Douglas.

"I'm exhausted," Lisa told Mark. "I'm glad that's all the sites. I just hope I can get some extra rest before we fly out on Sunday."

"Of course that isn't really all of the sites that MNH is responsible for," Mark told her. "For instance, we look after the Sound and have a café there. For now, we're concentrating on the historical sites, but we are hoping, eventually, to include the other sites as well. The café at the Sound doesn't currently use computers at all, but eventually we'd like to integrate it into the system for inventories and the like. I suppose it would be handy if they could sell site tickets down there as well."

Lisa nodded and added to her notes. "And, of course, there's always a chance that you'll add new sites or museums to your collection. The new system has to be able to accommodate such things in the future, as well."

Mark dropped Lisa off at home. "Shall I collect you on my way to Ronaldsway on Sunday?" he asked.

"That would be great," Lisa replied. "No point in both of us paying for parking for a week."

Mark laughed. "MNH has a few permanent spots down there that we're allowed to use when we travel on island business. Just don't tell anyone about them."

Lisa laughed. "Since I'm going to be taking advantage of one of them, I certainly won't."

A long hot bath with truffles and a new romance novel put Lisa in a wonderful mood for the evening. She was excited about the new project and had really enjoyed working with Mark so far. Saturday would be all about being lazy, she decided as she snuggled down under the covers.

6

Saturday was grey and miserable. Lisa did her laundry and then ironed everything that needed it. She wanted to make sure she had a full complement of professional-looking outfits for the week ahead. By lunchtime she was finished with her basic packing. The rest would have to wait until Sunday. She couldn't very well pack her hair dryer or her makeup before she'd used them the next day.

After lunch, she was just settling in with another good book when her doorbell rang. As she crossed to the door, it rang again. Has to be Darcy, she told herself. No one else was that impatient.

Darcy swept into Lisa's house the second she opened the door. "You have to get ready," she told Lisa. "Fix your hair and put on some makeup."

Lisa shook her head. "Go away, Darce," she said. "I'm having a relaxing day before I fly away for a week tomorrow."

"Oh, yeah, isn't that weird?" Darcy grinned at her. "You're going away for a week with the guy I'm dating."

"It's work," Lisa said.

"Oh, I know, no worries," Darcy waved an exquisitely manicured hand in the air. "Anyway, the guy you're dating will be here any minute. You need to get ready."

"Darcy, what have you done now?" Lisa demanded anxiously.

"I've found you the perfect man," Darcy told her.

Lisa laughed. "That's what you said last time," she reminded her friend. "That one was a dud, so you'll have to forgive me if I don't get excited about this one."

"You don't have to get excited," Darcy told her. "But you should. This one is really amazing. If I weren't already dating Mark, I'd be tempted."

Lisa rolled her eyes. "Like I believe that," she said with a snort. "Look, I told you I'm not looking for a man. Can't you just leave me alone?"

Darcy laughed. "You'll thank me one day," she told her friend. "When I'm acting as maid of honour at your wedding, you'll thank me for interfering in your life."

Lisa shook her head. "Whatever, but today really isn't a good day. I have to do laundry and iron and pack and get things ready for tomorrow."

"If I went and looked on your bed, I bet I'd find your suitcase already ninety per cent packed and ready to go," Darcy said.

Lisa sighed. Darcy knew her too well. "I still want a relaxing day," she told her friend. "Going out with a total stranger is not relaxing."

Darcy's reply was cut off by the doorbell. "He's here," Darcy told her. "And we didn't fix you up at all."

Lisa shrugged. Her hair was in a loose ponytail and she hadn't put on any makeup. She was wearing her oldest and most comfortable jogging bottoms and an oversized T-shirt. At least she'd taken the time to put on a bra. She sometimes didn't when she was relaxing at home.

As the doorbell rang again, Lisa crossed to the door and pulled it open. The man behind it made her gasp. He had to be at least six-four and his shoulders looked almost as broad as he was tall. He had a deep tan that set off his blond hair and brilliant blue eyes gorgeously.

"You must be Lisa," he said with a bright smile. "I'm Brad Johnson. I do hope that Darcy told you I was stopping by."

Lisa nodded and took a step backwards, pulling the door open as far as it would go. His shoulders barely fit through the frame.

"Hi, Brad," Darcy cooed from across the room. She crossed over and gave him a welcoming hug. "It's great to see you again."

"You too," Brad told her. He engulfed Darcy in a bear hug as Lisa pushed her door shut.

"I just arrived," Darcy was telling Brad. "So I didn't get a chance to tell Lisa anything about you."

"I suppose I can fill her in, then," Brad laughed. He turned to Lisa and gave her another dazzling smile. "Darcy was part of the crew that flew me back from an event in Birmingham. We got to talking and she thought I'd be perfect for you. I'm always up for new adventures, so here I am."

Lisa forced herself to smile. "What sort of event?" she asked.

"Weight lifting," Brad replied. "I'm really into fitness and body building."

"I would have guessed that," Lisa told him.

He laughed. "Yeah, I imagine it's pretty obvious," he acknowledged. "Anyway, I'm so excited to meet you. Darcy told me all about you. I hope you're ready to go."

"Ready to go where?" Lisa asked apprehensively.

"I thought it would be a fun first date if we tried hiking a few glens," Brad beamed at her.

"It's pouring," Lisa pointed out.

"You have Wellies, right?" Brad asked.

"Maybe, somewhere," Lisa said faintly. This giant hulk of a man wanted to go hiking in the glens in the pouring rain? He was gorgeous, but he was totally wrong for her. She looked over at Darcy.

"I'm sure I saw your Wellies in the back of your wardrobe," Darcy said. "Come on, I'll help you find them."

"He wants to go hiking in the rain," Lisa hissed to Darcy as she pushed her bedroom door shut.

"It's romantic," Darcy replied.

"It's stupid."

"He's gorgeous," Darcy pointed out.

"Yeah, if you like men who can bench press a car. He's really not my type. Besides, he's blond."

"I'm pretty sure that's fake," Darcy told her. "Anyway, just give him a chance."

"Hiking in the rain? You know I hate rain. And I'm not terribly fond of hiking."

"Okay," Darcy sighed dramatically. "I'll get rid of him, if that's what you want."

Lisa opened her mouth to agree and then sighed. Darcy was only trying to help and Brad seemed like a nice enough guy. A short hike in the rain wouldn't kill her, and it would get Darcy off her back.

"I'm going to go," she told Darcy. "But this is the last blind date, do you hear me?"

"No," Darcy grinned. "I'm not listening."

Lisa rolled her eyes as Darcy turned her back. Two minutes later Darcy emerged from Lisa's wardrobe holding her Wellies aloft. "Found them," she announced.

"Oh, joy," Lisa replied.

"Surely that isn't what you're wearing," Darcy said, looking Lisa up and down. "I can't believe that's what you were wearing around the house, actually."

"I was doing laundry," Lisa told her, blushing under her critical gaze. "There isn't much point in putting on anything nicer, though. It is wet and cold out there. Whatever I wear is going to get soaked and muddy."

Darcy was ignoring her, flipping through her wardrobe. "How about these?" she asked eventually, holding up a pair of black trousers. "They've certainly seen better days."

Lisa shook her head. "I've agreed to go hiking with your mountain-like friend. I'm not dressing up for the experience."

Darcy looked like she wanted to argue, but she didn't. "What about your hair and makeup?" she asked instead.

"Nothing more attractive than a woman hiking in the rain with makeup running down her face, right?"

Darcy laughed. "I suppose you're right," she said with a sigh. "At least brush your hair and pull it back properly."

Lisa stuck out her tongue at her friend, but complied. "Better?"

"A bit."

Brad was exactly where they'd left him in the foyer. He was busily doing squats as they emerged from Lisa's bedroom.

"Did you want to do any warming up?" he asked Lisa as she began to pull on her boots.

"I think I'm okay," she answered him, shooting Darcy a nasty look.

"You two have a wonderful time," Darcy said, giving them both a huge smile. "I need to dash home and get ready for my dinner date with Mark."

"Are you staying here tonight?" Lisa asked her. Darcy often stayed over when she had evening plans in the Douglas area.

"Maybe," Darcy said with a shrug. "I'll try to let myself in quietly if I do."

Lisa nodded and then forced herself to smile at Brad. "Let's do this," she said with as much enthusiasm as she could muster.

She found a raincoat on the hooks by the front door and zipped it up, pulling the hood over her head. Brad hadn't bothered with such things and he didn't seem to notice the cold wind that was blowing as they stepped outside, either.

"Brrr," Lisa muttered.

"It's a little fresh," Brad told her. "But once you get your blood pumping, it'll feel great."

Lisa nodded uncertainly. What would feel great was being curled up on her couch with a book. She just hoped this would be bearable. She gave herself a mental shake. Darcy was trying to be nice and she needed to give Brad a fair chance. He seemed like a really nice person. Maybe they had more in common than she realised.

"I thought we could start at Molly Quirk's and then hike over to Groudle. After that we'll have to see what we feel like."

Lisa followed Brad down towards the promenade. Gradually it dawned on her that he intended to walk to the glen.

"Um, how far is it to the glen?" she asked.

"Oh, maybe two or three miles," Brad told her cheerfully. "I know it's a bit wet and cold, but it isn't a bad walk, really."

"I would have driven if you wanted me to," Lisa told him.

"Oh, no," he said. "I never drive anywhere. I have a bike, for longer journeys, but cars are so bad for the environment I simply can't justify having one. I try not to fly either, but sometimes I just have to. I couldn't very well bike to Birmingham, could I?"

"I'm surprised you didn't take the ferry," Lisa replied. "Surely that's better for the environment?"

Brad wrinkled his nose. "It's hard to be certain," he told her. "They both use fossil fuels, but the ferry takes a lot longer. I let myself take one trip a year, but I'm thinking about cutting back."

"What is it you do?" Lisa asked curiously.

"I work at *Veggies*," he told her, naming the island's premier vegetarian restaurant. "I'm the assistant manager."

"I've never actually tried *Veggies*," Lisa told him. "What's your most popular item?"

"We get a lot of customers who order the fake meat stuff, you know, tofu flavoured like chicken or whatever, but I think that's cheating. We're working on adding more vegan options, and I'd love to go totally vegan one day."

"So you're a vegetarian?" Lisa checked.

"Oh, yes," Brad said enthusiastically. "And I've never felt better. After our walk, maybe we could go and get some dinner at *Veggies*."

"Maybe," was as far as Lisa was willing to go. "I might be too tired after all this walking."

"We've only just started," Brad told her. They were heading away from Douglas now, up the steep hill that led towards the glen, and Lisa stopped trying to make conversation in favour of breathing. After what felt like hours, they finally reached the wooded glen.

"At least there's some shelter from the rain," Lisa muttered as they began to make their way along the path through the trees.

"Isn't it wonderful?" Brad asked, turning slowly in a full circle and breathing in deeply. "I could live in here forever."

Lisa looked around at the wet woodlands and shook her head. "It's nice for a stroll, but I wouldn't want to live here," she told him.

"Where's your sense of adventure?" he demanded. "Think how amazing it would be, falling asleep every night under the stars and then waking up with birds calling and the sun rising."

Lisa saw the genuine passion in his face and couldn't bring herself to mention the bugs, the weather, or the lack of toilet facilities.

"That's another reason why I don't have a car," he told her. "I'm saving every penny I can towards property."

"You want to buy a house?" Lisa asked.

"Oh, no, I want to buy land," he said. "Somewhere off the beaten path where I can build a little cabin and live with only nature for neighbours."

Lisa nodded and forced herself to smile. This man was so not for her. "How nice," she said.

"It will be amazing," he told her. Brad spent the next half hour filling Lisa in on every aspect of his dream. By the time they'd walked from one glen to the next, Lisa knew far more than she wanted to about various natural building materials, composting toilets, and how to collect rainwater for all of your household needs.

"Of course, it'll be years before I'm able to fulfill my dream. Well, unless I find someone else who shares it with me and is willing to help finance it," he concluded eventually.

"Good luck with that," Lisa told him.

Brad's face fell. "You aren't even a little bit interested, are you?" he asked.

"Sorry," she replied. "But I'm not really the outdoorsy type. I like my creature comforts and I can't imagine not having electricity and running water. I work in IT, for heaven's sake."

Brad gave her a grin that looked forced. "I thought maybe, since you weren't the type to fuss with your hair and makeup, that you might be the sort of woman I need."

"I'm sorry to disappoint you," she said sincerely. "But I'm really not."

They continued their walk for several minutes in silence while Lisa mentally berated Darcy for putting her in this situation.

"I don't suppose you know any women that might be more my type?" Brad finally broke the silence to ask.

Lisa thought hard. "No one off the top of my head," she said. "I will give it some thought, though."

"I'd appreciate that," Brad said eagerly. "I just know that somewhere out there, there's a woman who wants the same things I want."

Lisa wasn't nearly as certain, but she didn't tell Brad that. Just then they rounded a corner, and Lisa sighed.

"What an amazing view," she said as she took in the babbling stream that ran alongside the path they were taking. It felt like they were hundreds of miles away from the rest of the world and she suddenly understood a little bit of what Brad was talking about.

"Nature is my favourite thing in the world," Brad told her. "Exercise comes second."

Lisa bit her tongue. Chocolate and books were probably her top two, but she didn't feel like she ought to share that with Brad.

They walked on in silence for a little while longer. Finally, Lisa realised she could hear road noises. It was something of a relief to her to see a car go past as they got closer to the road.

"Well, where do we go next?" Brad asked her. "We can hike along the coast towards Clay Head."

"I think I really need to get back," she replied. She looked at her watch. "It's nearly five o'clock," she said in surprise. "I need an early night. I have a plane to catch tomorrow."

Brad gave her a sad look. "Are you sure? We could just do another hour and then turn around."

Lisa shook her head. "We've already walked for well over two hours," she told him. "If we turn around now I won't get home until after seven. I really need to get back."

Brad frowned. "If you insist," he said in a sullen voice. "But we've come this far. It seems a shame not to keep going."

Lisa gave him a tight smile. "Here's an idea," she said. "You keep going. I'll ring a friend and see if I can get a ride back to Douglas."

Brad seemed to give the idea a lot of thought before he replied. "I don't know," he said slowly. "It seems wrong to leave you in the middle of a date."

"It's fine," Lisa assured him. "If you want to keep going, you should. I really need to get a ride home anyway, if I'm going to have time to get everything together for tomorrow."

Brad hesitated for only a moment longer. "If you're sure," he said.

"I'm sure," Lisa told him firmly. "You go on."

She watched for a moment as he strode away towards the coast, and then she sighed deeply. She pulled out her phone and rang Darcy's mobile.

"Come and get me," she told her friend as soon as she answered.

"I'm supposed to be meeting Mark in a couple of hours," Darcy wailed. "I have to get ready."

"Mark won't care how you look," Lisa told her. "And I'm soaked through and freezing."

Darcy laughed. "Where are you?"

Fifteen minutes later her friend arrived in her sleek black sports car. Lisa climbed in gratefully.

"I'd have been here sooner, but I stopped off for this," Darcy told her as she handed Lisa a cup of hot tea. Lisa took a sip and slumped back on the leather seat.

"I'm getting your leather all wet," she told her friend.

"Don't worry about it," Darcy replied. "It's about time for me to trade this one in anyway."

"Can we turn up the heat?" Lisa asked.

Darcy flipped a switch and the car began to fill with warm air. Lisa sighed deeply. "That's wonderful," she told Darcy.

"So was it awful?" Darcy asked nervously.

Lisa thought for a moment. "No, it wasn't awful," she admitted. "Brad is a really nice guy and some parts of the walk were beautiful."

"But?" Darcy demanded. "I know you, there has to be a 'but' coming."

Lisa laughed. "But he isn't the right man for me and I'm freezing besides."

Darcy nodded. "Should I ask what you did with him? I thought, for some reason, that I would be collecting you both."

Lisa laughed again. "He wanted to keep going," she explained. "I had had enough."

Darcy took Lisa back to her luxury flat near the airport and the pair chatted while Darcy got ready for her date. Darcy dropped Lisa off at home before heading out to meet Mark at a new little French restaurant that had just opened in Onchan.

"I'll probably crash here tonight," Darcy told her as Lisa got out of the car. "That way I'll get to see you in the morning before you leave."

"Mark is meant to be picking me up on his way to the airport," she told Darcy. "You can see us both off."

"Sounds good."

Lisa soaked her aching and frozen muscles in a hot bath until she began to feel more like herself. She made a bacon butty for her evening meal, wondering what Brad would say if he could see her happily chomping her way through it. She was curled up with a book a few hours later when Darcy came in.

"How was dinner?" Lisa asked her.

"It was lovely," Darcy answered with a huge smile. "Mark is such a gentleman. He's polite and smart and nice and kind." She sighed. "Maybe I've finally found a man who isn't going to play games with me."

She gave Lisa a mouth-watering account of their meal. "The food was amazing," she said with a sigh. "I love French food. Maybe I need a long weekend in Paris."

"Too bad Mark is pretty tied up with work at the moment," Lisa replied.

"Yeah, how long is this project going to take?" Darcy asked her.

"I'm hoping to have everything wrapped up before the end of November," Lisa told her. "But that might be optimistic. I haven't committed to a firm timetable yet. I need to get through the training sessions first."

"As long as you get it all done by Christmas, then maybe Mark and I can spend New Year's Eve in Paris," Darcy said dreamily. "If I plan it right, maybe I can get us booked on Finlo's flight. He always spends New Year's Eve in Paris."

Lisa shot her a suspicious look. "You aren't still hung up on Finlo, are you? That wouldn't be very fair to Mark."

"I was never 'hung up' on Finlo," Darcy protested. "But I do love the idea of seeing his face as I climb onto one of his planes as a passenger."

"I'm not sure Mark could afford to fly you both to Paris," Lisa told her. "I don't get the feeling that MNH pays all that well."

Darcy shrugged. "You have to get your project sorted out first," she reminded Lisa. "Then I'll sort out Paris."

A short while later the friends headed for bed. Lisa checked that she'd packed everything she could, adding her face wash cream that she only used at night to the growing pile on her chest of drawers. Mark was picking her up at one o'clock, so she'd have plenty of time in the morning to finish packing.

She and Darcy both slept late the next day. Once they were up, Darcy made pancakes for them, with lots of crispy bacon to go with it.

"I've now had bacon two days in a row," Lisa giggled. "And you tried to fix me up with a vegetarian."

"Brad's a vegetarian?" Darcy asked. "I didn't know you could grow muscles that big with vegetables."

Lisa shrugged. "I don't know. Maybe he's only recently gone veggie."

After their late breakfast, Lisa took a shower and got dressed in smart but comfortable clothes for the journey. She fixed her hair and added a light dusting of makeup before she finished her packing.

"Have a wonderful time," Darcy told her as they watched for Mark to arrive. "And remember you need to have the whole project done before Christmas so I can celebrate the New Year in Paris."

Lisa laughed, but she worried that Darcy was serious. She wasn't sure that Mark was a New Year's Eve in Paris kind of guy.

"Of course, we have Joney's wedding to get through before that," Darcy added. "Don't worry, I haven't given up on finding you a date."

Lisa just ignored her and watched for the car. It was overcast but dry as Mark pulled up in front of Lisa's house. When he reached Lisa's front door, Darcy opened it. Mark gave her a quick hug before turning to Lisa.

"All ready to go?" he asked.

"I am," Lisa told him. She checked again that she had her laptop and her notebook and then handed Mark her small suitcase.

"Where's your other case?" Darcy asked as Mark headed back out the door.

"That's all I'm taking," Lisa told her.

"But you're going away for a week," Darcy said. "I take more than that when I go away overnight."

Lisa laughed. "I have more than enough in that case for the week," she assured her friend.

Darcy followed Mark out of the house, still shaking her head. Lisa locked up her door and followed the pair down the short path to the street.

"I hope you'll ring me once or twice while you're gone," Darcy told Mark coyly.

"If I can find the time," he replied.

Darcy didn't look happy at the reply, but Mark was busy stowing Lisa's bag in his boot and apparently didn't notice.

Lisa climbed into his passenger seat and waved to her friend. "Try to stay out of trouble while I'm gone," she teased Darcy.

"I'll be good," Darcy laughed.

Mark was behind the wheel now and he started the car.

"And no more blind dates," Lisa called to Darcy as Mark began to pull away.

Darcy held a hand to her ear, as if she couldn't hear what Lisa had said. Lisa sighed.

7

"She didn't fix you up on another blind date?" Mark asked as they made their way to the airport. "Not after the last one."

"She did," Lisa told him with a laugh. "And wait until you hear about this one."

Mark almost had to pull over, he was laughing so hard, as Lisa told him about Brad and their hiking date. "He made you walk all the way to Molly Quirk's from your house?" he asked when she'd run through the highlights.

"He doesn't have a car," Lisa explained. "And it was such a nice day for a walk."

Mark laughed again. "I was helping out at Rushen Abbey for most of yesterday. It was wet and cold and miserable. I can't believe you went hiking in that weather."

"Darcy has a real knack for finding unusual men," she told Mark. "Sometime I'll have to tell you about some of the guys she fixed me up with at university."

"Why do you still let her do it?" he demanded.

Lisa shook her head. "I ask myself that all the time," she replied. "Actually, she did really well once. She introduced me to a terrific guy and we dated for quite a while. I suppose I'm hoping she'll find someone like him again."

"What went wrong?" Mark asked.

Lisa shrugged. "I wanted to come back to the island and he wanted to make his fortune in London. In the end, my family and my home won out over him."

"I can see that," Mark told her. "I had a girlfriend when I first came over. We tried the long distance thing, but that was a nightmare. After a few months, she came over for a few weeks, but she just didn't like the island. She couldn't wait to get back to London. When she left, we broke up. I wasn't going to go back, and she was never going to be happy here."

Lisa sighed. "Darcy and I have this wedding to go to in December and she's determined to find me a date for it. I just wish I knew where to meet nice guys that aren't body-building vegans or *Hungry Monsters* obsessives."

Mark laughed. "I'm going to see what I can do about that," he promised. "When we get back, I'll see who I know that's currently single."

Lisa shook her head. "No offense, but I'm not sure I want to be fixed up again."

"At least give me a chance," he replied. "I've got to be better at it than Darcy."

Lisa laughed and then shrugged. Hopefully he'd forget all about it once they got back.

At the airport, they quickly made their way to the Quayle Airways section of the building. They checked in with the pretty blonde receptionist, who took their bags and carefully marked them for their destination.

"Would you like a hot or cold drink while you wait?" she asked. "It's a little early for alcohol, but I can probably find a bottle of wine if you'd like a glass."

"I'd love a fizzy drink," Lisa replied. She had been kidding about trying to bankrupt Finlo by eating and drinking everything she could get, but she was thirsty and the woman had offered. A few minutes later, while Lisa sipped her drink, the man himself walked in.

"Hey, Cara, do I really have to fly to Blackpool today?" he asked the girl behind the desk.

"Yes, sir," she answered smartly. "Your passengers are already here." The girl gestured towards Lisa and Mark as Finlo turned towards them.

"Hey, Finlo, don't tell me you don't like Blackpool," Lisa said with a grin. "All those bright lights and happy people?"

Finlo grinned at her. "Lisa, why on earth are you going to Blackpool?"

"I'm working with MNH on their IT project," she explained.

"Ah, that's explains why you're travelling with a disreputable man like Mark Blake," Finlo replied.

"Hey, you gave us such a great deal, we couldn't turn you down," Mark told him.

Finlo frowned deeply. "Cara, did we give them a good deal?" he demanded.

The young girl looked flustered and tapped on her keyboard. "I'm not sure, sir," she said after a moment. "I don't generally handle billing, but everything seems in order. I'm not familiar with your normal rates for trips to Blackpool, though. I can ring Margo in billing if you want."

Finlo laughed. "I'm just teasing," he told the girl. "Relax, they probably got a fabulous deal. I'm sure William made the booking for them and he's Margo's favourite nephew." Finlo sighed extravagantly. "Never hire your family," he told Cara. "They just give crazy discounts to the rest of the family."

He turned back to Lisa and Mark. "Are you two ready to go?" he asked. "If so, we can get out there and see if we can get an earlier take-off slot."

Lisa quickly finished her drink and jumped up. "I'm ready when you are," she said.

"Terrific."

Mark was quick to rise from his seat as well. "The sooner we get there the better," he commented. "We still have to drive from Blackpool to Morecombe after we arrive."

"How's Darcy?" Finlo asked Lisa as they made their way across the tarmac towards the small private plane.

"You should ask Mark," Lisa told him. "They had dinner together last night."

Finlo chuckled. "I saw you two together at the House of Manannan party, but I didn't realise you were dating now," he told Mark. "Good luck."

"What that's supposed to mean?" Mark demanded.

"Darcy's a handful, that's all," Finlo told him.

Jack, one of Finlo's co-pilots, was waiting for them at the plane. "Climb on up," he told the pair. "We're just taking the little plane today, so no cabin service, I'm afraid, but you can help yourselves to the drinks and snacks."

Lisa climbed into the small plane and sat down in the first seat on the left. Mark followed her and sat across the tiny aisle from her. They both fastened their seatbelts, and then Lisa opened the small refrigerator that was right in front of her.

"Cold drink?" she asked Mark. "It looks like the usual assortment of fizzy drinks, but there's wine, too. Oooohh, look," she giggled. "Champagne." She held up the tiny individual-sized bottle of champagne. "Want to share one?" she asked.

Mark laughed. "One of us has to drive when we land," he reminded her. "You go ahead and have some wine or champagne if you want. I'm happy to drive, but I won't drink if I'm doing so."

Lisa shrugged. "I don't really want a drink," she told him. "It's only half two, after all. Maybe we should smuggle a few of these out with us, though. We could have a drink together tonight in my room."

Mark grinned at her. "That sounds like a better plan."

Lisa giggled and then pulled out two bottles of champagne. She slipped them into her handbag, glancing around guiltily while she did so. A second later, the airplane's door slid shut and Finlo's voice came over the tannoy.

"Yes, I can see what you're up to," he told Lisa. "But by all means, take a couple bottles of champagne. I've been to Morecombe. You're going to need the drink."

Lisa flushed and stuck her tongue out at the camera she now spotted, high up on the wall in front of her.

"Saw that, too," Finlo laughed. "Settle back and have a snack. It isn't far to Blackpool and we've just been told we can have an earlier take-off slot, so we're just about off. I have thirty-odd minutes of journey time to persuade the folks in Blackpool to let us land early as well."

"He probably has a hot date to get back for," Lisa told Mark with a scowl.

"What's the story with him and Darcy?" Mark asked.

Lisa frowned. "You really should ask Darcy that," she replied, looking out the window as if suddenly fascinated by the side of the building, which was all she could see.

Mark chuckled. "Okay, so that's a topic we can't discuss," he said. "What shall we talk about?"

"What's in the cupboard on your side?" Lisa asked.

Mark pulled open the cupboard in front of him, and Lisa gasped. It was full of miniature packets of biscuits, cakes, crisps and nuts.

"I should have brought my biggest handbag," Lisa muttered.

Mark laughed. "Haven't you ever flown with Quayle Airways before?" he asked.

"No. I've always flown standard commercial, even though Darcy's worked for Finlo for years. This is the first time I've needed to get somewhere that the commercial services weren't going."

"MNH tends to use Finlo wherever we're going," he told Lisa. "Finlo was right. He gives us great deals."

"I understand he can afford it," Lisa replied tartly.

Mark shrugged. "I suppose so," he said. "He seems to do okay."

"I've been to his penthouse flat," Lisa told him. "He's doing quite a bit better than okay."

The plane was now taxiing down the runway, so Lisa had to stay in her seat. She got Mark to pass her one of each of the varieties of small packets of treats, and inspected each one before deciding whether she wanted to try its contents or not. When the tray in front of her was filled to overflowing with things she wanted to try, she had to stop.

"This isn't all going to fit in my bag," she said sadly. "I'll have to put some of it back."

"Some of it might fit in my laptop bag," Mark said helpfully. He pulled his bag up and unzipped a side pocket. "Give me the biscuits and crackers and things that are flat," he told her. Lisa passed him a few packets and grinned as he slid them into the pocket.

After zipping it shut, he opened the top of the case. "There should be room for a few bags of crisps up here," he told Lisa, showing her the gap between the top of his computer and the top of the bag. Lisa passed him three bags of crisps, and he arranged them carefully to fill the space.

"I'm sure they're giving my laptop extra protection," he told Lisa with a smile.

Lisa opened her handbag and dumped as much of what remained into it as she could. The few packs that remained got tucked into her own laptop bag.

They were now flying over the sea and Lisa looked out the window and gasped. "We don't seem to be flying very high," she said.

"It's a small plane," Mark said, his tone unconcerned.

Lisa watched out the window for a while. "Oh, I can see land," she told Mark. She watched eagerly to see what she could recognise from the famous Blackpool landscape.

"I can see Blackpool Tower," Mark told her after a few minutes.

"Where?" Lisa asked eagerly.

Of course. She was on the wrong side of the plane. She sighed deeply a moment before the plane went into a steep turn and suddenly she could see the tower as well.

"Oh, hurray," she shouted. "I can see it now."

Mark laughed. "You really need to get out more," he teased her.

"I've never actually been to Blackpool," she told him. "My parents weren't big on holidays, really. When we did go anywhere, it was always to visit relatives in places like Chesterfield or Derby. We never took any proper holidays anywhere."

"We did continental holidays," Mark told her. "But my university mates and I used to drive up to Blackpool for long weekends once in a while. It's fun and appalling in equal measure."

Lisa nodded. "I hope, one day, to drag my kids here for at least one holiday. I know it's meant to be tacky and all that, but I really want to see it for myself."

"I wish we had time for a short visit today," Mark said, looking at his watch. "But I'd rather get to Morecombe before it starts to get dark."

Lisa nodded. "I know. This is business, not pleasure. At least I've seen the tower now."

A moment later they landed at Blackpool airport. They taxied to a stop and, after a brief wait, the door to the cabin popped open. Jack grinned at them.

"We're here," he said.

Lisa stood up and collected her bags. She climbed out the door carefully and made her way down the steps. Mark was right behind her.

"Careful with your bags," Finlo cautioned her when she reached the bottom of the stairs. "You don't want to crush all those cakes and crisps."

Lisa flushed and then lifted her chin. She wasn't going to feel guilty about taking a few treats from the plane. Finlo could certainly afford them and besides, her fare must have included some portion for refreshments on the flight.

Finlo escorted them to the terminal building. "Your checked bags will be here in a minute," he told them. "We're trying for a quick turn-around, so I'll leave you here, if that's okay."

Mark and Lisa sent him back to the plane with thanks and then waited for their bags before heading towards the car hire stands. Mark dug in his bag for the information about the car.

"It's this one," he told Lisa, leading her towards one of the hire desks. A few minutes later, he was handed the keys to the small car that they would share for the week.

"I'm happy to drive," he told Lisa. "But you'll have to navigate."

"Surely there's a sat nav?" Lisa asked.

There was, but programming it wasn't as straightforward as Lisa had hoped. After a few minutes of trying to enter their destination and getting repeated error messages, she took the map that Mark had printed from the Internet and told him she was ready.

"It can't be that hard, can it?" she asked.

It was actually quite a simple journey and Mark's map had exact directions running down the side of it that made it even easier. Lisa still sighed with relief as they pulled up in front of their hotel.

"Home sweet home," she remarked as Mark parked the car.

"For a little while, anyway," he agreed.

They grabbed their bags and made their way into the hotel's lobby. Lisa's first impression was that it was a very grand and old hotel. A moment later, her eyes began to pick up the signs of neglect and age that she missed on her first look around. It was clear that the hotel had once been impressively opulent, but now it was looking a bit worn around the edges and quite tired, really.

The man behind the check-in desk looked quite tired as well. "Can I help you?" he asked in a bored voice.

Moments later, with keys in hand, they headed for the lifts. Mark pushed the call button and they waited patiently for one of the cars to arrive. After several minutes, Mark shook his head.

"We're only on the third floor. How about we take the stairs?" he suggested.

Lisa was quick to agree. If the lift was as slow as it seemed, she didn't really fancy taking it.

Her room had seen better days as well, although it appeared spotlessly clean. Someone had obviously made an effort recently to smarten it up a bit and the coffee maker and hair dryer looked brand new, in stark contrast to the ancient CRT-type television that Lisa feared might even be black and white. She switched it on while she unpacked and once it warmed up enough to show a picture, she was relieved to find it was in colour.

It didn't much matter, she thought as she switched it off. She didn't plan on watching much TV while she was in Morecombe. She set her champagne bottles on the small table, along with her snacks and her laptop, and glanced at her watch. It was nearly five and she was suddenly starving. The pile of snacks was tempting, but she wanted real food.

Someone knocked on her door.

"I brought your food," Mark told her when she opened it. His hands were full of the packets of crisps and biscuits that he'd brought off the plane for her.

Lisa laughed. "Thanks, but I want real food right now. Want to come with me to find something to eat?"

Mark nodded. "I'd love to. I'm starving."

After taking five minutes to get ready, Lisa met back up with Mark. The pair headed for the lobby, ignoring the lifts and taking the stairs.

"Maybe the man at the check-in desk can suggest somewhere good," Mark said.

Of course, his first suggestion was the hotel's own dining room.

"I hope their food is good," Lisa told him. "I expect I'll end up eating there nearly every night after I finish work. For tonight, though, we have a little bit more time. There must be some place nearby that is good."

"There's an excellent chippy on the next corner," he suggested. "Or there's a great little Italian restaurant about three doors down from the chippy."

Mark and Lisa exchanged glances. "Chippy," they said in unison.

Their hotel was close to the beach, so they bought their fish and chips and then ate them while they strolled along the shore.

"It's a lovely night," Lisa said.

"It is. It rains so much at home that I'd forgotten how nice autumn can be when it's dry," Mark replied.

When they got back to the hotel, Lisa grinned at Mark. "You have to come back to mine for some champagne," she reminded him.

He laughed. "I suppose I could be persuaded."

Lisa had filled her ice bucket with ice and shoved the small bottles in before they'd left for dinner. Now she dried off one icy cold bottle and handed it to Mark.

"I'm afraid we only have teacups or water glasses," she told him as he opened his drink.

"Teacups are fine," Mark said.

"We do have a lovely selection of biscuits and cakes," Lisa laughed, waving her hand over the pile on the table. "Please do help yourself."

"But which go best with champagne?" Mark asked.

"I'm sure none of them," Lisa grinned. "But no one is here to make a fuss, so take what you like."

Mark grabbed a packet of custard creams and Lisa selected some plain digestives.

"Those aren't very exciting," Mark commented.

"But they taste great with champagne," Lisa told him, taking a sip of her bubbly drink.

"I looked at the map and directions for where we're going in the morning," Mark said. "It isn't very far. I think we could walk it, if the weather's fine."

"I'm willing to try," Lisa said. "I don't want you to have to drive us all over the place and I don't really like to drive in strange places. The more we can walk places, the better."

"I'll collect you at seven, if that's okay?" he asked. "We can grab breakfast in the hotel restaurant and then head over to SDDC so that we're there by eight."

"That sounds perfect," Lisa agreed. "But what does SDDC stand for?"

Mark shrugged. "I have no idea."

"Maybe we'll find out tomorrow," Lisa laughed.

The bed was more comfortable than Lisa had hoped for, and the pillows were feather, her favourite. She snuggled under the duvet and drifted off to sleep. It was going to be a hectic week.

Monday was dry and sunny, so, after a quick full-English breakfast at the hotel, Mark and Lisa headed to work. The walk took less then ten minutes and much of it was along the waterfront, which meant they had stunning views to enjoy as they strolled.

"I think we're early," Mark told Lisa when they'd reached the small office building that was their destination.

"Hurray, tomorrow I can sleep for an extra fifteen minutes," Lisa laughed.

The building was open. Mark held the door for Lisa and they made their way inside.

The middle-aged receptionist seemed delighted to see them.

"We have such an action-packed week ahead for you both," she told them. "I'm Debby, with a 'y,' and it's my job to make sure you're both happy while you're here. If you need anything, please don't hesitate to ring."

She gave Lisa and Mark her business card, carefully printing her mobile number on the back. "You can reach out to me anytime. I mean that."

After being assured that they'd slept well and had plenty of breakfast, she made a quick phone call.

"Danny will be right out," she announced.

"Danny's the sales representative we've been dealing with," Mark told Lisa.

Danny turned out to be a fifty-something bald man with a potbelly and an overly flirtatious manner.

"Lisa, it's so wonderful to meet you," he said, holding her handshake for several seconds too long. "I really think you're going to love what we've come up with for MNH. Our software is bespoke, of course, and we've worked really hard with Mark and his colleagues to create something really special."

"That's great," Lisa said with a tight smile. "I can't wait to get started."

"I'll just take you along and introduce you to the crew that's going to handle training this week, then," Danny replied. "Of course, you'll be having very different sorts of training."

He led the pair through the door behind Debby, still talking as they walked through it.

"Mark, you're going to be working with Janice. She has your whole system set up on computers in our training centre. You'll be able to use them as if the system is live. Janice will show you how to do every little thing you could possibly want to do with the system."

"Great," Mark replied.

The corridor was short, but Danny led them to the very end and then tapped on the last door. Lisa couldn't make out the muffled reply, but apparently Danny could, as he quickly pushed the door open.

"Ah, Janice, there you are," Danny said brightly as the trio made their way into the spacious room. There were about a dozen desks lined neatly in rows, with a computer humming on each one.

Lisa smiled politely at the woman, who was older than she had expected. Janice had to be sixty or more and she had the grey hair to prove it. It was cut short, which made her huge pair of glasses with black frames the main thing you noticed about her. She stood up as they entered and extended a hand towards Mark.

"You must be Mark. So glad you're here, and all that," she said in a raspy smoker's voice.

"I'm glad to be here," Mark replied politely.

"I'm Lisa," Lisa said, holding out her own hand.

"Great," Janice gave her hand a squeeze and then turned her attention back to Mark. "We should get started. We have a lot of ground to cover."

"Lisa, let me take you to Howard," Danny said, touching Lisa's arm.

Lisa spun around quickly, dislodging his hand and walking back out the door. Danny chuckled and followed her out. "Have fun today," he called back to Mark and Janice. Lisa didn't catch their reply.

Two doors back down the corridor the way they'd come, Danny knocked on another door.

"Yep," was the reply that was shouted this time.

Danny swung the door open and then gestured. "After you," he said.

Lisa walked into the tiny office and stopped only a foot inside the door. There was simply no room to go any further. A huge desk took up nearly every inch of space in the room. It had four computers spread across it and Lisa could just see a bit of movement from behind one of the giant monitors. Danny had followed her and was now standing way too close behind her for her to feel comfortable.

"Harold? This is Lisa. You're training her for the system for MNH," Danny said.

A face peered around a monitor. "That's this week?" the man demanded. "I thought that was next week."

"Harold, we went through this on Friday," Danny said, shooting Lisa a nervous glance. "You need to train Lisa this week so she can start installing the system next week."

Harold frowned. "I could use another week to finish getting it ready," he said.

Danny ignored that in favour of introductions. "Harold, this is Lisa. Lisa, this is Harold. I'm sure you'll learn a lot from each other. Please let me know if you need anything." Danny shot one more anxious look at each of them and then fled the room.

"Yeah, I need another week to get everything finished," Harold called after him. Danny never looked back.

As the door shut, Lisa looked at Harold and gave him a small smile. "It's nice to meet you," she said, unable to stop the words from coming out almost as a question.

Harold laughed and came out from behind his desk, squeezing between one end and the wall. The other end of the desk was flat against the far wall.

Lisa studied him. He looked no more than thirty and was pretty much exactly what people expected when told they were meeting a computer guy. He was skinny, in jeans and a T-shirt that said "Have you tried turning it off and back on again?" No taller than Lisa, he had thick glasses and curly ginger hair that badly needed a cut.

"Hey, it's nice to meet you as well," he told Lisa, offering a hand.

Lisa was relieved by the firm handshake that didn't linger.

"Need coffee?" Harold asked. "I have a pot brewing all the time when I'm here." He pointed to the corner behind the door and Lisa turned and spotted the coffee pot.

"Coffee sounds good," she replied.

"Here, you can use this mug all week," Harold told her, handing her a mug with the digits of pi circling it. The handle was in the shape of the pi symbol, which made Lisa smile, even if it was slightly awkward to hold.

"Embrace your geek side," Harold said with a laugh.

Lisa poured herself a cup of coffee and took a sip. "Oh, this is good," she said.

"Yeah, I buy the good stuff and I make it fresh all day long. I'm pretty much entirely fuelled by coffee."

Four hours later, Lisa realised how true that statement was. Coffee in hand, she'd joined Harold behind the desk. He'd fired up a computer and let loose, giving her every last technical detail she could possibly need for the new system. Almost on the dot of twelve, her stomach began to rumble loudly.

She leaned back in her chair and stretched. "I think I need lunch," she told Harold.

"I always bring mine," Harold told her. "But I'm sure Debby will send out for something for you if you need it."

"I'll go chat with Debby then," Lisa told him. She felt like Harold didn't entirely approve of the break, but she desperately needed it. Debby had a stack of menus from local cafés that would deliver to them and Lisa quickly selected a sandwich from one of them. While Debby sorted out the order, Lisa retired to the loo. Less than ten minutes later, she was back in Harold's office clutching her sandwich.

As she squeezed back behind the desk, Harold was just finishing the last bite of his own sandwich. Lisa could smell egg salad. Harold pulled out a small bag of crisps and munched through them as Lisa ate her sandwich and her own somewhat larger bag of crisps. She washed everything down with a can of fizzy drink. Harold stuck to his coffee, setting another pot brewing as he finished the first.

"So far everything seems to be just about perfect," Lisa told him as they ate. "What did you want another week to do?"

Harold laughed. "I didn't really want another week," he answered. "I just like to make Danny nervous. He doesn't know anything about computers. He's sales. I knew you were coming today and I made sure to have everything ready to go, but Danny doesn't know that. I like to see him sweat."

Lisa laughed. "He certainly seemed uneasy around you," she replied.

"And I like to keep it that way," he said with a grin.

After lunch, Harold went back to his blistering pace, taking Lisa through the system from every possible angle. "I'm trying to anticipate everything that could go wrong during install, and then work out how you can fix it," he told her.

Lisa took copious notes. "I'm going to go over all of this tonight and I'm sure I'll have lots of questions tomorrow," she replied.

Harold nodded. "Questions are good."

By five o'clock Lisa felt as if her brain were completely fried. She'd drunk at least twice as much coffee as she was used to from the pi mug, and she felt a bit giddy and slightly sick.

As Harold clicked through to yet another screen she hadn't seen before, she shook her head. "I can't," she told him. "I need a break. Can we pick back up right here in the morning?"

Harold grinned at her. "We're about two hours ahead of where I expected to be at this point. If we keep working at this pace, we'll finish before lunch on Friday."

"Maybe we could slow down, then," Lisa muttered as she packed up her bag.

"Nah, why would we do that?" Harold replied, giving her a grin when she shot him a dirty look.

Mark was sitting in reception, chatting with Debby, when Lisa emerged.

"Are you finished for the day?" she asked him.

"We finished about half an hour ago," he told her. "My brain couldn't take any more."

Lisa laughed. "I know exactly how you feel."

They walked slowly back towards their hotel.

"It feels so good to be outside," Mark said. "Janice isn't one for taking breaks."

"Must be company policy," Lisa replied. "Harold didn't even want to stop for lunch."

"Oh, Janice was happy to stop for lunch," Mark told her. "She doesn't have anyone to cook for at home anymore, since the kids are all grown up and her husband left her, so she made lunch for us both."

"Lucky you. I just got a sandwich from somewhere. What did she make?"

"It was some sort of soup. I'm not sure what all was in it, but it was definitely meant to be soup."

Lisa laughed. "Does that mean you didn't like it?"

"I sort of hated it," Mark admitted. "But I couldn't tell Janice that, of course, so I had to eat it."

"Is she planning to cook every day?"

"I think so," Mark said in a sad voice.

Lisa couldn't help but laugh. "Should we just grab dinner on our way back to the hotel?"

"I could eat just about anything right now."

They settled on a little pub that was about halfway between the

SDDC office and their hotel. Lisa sipped a glass of wine with her shepherd's pie while Mark enjoyed a pint of lager with his bangers and mash.

Back at the hotel, Lisa headed to her room and curled up with her notes and her laptop. She knew they had made good progress today, and she was determined to continue that going forward.

The rest of the week had a curious déjà vu feeling to it as she and Mark walked to SDDC together after breakfast each morning and then emerged, blinking and dazed, into the autumn air around five each evening.

The pair ate together each evening at a different place that they came across on their journey home. Conversations were inconsequential, as they were both preoccupied with what they were learning each day.

By Friday lunchtime, Lisa and Howard had pretty much covered everything that Lisa needed to know. "I suppose I can take the afternoon off," Lisa joked when Howard had sat back and announced that they were finished. "I just have a few questions after lunch," she told him.

Debby ordered celebratory pizza for everyone for lunch, so Howard and Janice as well as Danny and Debby joined Lisa and Mark that day. They had lunch in a small conference room that neither Lisa nor Mark had known existed.

"How are you guys getting on?" Lisa asked Mark when he'd joined her in the conference room.

"I think we're about done," he replied. "We've covered everything I can think of and a bunch of other stuff as well."

"We are definitely about done," Janice interjected. "I'm hoping to finish around two and then take the rest of the day off."

Lisa nodded. "I'd like to think Howard and I will be done by then as well. I'd love to sneak out at two."

"You can't be anxious to get away from me," Howard said loudly.

Lisa laughed. "You know I'm terribly sad about leaving you," she told the man. "I just think the sooner we make the break the better."

Howard sighed. "But where will I find another woman like you?" he asked dramatically.

Danny looked at them both, curiosity in his eyes. "Are you two, I mean, have you two been, is this, well, I suppose it isn't any of my business."

Lisa laughed and then turned back to Mark. "If we both finish by two, maybe we could drive down to the outlet mall and do some shopping this afternoon," she suggested.

Mark looked at Janice. "Maybe we won't finish before five?" he asked hopefully.

Lisa laughed. "I'll go by myself if you don't want to come," she told him. "Let's see how we do for time first, though."

It was closer to four than two when they were both finally finished for the day. Mark and Janice had finished first, but then Lisa and Harold did some playing around with the test system that was set up in the classroom. As much as Lisa wanted to finish early, she was more interested in doing her job properly.

"I think I'm ready to install the system," she told Harold eventually. "I just hope I remember everything on Monday."

"You'll be great," he told her. "You've been the best student I've ever had the privilege to work with."

"It's been great working with you as well," Lisa replied. "I've never had one-on-one tutoring for a project like this before. It makes such a difference."

She and Mark were quiet on their walk back to the hotel. They'd agreed to have dinner in the fancy restaurant in the hotel for their last night in Morecombe, so Lisa took a long bath and then put on the little black dress that was in the bottom of her case. She could add a jacket to make it look professional for work, but tonight she left the jacket off.

As she put on her makeup and fixed her hair, she had to remind herself of a few things.

"This isn't a date," she told her reflection sternly. "Mark is dating Darcy, and you and Darcy have never let a man come between you. Besides, Mark is dating Darcy. He isn't going to give you a single glance."

At dinner, Mark insisted on a bottle of wine, and soon the pair were laughing about all of the ups and downs of the week.

"I think my least favourite moment was when Janice brought in steak and kidney pie for lunch and I nearly broke a tooth on the crust," Mark told Lisa.

"My favourite moment was when Harold's shirt said 'No, I won't fix your computer,' and I had to ask him to fix the computer I was using."

The food was delicious and the pair found themselves talking for hours.

"I haven't felt this good in days," Lisa confessed. "I feel like I've been so totally focussed on work that I haven't thought of anything else. We should have another bottle of wine."

Mark shook his head. "I'm feeling quite lightheaded and I don't think I should have any more," he told her. "Janice was, um, difficult to appreciate and I'm way too relieved to be done working with her. I think I need to get a good night's sleep before we fly home tomorrow."

At Lisa's door they parted awkwardly. For a very strange moment, Lisa thought Mark might be thinking of kissing her, but that was impossible. He was Darcy's boyfriend.

8

The flight home was uneventful. Jack was piloting by himself on their return journey and he collected them on his way back from Liverpool. He'd taken a large group of football fans over for a game, so he was using a larger plane. That meant they had an air hostess for the trip, which limited the amount of snacks and drinks Lisa could sneak away with this time.

Lisa spent the weekend working through her notes. She was hoping that Darcy might stop by, but the island was hit by heavy fog and Darcy ended up spending the weekend stuck at Manchester airport.

Saturday night Lisa had found herself waiting nervously to see if anyone knocked on her door. It would be like Darcy to have arranged another blind date without bothering to mention it to her. Lisa finally went to bed later than normal, thankful that no one had turned up.

After a lazy Sunday, on Monday morning she headed over to the Manx Museum, arriving just before nine. Mark was waiting at the back entrance to let her in.

"I hope you had a nice weekend," he said politely.

"I spent most of it going over my notes," Lisa told him.

"Snap," he laughed. "I went over things so many times that I almost forgot to eat on Sunday."

Lisa shook her head. "I never forget to eat," she told him.

In the conference room, he introduced Lisa to Marjorie Stevens, the museum's librarian and archivist, and Thomas Clague, the director of Manx National Heritage. The foursome spent an hour going over the plans for the system conversion, agreeing easily on all of the key points.

"We could try installing the system everywhere and then going live all at once across every site," Lisa told them. "Or we can install the main software here and then add in each site, one at a time, until the whole network is live."

"Advantages and disadvantages of each?" Thomas asked.

"If they all go live at one time, you can immediately enjoy all of the new functions and features of the new system. Many companies, like banks for instance, always convert systems all at once. They can't function properly if one branch is using different software to the others. It's risky, though, and if things go badly wrong there could be a few days where everything is tangled up."

"Like that bank I read about that converted systems, and then no one could use their bank card to withdraw money for almost a week," Mark said.

"Exactly like that," Lisa told him. "It's safer and probably easier for me if we do a site at a time. Since your current systems don't talk to one another anyway, you aren't really losing anything and we can take our time and make sure we do each site exactly the way it needs to be done. We can also test each site as we go along, not adding another site until we're sure the previous one is working properly."

"I don't really know much about computers," Marjorie chimed in. "It sounds to me like you'd prefer the second option, and that's fine with me."

"It's fine with me as well," Thomas told her. "As long as the second option doesn't add too much to the timeline. I'm anxious to get this project finished."

"I don't anticipate it adding to the timeline at all," Lisa assured him. "The work is pretty much the same. It's just a matter of detail. And it won't actually be a single site at a time, either, really. I'll probably do two or three on any given day, depending on location."

By ten o'clock the group had agreed to the best plan for taking things forward.

"So when do you start?" Thomas asked Lisa.

"Right now," Lisa told him. "I can start installing the software on the machines here today. If everything goes to plan, the museum can start issuing tickets from the new system tomorrow morning."

"Wonderful, I look forward to frequent updates," he replied.

He and Marjorie departed, leaving Lisa and Mark to sort out the exact logistics. "You already have the software on your computer," Lisa said. "We just have to switch you to the live system once I get the server going."

Mark headed to his office, while Lisa got together with the head of the IT department to start working on the install. At midday, Mark found her on her hands and knees in the computer department, frowning at a power strip.

"That's not a happy face," he remarked.

Lisa shook her head. "I need room for one more thing and this power strip is full."

"Maybe you'll come up with a solution over lunch," Mark suggested. "You really should take a break."

Lisa glanced up at the clock in surprise. "I didn't realise it was that late," she said. "You're right, I need a break."

On Mark's invitation, the pair headed to the museum café to grab a quick bite to eat.

"They have a great menu," Lisa said, after they'd ordered. "I'm sure I won't mind eating here every day for the next fortnight or so."

"Is that how long it's going to take to get the museum finished?" Mark asked.

"Probably," Lisa said. "That's what I've budgeted, anyway. The new software needs to go on every machine in the building so that every member of staff has access to it. They might not need or want access, but at least they'll have the option. I know you've been working on lists of staff members and what access they are meant to have as the system goes in, so I'll need that list as I start installing things."

"What else needs doing?" Mark asked.

"I need to build the end user interfaces for each site. I'm going to customise each one to make it easy for staff to access the things they use most often. I started working on that with Howard when we were in Morecombe, but I need to finish things now. Your job is to start training the users as I have each site interface established."

"I have two lists," Mark told her. "One list is for people like Norma who always work at the same site and the other is our flexible staff that move around. I thought I'd start training with the first group, since they'll only need training with their own site-specific system, and then work my way through the people who will need training on every site."

Lisa nodded. "The interfaces won't be terribly different," she assured him. "It's all about making the end user experience as quick and easy as possible. I need to write basic instruction manuals as well, but I want to wait until the sites are starting to use the software before I do that. Things might change with the interfaces once people start using them."

Mark grinned. "Now let's talk about the weather or the football or something," he said. "Work can wait for twenty minutes."

Lisa laughed. "I can be a bit obsessive," she admitted. "Tell me about your childhood, then," she suggested.

Mark shrugged. "I grew up in London until I was eight. Then my dad took early retirement and we moved to Cumbria. Dad bought a little farmhouse and they raised me and my brother, along with chickens and a few goats."

"How lovely," Lisa sighed. "I always wanted a pet goat."

"Really?" Mark asked. "Why?"

"They just seem sort of cool," Lisa shrugged. "I don't know."

Mark laughed. "I suppose they were cool. They needed a lot of looking after, though, and they weren't terribly friendly."

"What did your dad do that let him retire that early?" Lisa asked.

"He was in banking," Mark answered. "Michael has followed in his footsteps and is doing really well. He'll probably be able to retire when he's fifty like our father did. I'll be working forever, but I don't mind. I love what I do."

"I love what I do, too," Lisa told him. "But if I could retire at fifty, I totally would. I'd love to have all that leisure time to read books and maybe learn to cook."

"I'd love more free time," Mark agreed. "But I love what I do too much to even consider retirement at this point."

"Did you always want to study history?"

"I don't know about always," Mark said slowly. "I did well at it in school, and I really wasn't great at maths or any of the sciences, but I sort of just fell into history when I was picking my A-levels. Once I started studying the subject seriously, though, I was hooked. What about you and computers?"

"Oh, I fell in love with computers when I was a kid. There just seemed to be no end of the amazing things they could do."

"And you grew up on the island?"

"I did. I went to Liverpool for university, but couldn't wait to get back here."

"The island does do that to people," Mark said with a smile. "I wasn't sure, when I first took the job here, that I was going to like it. I worried about feeling cut off from the rest of the world, you know? Anyway, I soon found out that the rest of the world doesn't much matter."

Lisa laughed. "No plans to leave in a hurry then?"

"No plans to leave, full stop," he told her.

After lunch, Lisa headed back to the computer lab. By five, she had accomplished as much as she could for the day. The museum was due to close, and she was mentally exhausted anyway. She stuck her head in Mark's office on her way out.

"I'm done for today, although I didn't finish as much as I wanted to," she told him. "I hate getting behind on the first day of a project."

"It happens," he told her. "Wait to worry until you're at least a week behind."

Lisa laughed. "I'll see you in the morning."

The next week seemed to fly past as Lisa worked her way through the museum, installing the new software on staff computers. She installed it on the computer at the entrance and they began issuing tickets for the various sites without any glitches.

She spent the weekend relaxing and trying not to think about work at all, curling up with a huge pile of romance novels and a large box of truffles. Darcy rang on Saturday afternoon.

"Hello, darling, I hope you aren't working too hard at the museum all the time," she cooed at Lisa.

"You know I always work very hard," Lisa told her.

"You really do," Darcy agreed. "I, on the other hand, am hardly working at all."

"Where are you?"

"Oh, Tenerife," Darcy said with a sigh. "It's a difficult life I lead, soaking up the sunshine and drinking daiquiris."

"Are you working all weekend?"

"I switched shifts with a few people and now I've ended up stuck here with Pete," Darcy explained.

Pete had only started working for Finlo in the last few months, and Lisa knew very little about him except that he was cute, but very young.

"Weren't you supposed to see Mark this weekend?"

"Oh, Mark's flexible," Darcy said casually. "I haven't seen him in ages, but I know you see him all the time, so at least he won't forget about me." She laughed. "But seriously, I tried to get him to go out on Tuesday night when I was back on island for an evening and he refused. He said he was too tired after work. It will do him good to be lonely all weekend."

Lisa bit back a dozen replies and then changed the subject. "At least if you're in Tenerife, you aren't fixing me up on more blind dates," she said.

Darcy laughed again. "That's why I'm ringing, actually," she told Lisa.

Lisa gasped. "No, no, no, don't you dare tell me there is some loser on his way over here right now. I'm tired and I've been working too hard to deal with that tonight."

"Relax, darling," Darcy replied. "I rang to give you plenty of fair warning. Next Saturday you are having dinner with a lovely man called Jack Williams. He'll be picking you up at seven and taking you to dinner at *La Terrrazza*, so make sure you look wonderful."

"What's wrong with him?" Lisa asked.

Darcy giggled. "Nothing! He's cute and very nice and I'm sure you'll thank me after this one. I think I'll be back on the island next weekend anyway, so I can come over and make sure you're properly dressed and whatever, but just in case I'm still hopping around the world, I wanted to warn you."

Lisa hung up, wondering what Darcy was doing. She didn't usually do so much travelling when she was in a relationship. It was different when she was dating Finlo, as the pair had travelled together all over the world, but Mark was on the island, and it wasn't like Darcy to switch shifts and take on extra flights when she had a man to come home to. Lisa hoped everything was okay between Mark and Darcy. If they were having problems, working with Mark might be awkward in the days ahead.

Of course, Darcy didn't have total control over her schedule. Maybe it was Finlo who was working to keep Darcy and Mark apart. He could easily keep Darcy busy and off the island if he wanted to do so.

Whatever was happening, there was no obvious sign of any awkwardness the next week. By the following Friday, Lisa was satisfied that the museum was fully up and running on the new system.

"All the interfaces are written," she told Mark on her way out on Friday evening. "We're right on schedule, assuming you've finished up with staff training."

"We're good," he replied. "Everyone has done their introductory training, as scheduled. We'll do final training on-site."

"In that case, on Monday we can start working on the sites," Lisa said.

"I knew we'd do it," he told her, giving her a high five. "We should go out and celebrate."

"We really should," Lisa agreed. They made plans to meet an hour later at a pub that was centrally located. Lisa stopped home to drop off her laptop and notebook and run a brush through her hair. As she touched up her makeup, she sighed. She was far more excited about dinner with Mark tonight than she was about the blind date Darcy had arranged for her for the following evening. It was a shame that Mark was dating Darcy. He was just about perfect otherwise.

The pub was quiet for a Friday night, but maybe it was just too early for the crowds. Mark and Lisa grabbed a table in the corner.

"I'm starving," Lisa told him. "Lunch was way too long ago."

Mark frowned. "I forgot to eat lunch today," he told her.

Lisa shook her head. "I wondered why you didn't come and pester me to eat," she told him. "I looked for you, but your office was dark."

"I had to go and collect some folks coming in from Wales at the ferry terminal. They're here to spend some time at Bunscoill Ghaelgagh," he told her.

"Stealing all the good ideas from the Manx language school to use back in Wales?" Lisa asked with a laugh.

"We're more than happy to share ideas with them," Mark replied. "Anything we can do to encourage more people to get interested in native languages helps all of us."

"So how did you miss lunch, exactly?" Lisa dragged the conversation back to where it had started.

"I don't know," Mark laughed. "But I intend to make up for it now."

They both ordered a hearty meal and Mark got a second round of drinks for them as well. Two hours later they were both stuffed and on their fourth round of drinks.

"I love this place," Lisa said, looking around the dimly lit pub that was still only about half full.

"It's one of my favourite pubs," Mark agreed. "They have good food and I can have a drink or two and then walk home."

"Where do you live?" Lisa asked.

"I have an flat on the prom," Mark replied.

"Ooooo, most of those are expensive," Lisa said. "Maybe your job pays better than I thought."

Mark shook his head. "I, um, had some money to invest," he said, turning red under her gaze. "And I'd bought a house when I first moved here, before prices went crazy. When I sold that house I made out quite well."

Lisa didn't ask any more questions. It seemed like a subject Mark didn't want to talk about. "It isn't raining, is it?" she asked instead.

"I don't think so," Mark replied, looking confused at the change in topic.

"I feel like a walk," she explained. "But I hate rain."

"Let's go for a walk, then," Mark said. He paid for the meal and the drinks, ignoring Lisa's protests.

"It's a celebration," he reminded her. "And you've worked really hard for the last fortnight. You've earned it."

Lisa couldn't think of a logic counterargument. "Okay, but then I get to buy dinner the next time we have something to celebrate," she told him.

"That's a deal," he agreed.

They walked slowly down the prom, listening to the waves as they reached the shore, and the seagulls as they screamed at one another along the beach. The natural sounds were an interesting contrast to the noises from the bars and restaurants along the prom. Lisa could hear music and loud conversations spilling out of open doorways as they walked. The day had been very pleasant for early October, but the evening was chilly. By the time they'd reached the Sea Terminal, Lisa realised she should have brought a jacket.

"It's cooling off fast," she said to Mark as they turned around and headed back down the promenade.

"Here, take my jacket," he told her, slipping off the suit jacket that he was still wearing from his day in the office.

"Oh, I can't," Lisa said, trying to step away from him.

"Don't be silly. I'm not cold and I have long sleeves," he insisted. He settled the jacket over her shoulders and Lisa couldn't resist sliding her arms in the sleeves. It was so lovely and warm that she sighed contentedly.

"Better?" Mark asked.

"Much," Lisa replied.

After a few minutes, however, Lisa began to feel uncomfortable in the warm jacket. There was a curious intimacy to the situation that bothered her. The jacket wasn't just warm, it smelled good. Lisa had never been close enough to Mark to notice his cologne, but now she decided she loved it. It had a warm, woodsy and spicy smell that she found herself inhaling deeply.

"I think I'd better get home and get some sleep," she said suddenly, startling both Mark and herself.

"I'll walk you home," Mark replied. "It's getting late."

Lisa was going to protest, but mostly because she wasn't in any hurry to return Mark's jacket to him, she didn't. At her door, he took his jacket back with a smile.

"Congratulations again on getting the museum finished," he told her. "Monday we start site-hopping, right?"

"Yeah, in the order we discussed."

"Sounds good," he agreed. "See you Monday."

Lisa let herself into her house, waving goodbye to Mark as she did so. Inside, she gasped. Darcy was lying on the sofa in the dark, illuminated only by the television she was watching.

"I didn't know you were back on the island," Lisa said, blushing furiously. "Mark and I had dinner. You could have come with us."

Darcy glanced up and then shrugged. "I'm tired," she said. "I flew for too many days in a row and had to handle more than my fair share of difficult passengers. I didn't feel like dealing with anyone tonight, not even Mark. I was just going to go home and go to bed, but I forgot that I'd told Kym she could crash at my place tonight. The last person I feel like spending time with tonight is Kym."

Lisa laughed and crossed the room to her friend. She gave her friend the best hug she could manage with Darcy still lying down. Kym was another air hostess with Quayle Airways. She was sweet and friendly but also rather vacuous and very high energy. She was the perfect friend for New Year's Eve parties or drunken nights at the pub, but not really someone you would choose to spend time with after a hard day.

"So when did you get back and how long are you staying?" Lisa asked.

"I'm staying long enough to help you get ready for your date tomorrow," Darcy said with a smile. "Which is all you really wanted to know."

Lisa shrugged. "Pretty much," she agreed.

Darcy laughed. "You could have pretended that you missed me."

"I always miss you," Lisa replied. "But you know that."

"I miss you too," Darcy said. "Can I crash here?"

"You know you can," Lisa replied. "You don't need to ask."

"Yeah, maybe I should stop fixing you up," Darcy said thoughtfully. "If you find a guy, he might not want me crashing in your spare room all the time."

"If he doesn't, he's not the guy for me," Lisa assured her friend. "Now let's get some sleep. Apparently, I have a hot date tomorrow night."

9

Both women slept late on Saturday before Darcy made them omelettes for a very late breakfast. After breakfast she went to the grocery store and came back to Lisa's house with bags full of goodies.

"What are you cooking?" Lisa asked as she unpacked cucumbers, yoghurt and honey.

Darcy laughed. "Face masks," she told her friend. "It's time to pamper ourselves and this is cheaper and easier than trying to get an appointment at the spa."

An hour later the friends were giggling together as they lay on the floor, faces covered in goo.

"It smells good," Lisa said, wrinkling her nose.

"You can eat it," Darcy told her. "But you shouldn't. It's doing more good on your face than it would in your tummy."

"What's it doing to my face?"

"Cooling and hydrating. And the less you talk, the better."

Lisa chuckled. "How long am I meant to keep quiet for exactly?"

"An hour."

Now Lisa laughed. "I can't do it," she told her friend. "I haven't seen you in weeks. I have to talk to you."

"I'm not talking," Darcy said. "I'm letting my mask work."

"But I want to hear what you've been up to," Lisa said in a deliberately whiny voice. "Your life is so much more exciting than mine."

Darcy shook her head. "No excitement, just work."

"But what about Tenerife?"

Lisa could see the slightest hint of a grin on her friend's face. "Okay," was all that Darcy said though.

"What does 'okay' mean?" Lisa demanded.

"Tenerife was okay," Darcy said with a sigh. "Can't you just lie still for a few minutes and let the mask work?"

"You said an hour," Lisa said. "I can't possibly lie still for an hour."

"Get a book," Darcy suggested.

Lisa thought about it. "Do I have to stay on my back?"

"If you sit up, the mask will run down your neck," Darcy told her.

"Maybe that's why it's running into my ears," Lisa said, getting up very slowly. "I need to fix this."

Darcy sighed and sat up slowly. "Mine is getting in my ears as well," she admitted. "I reckon I didn't make it thick enough."

In the loo, they both washed their faces.

"Well, that was fun," Lisa said with a grin. "What next?"

"Your skin is glowing," Darcy told her. "It was worth it."

Lisa studied her face in the mirror. It was just possible that Darcy was right. Her skin did look softer, and maybe it did have a bit of a glow to it.

"Let's go shopping," Darcy suggested. "You need something nice to wear for tonight."

"I have plenty of clothes," Lisa said. "I'll find something that will do."

"I'm not going to argue," Darcy told her. "But I still want to go shopping. I need something new for tonight to cheer me up."

"What's wrong?"

Darcy sighed. "Nothing, really, I'm just a little bit down. Nothing a new pair of shoes and a fabulous new frock won't fix."

Lisa didn't have any other plans for her Saturday, so she was happy to agree to Darcy's plan for retail therapy. Half an hour later she was showered and dressed and waiting for Darcy. Darcy was only a few minutes behind her.

"You are eager to get out," Lisa laughed. "I've never known you to do your makeup that quickly."

"I'm just going to wash it all off and start over before my date tonight," Darcy replied. "So I just did the bare minimum."

"Your minimum is a lot more than my usual," Lisa told her, comparing her friend's perfectly made-up face to her own. Lisa had brushed on a bit of eye shadow and blusher and then added lip-gloss and considered herself done.

"I'll do your makeup for tonight," Darcy told her as they made their way out of Lisa's house.

"Of course you will," Lisa said with a sigh.

At one of Darcy's favourite little boutiques, Darcy tried on half a dozen sexy little dresses. She finally settled on a metallic purple mini that should have looked terrible with her red hair, but somehow didn't. The store had matching shoes that Darcy loved.

"My feet hurt just looking at those shoes," Lisa told Darcy as they emerged from the shop.

"They aren't bad," Darcy said with a shrug. "I'm used to heels."

A few doors down, Darcy wandered into another clothing store. Lisa flicked through the racks mindlessly, waiting for her friend.

"This is really cute," Darcy said from across the store.

Lisa turned and looked at the dress Darcy was holding. It was a soft magenta colour, perfect for autumn.

"I can't see you in that at all," Lisa said. "It's too long and way too modest."

Darcy laughed. "Not for me, silly, for you."

Lisa shook her head. "I don't need any more clothes."

"At least try it on," Darcy suggested. "I think it's the perfect colour for you."

Lisa sighed. She knew if she tried it on and it came even close to fitting, Darcy would try to persuade her to buy it. But Darcy was right. It was a gorgeous colour.

She took the dress from her friend and then sighed again. The fabric was soft and it almost felt like an old, favourite T-shirt that had been washed until it was incredibly comfortable.

"You should try it on," Darcy told her. "It's your size."

Lisa headed towards the dressing room, mentally making faces at her friend. Darcy was, as usual, correct. The colour was incredibly flattering and the dress itself seemed tailor-made for Lisa's somewhat less than generous curves. It wouldn't have suited Darcy at all, and somehow that made Lisa even more tempted to buy it.

"What do you think?" she asked Darcy as she walked out of the fitting room.

"It's perfect on you," Darcy told her. She frowned. "I couldn't wear it. I'm too curvy."

"It is a great colour," Lisa said with a sigh. She'd received a generous bonus when she'd wrapped up the Westlake project. She could certainly afford the dress.

"And there are matching shoes," Darcy told her, holding up a pair of low heels that were just Lisa's style.

"Oh, goody," Lisa replied, sticking her tongue out at her friend.

Darcy laughed. "Go get changed and I'll buy you a cake."

Lisa didn't need any more motivation than that. She changed quickly and then joined her friend.

"You are getting it, right?" Darcy demanded.

"Yes," Lisa sighed. "I'm getting it."

"And the shoes?"

"And the shoes," Lisa said, slipping on a pair in her size to make sure they fit. They fit, and they were almost comfortable. What more could she ask for from "date shoes" than that?

There was a little coffee shop next door, so after Lisa paid, they grabbed a table there.

"We never had lunch," Lisa reminded her friend as she looked over the menu.

"We had breakfast at eleven," Darcy said.

"Well, yeah, but still," Lisa laughed. "I'm starving."

"Just remember you're going out for a nice meal tonight. Don't stuff yourself too much now."

Lisa nodded. She loved *La Terrazza,* so she even listened to her friend. "I'll have a cup of tea and a scone," she told the waitress.

Darcy just ordered tea.

"Aren't you hungry?" Lisa demanded.

"A little," Darcy shrugged. "But I'm saving room for later."

"I'm assuming you're going out with Mark?"

"Yeah, he's taking me to that new restaurant in Castletown."

"I've heard good things about it," Lisa told her. "And I've heard it's very posh."

"Yeah, well, so am I."

"Was there anything special bothering you, or did you just work too hard the last few weeks?" Lisa asked as they sipped their tea.

Darcy sighed. "I did overdo it a bit," she admitted. "And then, Joney and Nigel were on my flight back to the island."

"Oh, dear," Lisa said.

"Yeah, Joney made a big thing about how embarrassing it was to have a 'friend' having to wait on her hand and foot," Darcy said.

"And then she made sure you had to wait on her hand and foot, right?" Lisa asked.

"Exactly," Darcy said with another sigh. "Even Nigel started looking embarrassed after the twenty-third time she'd called me over to ask me for something. I suppose I'm lucky it was only an hour flight."

" I hope you put salt in her tea or something," Lisa said angrily.

Darcy shook her head. "It was tempting, but I love my job too much. Believe me, she would have complained."

"What's Nigel like, then?" Lisa asked. There had been a lot of gossip about the man, but he rarely visited the island.

"I think he's perfect for Joney," Darcy said, making a face.

Lisa laughed. They drank their tea and chatted about nothing much else before heading back to Lisa's house. Once there, Darcy took another shower and then began to get ready for her date. Lisa read a book for an hour before starting her own, considerably less involved, "date-night" routine.

Once she was dressed, Darcy fixed Lisa's hair and makeup for her and then Lisa poured them each a glass of wine while they waited for their dates to arrive.

"This reminds me of a hundred other nights just like this from the last ten years," Darcy laughed as they toasted themselves.

"I hope we aren't still doing this in another ten years," Lisa replied. "I've never really enjoyed dating, and I won't miss it if I ever find a husband."

"I'll miss this part," Darcy said.

"This part is fine," Lisa told her. "It's the dating part that's miserable."

Darcy laughed. "You've been dating the wrong men."

"Tell me about it."

A knock on the door had Lisa's heart racing. Mark gave her a huge smile when she opened the door.

"Hey, you look great," he told her. "That's a gorgeous dress."

Lisa flushed. "Thanks," she replied. She'd just let him in and pushed the door shut when someone else knocked. As Mark and Darcy said their hellos, Lisa opened the door again.

The man at the door gave her a huge smile. "Lisa?" he asked.

Lisa nodded and stepped back to let him in. He bounced in energetically and then offered Lisa his hand.

"I'm Jack Williams, of course, but then I'm sure Darcy's told you all about me."

"Not really," Lisa said, giving him a forced smile. He was only an inch or two taller than she was and he looked to be closer to fifty than forty, with greying and thinning hair and glasses. He was wearing a black suit that was tight on him, with what looked like black cowboy boots.

"Well, I'll have to fix that over dinner, won't I?" he asked, laughing heartily.

"It's nice to see you again, Jack," Darcy said, walking forward to greet him.

"Wow, hey, Darcy, I didn't know you were here. Wow, that is some dress you're wearing. You look amazing."

"Thanks," Darcy smiled. "This is Mark, and we're off to Castletown. You two have fun tonight."

Darcy and Mark were gone too quickly for Lisa or Jack to reply.

"Well, ready to go?" Jack asked Lisa. She nodded, feeling like things weren't going well, but not exactly sure why.

Outside, Jack held open the door to his late model luxury sedan. "I hope you like the car," he told her. "It's worth a fortune, of course, but it's the company's really. I was top salesman last year so I got an upgrade from the standard company car to this one. Isn't it wonderful?"

Lisa nodded, and then felt like she should speak. "I don't know much about cars," she said in an apologetic tone.

"You should," Jack replied. He spent the twenty-minute drive to Laxey talking about horsepower and performance specifications while Lisa murmured "really" and "I didn't know that" at appropriate intervals. By the time they arrived in the small village, Lisa was ready to go home.

Jack drove around the streets of Laxey for several minutes, looking for the perfect place to park his car. "Can't leave this baby just anywhere," he told Lisa. Eventually he found a spot that satisfied him and he slowly maneuvered his way into it. After she got out, Lisa waited patiently as he checked that all of the doors were locked and that the security system had engaged.

The host smiled at them as they walked into the restaurant. "Ah, Ms. Mylchreest, how lovely to see you again," he told Lisa.

"It's nice to see you as well, Timothy," she told the man. She ate at *La Terrazza* at least once a month, more often if she could find excuses for doing so. She'd recently treated Darcy to dinner there for Darcy's birthday and she was determined to bring Darcy back soon to celebrate the end of the Westlake project. She'd been too busy to think of it before now, but she felt like she deserved it.

"I have a booking," Jack announced. The host found his name in their reservation book and then escorted them to a small table in the corner.

"I don't think this will do," Jack said haughtily. "I don't want to be crammed into a dark corner."

Timothy smiled politely and then looked around the room. Every table was full, and it seemed to Lisa that every eye in the room was on her. She flushed with embarrassment.

"I'm sure this will be fine," she said to Jack. "It isn't like they have other open tables."

Jack frowned. "When I take a lady out for an evening, I expect a perfect experience. This table does not meet my standards."

Lisa bit back a dozen replies, settling for sliding into a chair instead. "It meets mine," she said with forced cheer. "Timothy, I need wine."

Timothy grinned at her and then hurried away, leaving Jack standing grumpily next to her.

"You shouldn't have done that," he admonished her as he slid into the seat opposite. "We deserve a better table or at least a discount of some sort."

Lisa narrowed her eyes. "You weren't just fussing in order to get a discount, were you?" she asked.

Jack flushed. "Of course not. I don't need a discount." He looked around the room and then leaned in towards Lisa. "I don't like to brag," he said quietly. "But I'm going to be a millionaire before I'm fifty."

Lisa smiled tightly. "How nice for you."

"I'm nearly there," he added.

Nearly fifty or nearly a millionaire, Lisa wondered.

A waiter appeared at her elbow. He handed her a glass of chilled white wine. "With compliments of the management," he told her with a small bow.

Lisa smiled and took a sip. "Delicious," she said.

She picked up her menu while Jack scowled at the waiter and then gave him his own drink order.

"I don't see why you get a free drink," he grumbled after the waiter left. "You didn't complain."

Lisa bit her lip and studied the menu. She'd tried just about everything on it at least once. She wondered what Jack would say if she ordered the most expensive thing she could find.

"I think I'll try the chicken," Jack announced.

"Which chicken?" Lisa asked.

"The one on special," Jack told her. "Did you see the menu with specials? They're usually much better deals than the regular menu items."

Lisa forced herself to smile as Jack handed her the sheet with specials on it. They had one of her very favourite items on the list, and she decided she might as well make Jack happy by ordering it. Besides, she thought, maybe specials could be prepared faster than regular items. Anything that made the date end sooner would be good.

The waiter returned with Jack's ice water and took their order. Once he'd departed, Jack leaned back in his chair and smiled.

"Where was I? Oh, yes, I was telling you about how successful I am." He shook his head. "I'm not bragging, really, but I think it's important to share such information early on in a relationship, so that everyone knows where they stand. Don't you agree?"

"Sure," Lisa shrugged. Jack could talk about himself all night if he wanted to. She would tune him out and enjoy her meal.

"Right, well, like I said, I'm well on track to be a millionaire by the time I hit the big five-oh. I had a very successful year last year and this year is already looking better. Three more years like that and I'll have assets worth a cool million."

"That's quite an accomplishment," Lisa replied, downing her drink.

"Of course, that's including the company car that isn't actually mine, but as I get use of it, I'm counting it."

"Of course you are," Lisa grinned and then caught the waiter's eye. He nodded at her.

"It helps that my flat has tripled in value since I bought it," Jack continued. "I've taken some of the equity out to pay for holidays and things, but it's still mine."

Lisa nodded and then beamed at the waiter as he delivered her second glass of wine.

Jack frowned. "I'm keeping track," he told the waiter. "You said the first one was free."

The waiter nodded. "All of Ms. Mylchreest's drinks are on the house tonight," he told Jack.

Jack grinned. "Terrific," he said. The waiter withdrew and Jack picked back up where he'd been.

"So, anyway, once I pay off my mortgage, my flat will be worth a ton. My original goal was to be a millionaire by forty, and when I missed it, I was quite depressed for a while, but now I'm back on track and this time I'm going to get there."

"A million pounds is a lot of money," Lisa said. "It will be an achievement to be proud of, for sure."

Jack nodded. "Actually, I'm aiming for a net worth of a million dollars, US," he told her. "A million is a million."

And a million US dollars is a lot less than a million pounds, Lisa thought to herself. "Indeed," she murmured.

The waiter arrived with a plate of garlic bread. "Complimentary starter," he told the pair.

Lisa loved their garlic bread, but she hadn't ordered it. Doing so would have felt rude somehow. Now she grabbed a piece and took a huge bite. Jack simply sipped his water.

"Don't you like garlic bread?" she asked him.

"No, not at all," he said. "I have breath mints in the car for you when I take you home."

Lisa nearly choked on her bread. Was he implying that she'd need to have a breath mint before he kissed her goodnight? That was so not on the agenda that it didn't merit thinking about.

"So where is your flat?" Lisa asked politely.

"Maybe I'll just have to show you later," the man said teasingly.

Lisa smiled weakly. "No, that's okay. I was just curious," she told him.

"Of course it is much too soon to be thinking about taking things to that level," Jack assured her. "But since you asked, I'm in the Onchan Beachland development."

Lisa nodded. "I thought I heard that they had some problems," she said, trying to remember what she'd heard. "Something about flooding issues?"

"Some of the ground floor flats did flood last year," Jack said. "But they've made some important changes since then."

"Which floor are you on?" Lisa asked.

"The ground," Jack said, clearly reluctantly. "But my flat wasn't too badly damaged, and they've almost finished the repair work anyway."

Lisa focussed her attention on the garlic bread while she tried to remember what else she knew about that particular development. It had been built by a company that was notorious on the island for cutting corners. Nothing they did was illegal or unsafe, but they were known for using the cheapest possible materials that let them provide a living space that looked flashy, but was only just up to basic standards. Quality wasn't on their list of options. Perfect for Jack, she thought.

The food arrived before Lisa could think of another topic to discuss and the pair ate in silence for a time. Jack interrupted the quiet that Lisa had been enjoying.

"So what's the story with your friend?" he asked.

"Do you mean Darcy?"

"Yeah, Darcy, what's the story with her?"

"I'm not sure what you mean," Lisa said, inwardly sighing deeply.

"She's gorgeous, right, so what's she doing with that guy Mark?"

"What's wrong with Mark?"

"He just didn't seem like her type," Jack said with a shrug. "She could do better."

"Mark's a really great guy," Lisa replied. "He's smart and he's fun to be with and he's gorgeous. What more could Darcy want?"

Jack shrugged. "I suppose I was just surprised to see her with a guy like him. I met her when she was working on my flight back to the island and she and the pilot seemed quite cosy. They seemed like the perfect match."

"When was this?" Lisa asked.

"A couple of weeks ago," Jack said. "The pilot was some guy called Finlo and I got the feeling he was rich and successful as well as being good-looking. He and Darcy looked like the perfect couple together."

"Maybe Darcy prefers quality over flash," Lisa told him.

Jack laughed. "She was wearing a bright purple mini-dress tonight," he reminded Lisa. "That girl is all about flash."

Lisa laughed in spite of herself. Jack was right. Darcy usually did go for style over substance. But maybe Mark was a move in the right direction for her. Maybe Darcy was maturing.

Jack waved away the offer of coffee and the pudding menu. "I'm stuffed," he announced. "I couldn't eat another bite."

Lisa had to agree, but then she'd eaten an entire plate of garlic bread by herself, as well as her meal.

The drive home was a quiet one. Jack made a few more remarks about how wonderful his car was and Lisa muttered polite replies, but as far as Lisa was concerned the date was over and it was obvious they hadn't hit it off.

At Lisa's house, Jack walked her to the door. "I had a wonderful time," he told her. "Maybe we could try my favourite restaurant next weekend."

Lisa shook her head. "I don't think so," she said. "You seem like a nice guy, but you aren't really my type."

"What?" Jack said, his tone shocked. "If I'm not your type, what exactly are you looking for?"

Lisa sighed. "Look, I don't want to argue, I just don't want to see you again."

Jack sighed. "Darcy told me you were very particular, but really, you aren't exactly my type, either, but I'm willing to make concessions. Maybe you should think about reevaluating your standards. You aren't getting any younger, you know."

Lisa stared at him, open-mouthed. A hundred angry replies fought with each other to be first to blast out of her mouth. Her front door opened before she had a chance to say anything. Darcy smiled out at her and Jack.

"There you are," Darcy exclaimed. "I feel like I've been waiting all night for you to get home."

Lisa looked at her friend and shook her head. "Why are you here, exactly?" she asked.

Darcy laughed. "I had Mark drop me off here after dinner," she explained. "I didn't feel like staying in my flat on my own."

"You must've eaten quickly," Lisa remarked.

"Yeah, sort of," Darcy told her. "Actually the restaurant we wanted to go to was having a private function, so we ended up just grabbing a pizza and taking it back to my flat. After that, I had him bring me here."

"Hello," Jack said waving his hands in the air. "I hate to interrupt this, but we were having a conversation."

"As far as I'm concerned, that conversation was finished," Lisa said firmly. "Thank you for a lovely meal. Good night."

She nodded at Jack and then pushed past him into her house. He looked as if he was going to protest, but she shut the door before he had a chance to say anything.

"That seemed a little bit rude," Darcy said to her friend.

"He'd just finished telling me I wasn't getting any younger," Lisa told her.

Darcy laughed. "Was that after you told him you didn't want to see him again?" she guessed.

"Exactly!"

Darcy sighed. "What was wrong with him, then?" she asked.

Lisa shook her head. "Let's just not even go there," she said with a sigh.

Darcy laughed. "Come and have a glass of wine and tell me everything," she said.

Lisa followed her to the kitchen, where Darcy opened a bottle of wine and poured them each a glass.

"Popcorn," Darcy exclaimed. "We need popcorn."

She found bags of microwave popcorn in the cupboard and set one going. While she was sorting the snack out, Lisa drained her glass of wine.

"Oh, dear," Darcy said as she refilled the glass. "You did have a bad evening. But let me tell you one little interesting thing about mine first."

"What happened?" Lisa asked.

"I told you the restaurant was closed for a private function," Darcy said. "Guess who was hosting said function?"

Lisa frowned. "Joney and Nigel?" she guessed.

Darcy laughed. "Exactly. And I'm not sure why I'm laughing, because it was pretty awful, actually. Mark and I walked up to the door and this man was just telling us that the place was closed to the public when a limo pulled up and Joney and Nigel got out. Of course, Joney had to make a huge fuss."

"Of course," Lisa rolled her eyes.

"She went on and on about how embarrassed she was to have not invited us to her little event."

"Why didn't she invite us? She's invited us to her wedding."

"Yeah, well, essentially, although this wasn't how she put it, tonight's event was a charity fund-raiser and she assumed we're too poor to donate enough to make her look good."

"The cow," Lisa said. "I'm surprised we got wedding invitations. I'm sure our presents won't be up to her standards, either."

Darcy laughed. "I think she just wants warm bodies at the wedding," she told Lisa. "But tonight was all about money. From what I could see, all of the guests were Nigel's work colleagues, you know those guys in suits that work in banking. About a dozen people went in while I was talking with Joney and she didn't seem to know any of them."

"I hope she had a miserable evening, then," Lisa said.

"I'm more interested in hearing about your miserable evening," Darcy replied.

Lisa gave her friend a rundown of the evening. Darcy laughed as Lisa told her about Jack's money plans.

"It's easier to hit your goals if you change them to lower ones," Darcy said. She had poured the hot popcorn into a large bowl and now both women grabbed handfuls and munched through them.

"I'm sorry," Darcy said. "I've done a terrible job of finding you a man."

"Time to give up," Lisa suggested.

"Time to regroup," Darcy told her. "I need to think outside the box. I'm clearly looking in the wrong places and not taking enough time over this."

"I wish you'd just quit looking," Lisa told her, washing popcorn down with more wine.

Darcy laughed. "I've even got Mark looking," she told Lisa. "He's going to talk to a few friends and see what he can do."

For some reason Lisa didn't like that idea, but she bit her tongue. It was getting late and she hated arguing with Darcy.

"I need some sleep," she told Darcy.

"Me too," Darcy replied. "I'm flying out at two tomorrow for another fortnight of hopping all over the place."

"You'll be gone the whole time?" Lisa asked.

"Probably," Darcy shrugged. "I'm flying with Pete again, as Finlo is avoiding me. Pete likes to keep heading further out. He likes going new places and staying in hotels at the company's expense."

"And so do you," Lisa said.

Darcy nodded. "Although I think I'm getting old," she told Lisa. " I'm enjoying it less and less all the time."

Lisa thought about several replies, but none of them felt quite right. Instead she gave Darcy a hug and said goodnight.

She treated Darcy to brunch at a nearby hotel the next morning before Darcy had to head back to her flat.

"I need time to run a load of clothes through the washer and dryer before I go, or I won't have clean undies for the fortnight," she told Lisa.

Lisa used the rest of Sunday to plan the site visits for the week ahead. She was looking forward to getting started on them, she told herself. Seeing Mark had nothing to do with her eager anticipation of Monday morning.

10

Mark picked Lisa up at nine on Monday morning. They'd spent some time the previous week discussing the order in which they were going to convert the sites. In the end they'd agreed to start with the House of Manannan.

"It's going to be the most complicated, so I'd rather get it over with first," Lisa said. "If any site is going to find bugs in the system, it's that one."

It only took Lisa an hour to install the new system. As they didn't want to start using it in the middle of the day, instead of switching it on, she and Mark headed to Peel Castle. Lisa spent the rest of the morning installing the new system there, as well.

"There isn't much more we can do until morning," Lisa told Mark after she'd finished the install. "The installation has gone very smoothly, so now we just have to see how things go once the system is live."

With their afternoon free, the pair grabbed a quick lunch before Mark persuaded Lisa to let him take her on a proper tour of the House of Manannan.

"You should understand the site better," Mark told her. "Just in case there are any problems tomorrow."

Lisa might have felt guilty about spending the afternoon sightseeing if they weren't already several days ahead of schedule. As it was, she left the museum staff playing with the new system as they headed off on their tour.

"I'll be back in an hour or so," she told them. "I'd like you to have lots of questions for me when I get back."

She and Mark joined a couple of small family groups that had just arrived and Lisa enjoyed watching how the children reacted to the different exhibits almost as much as she enjoyed the exhibits herself.

As the lights went down in the first room, and the animated characters began to move, the youngest of the children were quick to climb into laps for reassurance. Older children whispered excitedly as the soundtrack began and the story unfolded. Lisa watched as the dog by the fire wagged his tail throughout the story. A few minutes later the lights came back on and the group moved to the next section.

Lisa enjoyed learning more about life on the island as the Vikings arrived and stayed to intermarry with the island's residents. In the middle of the museum was a full-sized model of a Viking ship, and the children in the group were delighted and amazed to find it sitting in a pool of real water. The ship seemed to be sailing right through the huge glass windows at the front of the museum, an effect that impressed Lisa as least as much as the children.

The tour through history continued on the upper level, where Lisa learned about shipping and the herring industry. The smell of smoking kippers filled one room and had Lisa wishing she'd eaten more lunch. The last section was all about Peel Castle, and Lisa was excited at the prospect of spending some time there the following day.

After the tour, the staff at the front desk had a few questions that Lisa spent the rest of the afternoon answering. When Mark took her home, she was happy that the day had been well spent.

"Should we stop somewhere for pizza?" Mark asked her on the drive.

"That would be great," Lisa replied. "I'm too tired to cook."

Mark laughed. "That's pretty much me every day."

"I'm not really much of a cook," Lisa admitted. "I always have good intentions, but usually I end up having cereal or ordering take-away from somewhere."

Mark nodded. "There's a few places in my building that do good take-away and I'm pretty much a regular at all of them."

As the evening was cool but dry, Mark parked at Lisa's house and the pair walked down to the prom. They stopped at one of the island's most popular pizza places and grabbed a table. It was quiet on a Monday night, and they sipped lager and watched the waves on the beach as they waited for their food.

"I can't imagine living anywhere else," Lisa said as she watched a small child chasing a seagull down the sand.

"Me either," Mark told her. "I'd never been here when I got short-listed for the job with MNH, and when I came over for the interview, I fell in love. I sat by the phone for a fortnight, waiting for them to ring to tell me I had the job. I don't know what I would have done if they'd hired someone else instead."

After their meal, they walked back to Lisa's house.

"I'll pick you up at nine again, okay?" Mark asked.

"Do you want me to drive for a change?" Lisa asked in reply. "You always end up driving and it really doesn't seem fair."

"I don't mind," Mark told her. "If you'd rather drive yourself, that's fine, but I really need to have my own car on site just in case there's a problem somewhere else and I need to get there in a hurry."

Lisa nodded. "I'm more than happy for you to drive," she told him. "I just don't want you to think I'm taking advantage of you."

"No problem there," he assured her.

Lisa had trouble sleeping that night. Taking the system live in the Manx Museum had been mildly worrying, but going live at the first two remote sites was both more exciting and more frightening. She was quiet in the car the next day.

"You're not usually this uncommunicative," Mark told her during the drive. "I've tried to start three conversations and you've been monosyllabic in your replies to every one. What's wrong?"

Lisa flushed. "I get nervous when a new system is going live," she replied. "We've been working towards this for almost a month now and I'm afraid it's all going to go pear-shaped this morning."

Mark patted her arm reassuringly. "It's going to go great," he said firmly. "And if it does all go wrong, there's no doubt in my mind that you can fix it."

Lisa gave him a smile. "Thanks," she said. "I'm glad you have so much confidence in me."

At ten o'clock the museum opened its doors to the handful of tourists who were waiting outside. Lisa held her breath as the first tickets from the new system came out of the printer. She couldn't stop herself from following the ticket holders to the entrance gates, where they scanned their tickets and the gates slid open. She let out a huge sigh of relief when every ticket printed perfectly and the gates opened for each person in turn.

"Well, that was anticlimactic," the girl at the ticket desk laughed.

Lisa rang Peel Castle to get a report on their first customers. They hadn't experienced any difficulties either. Lisa spent the rest of the morning working with the House of Manannan staff on completing the gift shop inventory. Ninety-five per cent of the items they sold had already been added into the new system, but a handful of items that had something unusual about them had given the staff problems. Now Lisa helped them work out the best way to enter them into the computer.

Lunch was a quick but filling meal at the pub across the street from the museum.

"We should go out and celebrate properly now that the sites are going live," Mark told her over a traditional Ploughman's lunch. "Are you free Saturday night?"

Lisa laughed. "I am, unless Darcy has arranged another blind date for me," she replied.

"I think Darcy is leaving the next one up to me," he replied. "And I think I have just the man for you."

Lisa rolled her eyes. "I don't even want to know," she said.

"He's not free this weekend, though, so I think you and I should celebrate. Let's go to *The Overlook*."

Lisa raised an eyebrow. "I've never been there," she said. "I've heard amazing things about it, but it's very expensive."

"It's my treat," Mark replied. "It's the least I can do after all your hard work."

"I'm just doing my job," she reminded him.

Mark laughed. "Okay, I just want to have a meal at *The Overlook* and I need an excuse," he told her. "Please come with me?"

Now Lisa laughed. "Since you put it that way, how can I refuse?"

Back at the museum, things were still running smoothly.

"Why don't we head over to the castle and check out things over there?" Mark suggested. Lisa was quick to agree.

They weren't having any trouble at the castle, either, but then, they'd had fewer visitors and their ticketing system was far less complex.

"We did sell a few tickets for tomorrow for Castle Rushen," the girl behind the ticket desk told Lisa excitedly. "It seemed to work perfectly."

Lisa put up her laptop and checked the system. Sure enough, it showed two tickets for Castle Rushen for the next day.

"Why don't I show you some of the most interesting parts of the castle while we're here?" Mark suggested.

For the next hour, he took her around the site, pointing out where the Derby apartments had been located and where the Pagan Lady had been buried.

"The necklace she was buried with had beads from around the world on it," Mark told her. "You've seen it at the museum in Douglas, of course."

"It's a shame there isn't more of the castle still standing," Lisa said as she surveyed the site.

He walked her through the chapel and down into the crypt below it.

"Okay, this is creepy," Lisa said. "I keep waiting for the ghosts to start moaning."

Mark laughed. "As far as I know, there aren't any ghosts down here," he told her. "The Moddey Dhoo lives in the gatehouse."

"That sounds vaguely familiar," Lisa said with a frown. "Tell me more."

"The Moddey Dhoo is a large black dog, as large as a cow, perhaps, that protects the castle," Mark told her. "In the past, guards always travelled the castle in pairs at night to keep it away."

"It only appears to people when they're on their own?" Lisa asked. "That sounds fishy to me."

Mark shrugged. "I've never seen it," he told her. "There is a story about a young guard who had a few drinks too many and insisted on walking alone through the castle. Apparently, the other guards heard screaming, and when he emerged he was shaking and couldn't speak. The story goes that he died three days later without ever speaking again."

Lisa looked at the small guard chamber near the castle entrance. "It doesn't look all that scary in there," she told Mark.

Mark shrugged. "I don't like being alone in either castle at night," he said. "Both places feel sort of spooky after dark."

Lisa nodded. "I don't think I'd like to be here alone at night, either," she agreed. "Does Castle Rushen have a ghost as well, then?"

Mark laughed. "Yes, but I don't have to worry about seeing that one."

Before Mark could continue, Lisa's phone rang. Marjorie, back at the Manx Museum, had a question about the report she'd just run off the new system. Lisa got her laptop back out and talked Marjorie through a few things before it was time to head home.

Mark dropped Lisa off at home after the short drive from Peel. He had a late meeting at the museum, so she fixed herself a sandwich and ate it in front of the television. Tomorrow they were due to install the new software at Rushen Abbey, which would be a relief for the staff there who were still struggling with their unwieldy old system.

Lisa was pleased that the next day was dry. Maybe she'd have a chance to have a walk around the abbey on this visit. Mark was prompt, and the drive to Castletown was a fairly short one.

"Oh, I'm so glad you're finally here," Jane told Lisa as she walked in. "I can't wait to get rid of the old system."

Lisa laughed. "I'm glad we're able to help you. I'll be installing today and you'll be going live tomorrow. I'm hoping to get a good start on things now, before you get busy."

"Well, I won't get in your way, then," the other woman replied.

Lisa got down to work, pausing only briefly whenever Jane needed to access the old system. Ninety minutes later, she was done.

"There's nothing else to do now, except wait for tomorrow and see what happens," Lisa told her.

"Are you sure I can't just switch systems now?" the woman asked.

"Sorry, but you can't," Lisa replied. "I have to tell the main system that you're live and I'll do that as of midnight tonight. You'll just have to endure the old system for a few more hours."

Jane nodded. "Okay, I suppose I can manage, if I have to."

The skies were clouding up, so Mark insisted that he give Lisa a quick tour of the ruins, just in case it started to rain later in the day.

Lisa studied the model of the site and then tried to picture it full-sized as they walked along. A walk through the gardens completed their tour.

"I wish we had time to walk to Silverdale Glen," Mark told Lisa.

"Oh, please, no more glens for a while," Lisa said with a laugh.

Mark laughed too. "I'd forgotten about your recent glen-walking adventures," he said. "But the Monk's Bridge is worth seeing."

"Another day," Lisa suggested. "For now, I'm starving."

Mark smiled. "I think it is time for lunch," he said.

They had lunch at a little restaurant near the abbey before heading into Castletown itself to go to the Nautical Museum.

Once there, Lisa quickly installed the new system for them, and then she spent some time helping them complete their gift shop inventory. Because of the nature of the site, they had several items in their gift shop that weren't for sale anywhere else. Lisa helped the staff categorise and record these items while Mark talked with the site manager about the upcoming restoration work on the *Peggy*.

"We went around here when we made our first visit, didn't we?" Mark asked after Lisa had finished helping with the merchandising.

"We did," Lisa replied. "Although I wouldn't mind seeing those hidden compartments again."

Mark laughed. "That's everyone's favourite part of this place, aside from the *Peggy*, of course."

"If he wasn't smuggling, what could he have used them for?" Lisa asked as Mark pulled open the hidden panels and trapdoors in the main room of the house.

"Storage?" Mark suggested. "Or maybe he was hiding things to protect them from thieves. We don't really know for sure, but smuggling is as good a guess as any."

Lisa grinned. "I'd love to have something like this in my house," she said. "I could hide all my valuables in there and never worry about them."

"Unless your burglar ever visited here," Mark said.

"Well, yeah, I suppose so," Lisa said with a frown. "Maybe it isn't such a great idea."

"I'd love to have something like this just for the sheer joy of owning it," Mark told her.

"There is that," Lisa agreed. "It's beautifully put together."

Mark dropped Lisa at home after that.

"I'd love to stop for a bite somewhere," he told her, "but I have a class tonight."

"You're taking a class? In what?"

"Not taking, teaching," Mark replied. "I teach a few classes at the institute now and then. Tonight is one of my nights to teach."

Thursday morning Lisa was nervous again. "I hope Rushen Abbey goes okay," she told Mark in his car on the way to the site. "They were so excited about the new system."

"I'm sure it will be fine," Mark told her, patting her arm. "Relax."

Lisa shook her head. "I won't relax until they've sold a few tickets and everything has worked."

At the abbey, a steady rain was falling. Mark and Lisa dashed from the car and into the building.

"We might not have a lot of customers today," Jane told Lisa.

"I hope you get a few," Lisa said. "Otherwise we can't test the system."

Ten o'clock came and went without anyone arriving. Lisa fielded a few phone calls from the other sites that were live as she waited for the first tickets to be sold at the abbey.

"I hope there isn't anything wrong elsewhere," Mark said after Lisa hung up from her third call.

"Nothing much," Lisa told him. "Peel wanted to double-check how to change the paper in the printer. House of Manannan had a customer that stuffed their ticket in a pocket and then the machine couldn't read it because the bar code had a crease in it. They simply needed to reprint it for him. And the Nautical Museum was just reporting that they'd sold three tickets and everything worked perfectly."

"Come on, let's take a walk around the inside displays again," Mark suggested. "I hate watching you just sitting there staring at the door."

Lisa grinned. "I'm okay, but maybe a walk will do me good. I'm afraid I might jump all over a customer if one comes in."

Mark shook his head. "With this rain, it doesn't seem likely that we'll see anyone this morning."

Lisa and Mark wandered through the exhibits, with Lisa taking her time to read every sign and listen to every presentation. An hour later they were back at the front desk, where Jane was beaming.

"We sold five tickets while you were gone," she told Lisa. "Three for this site and two for Castle Rushen."

"And everything worked okay?" Lisa asked.

"Everything worked perfectly," Jane told her. "Just like in the training sessions."

Lisa blew out a sigh of relief. "Now we just have to hope someone buys something from the gift shop so we can check that everything there is working correctly, too."

She didn't have long to wait. Only a few minutes later a young couple came in. They purchased site tickets and then decided that they needed an umbrella as well. The gift shop's software seemed to work perfectly as well.

Lisa took out her laptop as soon as the tourists had moved away. She clicked through a dozen screens, checking and rechecking that everything looked correct.

"Wow," Jane was peering over her shoulder. "That's all the tickets we've sold today," she said, pointing to the screen. "Can you see the umbrella as well?"

Lisa grinned. "If everything is working correctly, I can." She clicked on a different report and then pointed. "There it is, listed under sales from the Rushen Abbey gift shop today."

Mark grinned. "Do you feel better now?" he asked Lisa.

"Much," Lisa smiled back at him. "I suppose we should head over to the Nautical Museum and check on them, though."

"Let's do that, and maybe get lunch as well," Mark agreed.

They went to the same little restaurant near the museum for lunch, and Lisa loved the food yet again.

"Now I just want to go home and have a nap," she told Mark. "I'm lovely and full."

"If things are going well here, you could take the afternoon off, couldn't you?"

Lisa shook her head. "Tempting as that is, I have a lot of things I should be doing," she told him. "We're several days ahead on the project and I want to stay that way."

After checking in with the museum, the pair headed back to Douglas. Lisa spent her afternoon running reports from every site that was live, looking for problems or inconsistencies. She fielded a handful of phone calls from the live sites as well, with questions about various issues.

Mark stuck his head in her temporary office at the end of the day. "So no site visits tomorrow?" he checked.

"No, tomorrow is all about finalising the programming and interfaces for the rest of the sites. Assuming I finish everything, Monday we can pick back up with installations. If the sites were closer together, we could possibly finish everything next week. As it is, though, I think we'll need a few days into the following week as well."

"That still has us finishing up well ahead of schedule," Mark told her. "I can't believe how smoothly it's all gone."

Lisa shook her head. "Don't say that yet. We have a long way to go."

Friday was spent on reports and programming. Mark offered to go to lunch with her, but Lisa didn't want to take the time. Instead, he kindly brought her a sandwich and insisted that she take ten minutes out to eat it. At the end of the day, he reappeared.

"I'm having dinner with some friends tonight," he told her in an apologetic tone. "We get together once a month."

"That sounds like fun," Lisa replied. "Enjoy."

Mark started to walk away and then turned back. "You probably won't be interested. That is, I don't want you to feel like you have to, but, I mean, well," he stopped and shook his head. "Never mind," he said, taking a few steps away.

"Mark, what was that all about?" Lisa called after him.

Mark flushed and turned back towards her. "I'm giving a paper tomorrow at a sort of mini-conference here in the museum. I wondered if you might like to come and hear it."

"What sort of conference?" Lisa asked.

"It's mostly historical. I'm talking about the museum's plans for future exhibits, but most of the contributors are talking about their most recent research. Marjorie will be talking about seventeenth- and eighteenth-century wills, for example." He shook his head. "Never mind. It was just a thought."

Lisa grinned. "I'd love to come," she said impulsively. "It might be fun, and I don't have anything else to do."

"As long as it's not interfering with anything important," Mark said.

Lisa laughed. "You know I don't have a life," she said.

Mark gave her the details and Lisa noted them in her phone. "I suppose I'll see you tomorrow morning, then," she said.

"After the conference, are we still on for dinner at *The Overlook?*" Mark asked.

Lisa nodded. Her Saturday was suddenly looking very interesting.

11

Lisa ate cereal with milk in front of the television on Friday night, then curled up with a book until she was tired enough to sleep. Her sleep was restless, though, and she woke up feeling grumpy and worried about the day ahead. She'd never been to this sort of conference before, so she had no idea what to expect. And she'd never eaten at *The Overlook*, which was meant to be very fancy.

She rang Darcy's mobile. "Hey, have you ever been to an academic conference?" she asked her friend.

"You woke me up to ask me that?" Darcy asked. "I don't think I've ever been to an academic conference. Why?"

"Mark invited me to come and hear him speak this morning and I was wondering what to expect," Lisa explained.

"I suppose you'll have to wait and see," Darcy told her, yawning audibly.

"What about *The Overlook*? Have you been there?"

"Oooooo, who's taking you to *The Overlook*?" Darcy demanded. "It's incredible."

Lisa flushed, even though her friend couldn't see her. "Mark is," she said. "We're celebrating the success of the new system."

"If you were anyone else, I'd be jealous," Darcy told her. "I love *The*

Overlook, but I know you've been working really hard and I suppose you deserve it."

"But what am I going to wear?" Lisa asked.

"Borrow something from me," Darcy suggested. "There's a little black dress of mine in the wardrobe in your spare room. It would look fabulous on you."

"Are you sure?" Lisa asked.

Darcy assured her that she was more than welcome to anything in the spare room wardrobe. Lisa quizzed her friend on the menu and then they chatted a bit about Darcy's week before Lisa had to go and get ready for the conference.

She showered and dressed carefully in a long skirt and a light jumper. The weather was still fairly mild for late October, but it was definitely cooler than it had been. She added a pair of black leather boots and then headed out to the museum. She was annoyed with herself for feeling nervous as she took the short walk through Douglas.

At the museum, she followed Mark's instructions and headed to the lifts. On the top level of the building there were several spaces that could be used for lectures or conferences, and that was where today's event was being held.

In the education level's foyer, a large table was set up. Lisa smiled as she recognised the two men behind it.

"Henry and Doug, it's great to see you, but who on earth is manning the front desk?" she asked.

Henry laughed. "They had Sue come up from Castle Rushen to help out this morning. She was going to do this job, but then she decided she'd rather do tickets so she can check out the new system."

Lisa nodded. "Well, let's hope she likes it. I'm installing it down there soon."

"Mark told us you might be coming," Henry told her. "Here's your packet of information."

Lisa took the envelope and looked inside. There was a programme for the day as well as a couple of sheets with brief biographies of the speakers.

"Thank you," she said to Henry as she moved away from the table.

She looked over the papers and then slid them back into their envelope. There were tables with tea, coffee and biscuits laid out in the foyer, but Lisa ignored them. The schedule showed a short break in the middle. Maybe she'd grab something then.

All of the talks were being given in the A.W. Moore Lecture Hall, so she headed towards the sets of double doors that were open. That had to be the right room.

Inside the lecture hall, she surveyed the small crowd. She'd just decided to grab a chair in the back row when she spotted Mark. Their eyes met and he grinned and crossed the room to her.

"Come and meet everyone," he suggested when he reached her side.

Lisa found herself in the middle of a large group, feeling overwhelmed as Mark made the introductions.

"I think you already know William Corlett," Mark told her. "He runs the institute."

"Nice to see you again," Lisa murmured to the man that she'd been introduced to on a handful of occasions, but had never really spoken to. He was Finlo's cousin, though, so that made her slightly wary of him.

"I've been wanting a chance to speak to you," William told her. "Mark's been telling us about what you've been doing for MNH. I'm hoping you might be able to work some similar magic for us. We really need a single database system that lets us track researchers and research as well as...."

"Darling, let's let Lisa enjoy the conference for today," the pretty brunette standing next to William interrupted. "I'm sure you need to ring her boss to talk about hiring her anyway." She turned to Lisa. "I'm Katie, William's wife," she told Lisa. "Don't mind him. He's a bit obsessive about work sometimes."

Lisa laughed, immediately liking the young woman. "You're American," she said in surprise.

"I am, indeed," Katie replied. "I came over to do some research and fell in love with William while I was at it."

Lisa smiled. "How terribly romantic," she sighed.

William slipped an arm around his wife. "She's giving one of the papers today," he told Lisa proudly. "She's a brilliant historian."

"You might be a tad biased," Katie suggested to her husband as she rested her head on his shoulder.

"Nope, not me, not even a little bit," William said, shaking his head.

Mark introduced Lisa to the rest of the day's speakers and their significant others. When Thomas Clague came into the room, it was clearly time for the conference to begin.

Lisa slid into a seat next to William Corlett and watched as the five speakers took their places at the long table at the front of the room. She slid her programme out and took a look. Katie was speaking first, followed by Marjorie and then Mark. There was a break scheduled after Mark's talk. Lisa settled back into her chair, wishing she'd had some coffee to help keep her awake if she got bored.

Whether or not Katie was a brilliant historian, she was a skilled speaker, and Lisa found herself drawn in as Katie talked about the island during the English Civil War period. By the time she'd finished her remarks, Lisa was determined to have another look at the museum exhibits that pertained to that period and maybe take another trip to see the special exhibit at the House of Manannan as well.

Marjorie was almost equally interesting to listen to and Lisa thoroughly enjoyed learning more about wills from the distant past. After Marjorie had answered a few questions, it was Mark's turn to speak and Lisa found herself unaccountably nervous on his behalf.

William seemed to notice. "Don't worry, he'll be great," he whispered to Lisa.

Lisa nodded at him and then focussed on Mark. He seemed nervous himself as he started, but he slowly got into his stride and the talk itself was packed with interesting information. Lisa hung on every word and felt a huge rush of relief when he finished. After a few questions, it was time for the break.

Lisa was suddenly starving, but she waited for Mark to join her before they headed out to find drinks and biscuits.

"So, are you enjoying your morning so far?" Mark asked once they had drinks in hand.

"Everyone's been fascinating," Lisa replied. "I'm surprised how interesting it all is."

Mark laughed. "We have to find a way to convey that to the rest of the island," he told her. "These conferences always welcome the same group of people, most of them historians themselves. We'd love to get some of the general public to turn up, but they don't seem interested."

"Maybe they just don't know what to expect. I didn't."

Mark nodded. "I think we need to work on our advertising," he said.

Before Lisa could reply, the Corletts and a few others joined them. The fifteen-minute break flew past in a blur of conversation and biscuits before it was time to find her seat again for the last two talks.

Full of biscuits and milky tea, Lisa found the last two speakers somewhat less enthralling than the earlier ones had been. Nevertheless, she felt as if she learned something from every talk. As the morning broke up, it seemed as if everyone in the room wanted to talk to Mark. Lisa stood by his side as he answered questions and exchanged greetings with everyone. He introduced her to dozens of people but Lisa couldn't remember most names a moment later. Finally, the room cleared and Mark turned to her.

"Lunch? I'm starving, but I'm always hungry after I speak. It must be the adrenaline or something."

Lisa shook her head. "I was just going to have a can of soup for lunch. We're still going out tonight, right? I want to be very hungry for *The Overlook*."

Mark grinned. "You're right, of course. A big lunch would be a bad idea. But we can get something light here in the museum café that won't spoil our dinner."

Lisa couldn't resist, so the pair made their way to the small café. It was only about half-full and Mark suggested a small table in the corner.

"So what did you really think of the conference?" he asked Lisa once they'd ordered.

"I really enjoyed it," she replied. "You'll have to send me information when you do another one. I suppose I'll be finished with the installation by then."

Mark nodded. "We only do two or three a year, so yeah, you should be done with the installation before the next one."

Lisa ate her potato-and-leek soup with the thick slice of freshly baked bread that had accompanied it. "What time is dinner?" she asked Mark as she buttered the last bite of bread.

"Our booking is for seven," he told her.

Lisa glanced at her watch. "I suppose I'll have time to get hungry again," she said. "This bread is really good, but it's very filling. I shouldn't have eaten so much."

Lunch over, Lisa headed for home. She did laundry and gave the house a quick tidy-up before running herself a bubble bath. While she soaked, she let her mind drift. After several minutes, she became aware that it was drifting towards Mark with alarming frequency. Mark was gorgeous, intelligent, and fun to spend time with, but he was dating Darcy and she shouldn't be thinking about him.

With a sigh, Lisa drained the tub and dried off. She dug out the black dress that Darcy had suggested. It was far more modest than Darcy's usual choices and it actually fit Lisa quite well, even if it would have looked very different on Darcy. Lisa looked in the mirror and grinned. If only Darcy were here to do her hair and makeup. Of course, if Darcy were there, she'd be the one going out with Mark, not Lisa.

By the time Mark arrived, Lisa had redone her makeup three times. She still wasn't happy with the last attempt, but she'd run out of time, so she would have to live with it.

"You look gorgeous," Mark told her when she opened the door.

"Thanks, you look pretty good yourself," Lisa replied. Mark was wearing a dark grey suit, and Lisa suddenly felt a little intimidated by him.

"Shall we?" he asked, offering Lisa his arm.

She took it tentatively, letting him lead her down the short path from her door to the waiting car. He helped her into the taxi and then shut the door behind her before walking around the other side.

Lisa stared out the car window as they drove slowly through the streets of Douglas. At the restaurant, a valet opened Lisa's door and helped her from the car. She took Mark's arm and let him lead her towards the building.

"I feel like a little kid playing dress-up," she hissed to Mark as they made their way up the steps to the restaurant.

Mark smiled at her. "If you eat all your dinner, I'll take you for ice cream after."

Lisa laughed, which helped ease some of the tension she was feeling. Inside the restaurant, a man in a tuxedo ushered them to their table, which had a stunning view over Douglas Bay. He recited the specials and then left them with their menus.

Lisa spent several minutes reading through the menu. When she finally closed it and looked up, Mark was studying her with an amused expression on his face.

"What?" she demanded.

"I hope it all looks good," he told her. "What are you going to have?"

Lisa mentioned the chicken and Mark suggested a steak.

"There aren't any prices on my menu," she told him with a frown.

"There aren't any on mine either," he replied. "But everything is about the same price, so order whatever sounds the best."

Lisa opened the menu again and reread several mouth-watering descriptions. "It's too hard," she said, aware that she sounded whiny. "Everything sounds good."

When the waiter arrived, Mark insisted on ordering a bottle of champagne. "We're celebrating," he reminded Lisa.

When the man returned with the champagne, he and Mark had a lengthy conversation about the menu. By the time they'd finished, Lisa knew exactly what she wanted to eat, and she was only a little bothered about the prices.

Mark insisted on starters, ordering three different ones so that they could both try some different things. Lisa drank some of her champagne and tried to relax. This was meant to be a fun evening, even if it felt awkward and uncomfortable for some reason.

Lisa stared out at the amazing view. "I could sit and watch the sea all day," she said to Mark.

"That's what I like best about my flat," Mark told her.

"You have a view of the sea?" Lisa asked him.

"I'm right on the prom," Mark told her. "I have fabulous views."

"You mentioned that before, being right on the prom, but I didn't realise you had sea views as well," Lisa said. "Which complex do you live in?"

"Seaview Towers," Mark replied.

Lisa was surprised. Flats in the building were hugely expensive, and, aside from Howard, the computer gaming genius, she'd never actually met anyone who could afford to live there. Even Finlo Quayle, with his successful airline, didn't have a flat in that particular building.

"Uh oh," Mark said. "I know what that look on your face means. You're trying to work out how I can afford to live in a building like that on what I must make working for MNH."

Lisa flushed. He had pretty much read her mind. "I've never been in the building," she said. "But I have heard it's very expensive."

"It's not inexpensive," Mark replied.

Lisa stared at him, wondering how to get him to explain without being rude and asking awkward questions.

After a moment, Mark took pity on her. "I told you my father worked in banking," he told her. "And I told you he took early retirement. He was very, very successful at what he did."

Lisa took a sip of champagne and waited to see if Mark would tell her the rest of the story.

After his own sip of champagne, he continued. "He met my mother when he was older, and he wanted to be sure that my brother and I would be taken care of in case something happened to him. He established trust funds for both of us when we were very young. They're still in effect now."

He shrugged. "When I moved to the island and decided that I wanted to stay, I used some of my trust fund money to make a down payment on a house. Eventually, I sold that house and bought my flat."

Lisa nodded, but her mind was racing. She knew when she was looking for houses, that two-bedroom flats on the ground floor of that building were going for more than three times the price of her small detached home. Larger units and units above the fourth floor were considerably more expensive.

"I've never even been inside the building," Lisa said. "I've been told the views are spectacular, though."

"Sometime I'll have to have you over and you can see for yourself,"

Mark said with a smile. The starters arrived then, to save Lisa from having to reply.

The food was every bit as delicious as Lisa had been promised, and by the time she finished her main course she was feeling absolutely stuffed.

"I hope you saved room for pudding," Mark said with a grin. "Their puddings are amazing."

Lisa groaned. "I'm not sure I can eat another bite," she said.

"Crème brûlée is pretty light," Mark suggested. "And it's very good."

Lisa grinned. "Okay, then, I'll try it," she said. She drank what was left of her glass of champagne.

"Should we get another bottle?" Mark asked.

"Oh, good heavens, no," Lisa exclaimed. "I'm feeling quite giddy as it is."

Mark grinned. "We are celebrating," he reminded her.

"Pudding will be celebration enough after that meal and the champagne," Lisa assured him.

After the delicious pudding, Lisa took one last look at the amazing view and then followed Mark out of the restaurant. He gave the taxi driver her address and the car made its way through Douglas. Lisa felt a strange tension in the taxi. If this had been a date, she would have suspected that Mark was thinking about kissing her goodnight. But tonight wasn't a date. They were just friends. She shook her head. She shouldn't have drunk all that champagne. It was filling her head with all sorts of stupid ideas.

"I'll just walk you to your door," Mark said when the taxi arrived at Lisa's house.

"Oh, I'm fine," Lisa told him, jumping out of the car. She was up the path and unlocking her door before Mark was fully out of the taxi.

"Thank you," she shouted back at him. "See you Monday."

She shut the door behind her and leaned against it, listening intently as the taxi pulled away. No doubt Mark thought she'd taken leave of her senses.

In bed she found herself tossing and turning, unable to get to sleep. She had a lot on her mind, and she didn't want to think about any of it.

12

Sunday was spent on household chores. Lisa went grocery shopping and then, trying to keep herself busy, she washed all of the bedding and towels in the house. By the end of the day, both her bed and the guest room had fresh linens and towels and Lisa was hopeful that she would be tired enough to sleep at bedtime.

She slid into a bubble bath with a box of truffles and a book, and emerged an hour later feeling slightly sick from too much chocolate and very dissatisfied with the romance novel she'd grabbed.

"No one would be that stupid," she told the book as she dropped it in a box to take to a charity shop.

Darcy rang as she was getting ready for bed. "So how was *The Outlook*?" she asked.

"Incredible," Lisa told her. "If I could afford it, it would be my new favourite restaurant."

Darcy laughed. "It is really good, but some day you need to come with me to London. When Finlo and I were dating, we found this terrific little place that was so much better."

"I don't believe it," Lisa said firmly. "Anyway, how are you?"

"I'm good, but I'm not going to get back to the island for a while,"

Darcy told her. "We just picked up a two-week sightseeing tour for some rich American who wants to fly his new wife all over Europe."

"But you haven't been home for ages," Lisa complained.

"I know, but this is seriously light duty and the pay is fabulous," Darcy said. "We'll probably only have to fly every other day and the rest of the time we're living on expenses. Pete's as thrilled as I am."

"You're spending a lot of time with Pete," Lisa said casually.

"He's fun, but he's way too young for me," Darcy replied. "Anyway, he makes a nice change from Finlo. He's at least as good-looking, but nowhere near as arrogant."

"It would take some doing for him to be as arrogant as Finlo," Lisa said dryly.

Darcy laughed again. "So what do you have planned for this week?"

"More site installations for MNH. Everything's gone well so far, and I'm crossing my fingers the rest will just fall into place as well."

"Of course it will," Darcy told her. "You're a genius at what you do."

Lisa laughed. "Not quite, but it has been a fairly straightforward project."

"I hope Mark is helping loads."

"Yeah, he's great," Lisa mumbled, not wanting to discuss Mark.

Darcy didn't seem to notice. "Okay, I hate to say it, but I have to dash. We're collecting our happy couple in a few hours and Pete wants to go over the flight plans over dinner."

"Since when do you go over flight plans with the pilots?" Lisa asked.

Darcy just laughed and disconnected.

Monday morning, Mark picked her up and they headed north. Mark filled the car journey with a brief history of mining on the island so that by the time they'd arrived at the Laxey Wheel, Lisa felt as if she knew everything there was to know about it.

Installing the software in the small ticket booth took very little time, even working in between the handful of customers who interrupted. Lisa spent some time doing a bit more software training and then she and Mark headed into Ramsey and the Grove Museum.

"How did Norma do with her training?" Lisa asked Mark on the drive.

"She did okay with the special interface you designed for her," he told her. "But she still isn't happy about it."

Lisa nodded. "I didn't think she would be," she admitted. "Some people don't like change, no matter what. I just hope she manages to use the new system successfully."

While Lisa installed the software, Mark chatted with Norma, telling her all about the wonderful advantages of the new system.

"You're all set," Lisa told her once she'd finished. "It will be live tomorrow."

"So I don't do anything with it today?" Norma asked.

"Nothing today," Lisa confirmed. "Would you like me to walk you through it all again?"

"Yes, please," Norma told her. "I think I've already forgotten everything young Mark told me in our classes."

"Maybe we should grab some lunch first," Mark suggested. "A tour bus just pulled up, so you'll be busy for a while, anyway," he told Norma. "Lisa and I will get lunch at the café and then come back and do some more training with you this afternoon."

"That sounds good," Norma agreed.

Lisa glanced outside at the crowd that was gathering. "That's a lot of people all at once," she told Mark. "I hope Norma likes crowds."

"She'll be in her element, taking them through the history of the building. Advance group ticket sales are handled by the museum, so she won't have to worry about that, either."

The small café on the grounds of the museum was quiet when they arrived.

"Hey, Mark, I hear a tour bus just arrived," the young waiter greeted them.

"It did indeed," Mark answered. "I'm sure you'll be busy serving up tons of tea and cakes in about an hour."

The young man nodded and then handed them menus. "Give me a shout when you're ready," he told them. "I'm just going to give Don a quick hand in the kitchen, gathering up extra mugs and the like. The soup's tomato basil," he added as he left the room.

"Oh, yes, please," Lisa said. "It's soup weather today."

"It's definitely more autumnal today than it has been," Mark agreed. Lisa glanced over the list of sandwiches and salads but saw nothing that tempted her away from the soup.

"I'll just grab Joe," Mark said, putting his menu down.

Half an hour later, full of hot soup and tea, Lisa and Mark returned to the museum foyer.

"Is the café getting busy now?" Norma asked fretfully. "Because it's supposed to be my lunch break, but I don't want to have to fight through a crowd."

"We were the only ones there when we left," Mark told her. "You go and get some lunch. Who's meant to take your place at the door?"

"Ginny, but she's usually late," Norma tutted.

Mark laughed. "You go. I can handle the door for a few minutes until Ginny gets here. She'd probably appreciate a review of the new system as well."

Ginny was only a few minutes late, and it only took Lisa a short time to walk her through the new system again.

"I remember a lot of it from the training session," she told Lisa. "And I'm only on the door for an hour every other day, but thanks."

Once Norma was back, Lisa had to work a lot harder. The older woman didn't seem to remember anything from her training sessions with Mark and she was stubbornly insistent that she didn't need to write anything down as Lisa walked her through the steps needed to generate tickets and take payments. After two hours, Lisa needed a break. The arrival of a small group of tourists gave her a chance to take one.

"I think you've just about got it," she lied to Norma. "I'm going to take a short break and grab something from the café while you do this tour. When I get back, we'll go over it one more time."

Mark had disappeared at least an hour earlier, muttering something about making a few phone calls. Now Lisa wondered where he was hiding.

In the café, she treated herself to a pot of hot chocolate and a generous piece of homemade shortbread. While she was sitting there, she took out her notebook and wrote very careful instructions for Norma. If the woman didn't want to take notes, Lisa would give her some herself.

She'd just finished when Mark dropped into the chair opposite hers.

"Sorry, I didn't mean to leave you alone with Norma all afternoon," he told her. "There's a problem with some objects we're borrowing for a new exhibit and I've spent the last hour on the phone with two different museums in London trying to work things out."

Lisa had never seen Mark looking quite so stressed and miserable before. She reached over and rubbed his back. "I hope it's all worked out now?" she asked.

"More or less," Mark sighed. "As much as can be at this point, anyway. I'm waiting for a bunch of people to ring me back."

"And I'd better get back to Norma," Lisa said with a sigh. She stood and grinned at Mark. "Hot chocolate can make things seem brighter," she told him.

Mark laughed. "I suppose it can't hurt."

Back at the ticket window, Lisa handed her instruction sheet to Norma. "I'm hoping you can help me out," she told the older woman. "I need to write up instructions for all of the sites, especially those where people are having trouble with the new system. I need someone who's learned it all to test out what I've written. Can you go through a few practice sales using my notes and let me know what I've missed?"

Norma frowned at her. "I told you I don't need instructions," she said petulantly.

"I know that," Lisa assured her. "But you wouldn't believe how many of your co-workers do."

"Which ones?" Norma asked.

"I mustn't tell you," Lisa said in a whisper. "But I'm sure you can guess."

Norma nodded sagely. "I can at that," she said. "Okay, let's see how these instructions work."

For another hour Norma did her best to crash the new system as Lisa walked her through everything she needed to know. The instructions were a huge help, even if Norma did keep insisting that there were mistakes in them.

"I thought we went to the number of tickets field next," Norma said, ready to cross through Lisa's carefully written instructions.

"Not until you've verified the sites," Lisa replied patiently.

Finally, as the day was winding down, Lisa felt like Norma was as good as she was going to get. Tomorrow would be the big test.

Mark was distracted when he drove her home. "I think I might have to spend some time in my office tomorrow," he told her. "I suppose you'll want to be in Ramsey?"

"Absolutely," Lisa replied. "I intend to stand right next to Norma all day. Otherwise, I'll be troubleshooting for her from somewhere else."

"I'm sorry, but I think maybe you should drive yourself up to Ramsey, then," Mark said. "I'll try to get up there by midday, though."

"That's no problem," Lisa replied. "I've been surprised by how much time you've been able to give to the project as it is. I'm sure you have lots of other things you need to do."

"I made the effort to more or less clear my calendar so that I could work with you," Mark told her. "But that didn't allow for things going wrong elsewhere."

"So I'll see you tomorrow afternoon, or I won't," Lisa said as she climbed out of Mark's car. "I just hope things work out for you."

Lisa spent Tuesday figuratively holding Norma's hand. The new system worked perfectly, and by the end of the day Lisa was feeling more confident that Norma was going to be able to manage.

"You're coming back tomorrow, right?" Norma asked at the end of the day. "I think I've nearly got it, but I really could use one more day with you helping."

Lisa forced herself to smile at the woman. "I'll be back first thing in the morning," she promised. "I'm not sure I can stay all day, though. I have lots of other sites to get up and running."

The other sites that were live had checked in with Lisa throughout the day and there hadn't been any major glitches so far. She headed for home wondering how Mark's day had gone. It seemed strange that she'd gone all day without talking to him. They'd spent every working day together for over a month, after all.

He rang her at home that evening. "I'm sorry I didn't get up to Ramsey today," he said. "I hope Norma wasn't too much trouble."

"She was fine," Lisa said. "But she wants me back again tomorrow."

"I'm going to be tied up tomorrow again," Mark said in an apologetic voice. "Otherwise I'd go and hold her hand while you got on with the next sites."

"Cregneash is next," Lisa reminded him. "I'm hoping to get down there Thursday to get the install done. I'm not sure if I'll try to add on the Grammar School as well or leave the three remaining Castletown sites for next week."

"I'll ring you tomorrow afternoon and you can tell me what you've decided," Mark said. "I'm hoping to be free for Thursday and Friday, but I can't promise at this point."

Lisa went to bed feeling sad and confused. She liked Mark a lot and she'd really missed his company. Norma had been hard work as well, and she'd have liked to have had Mark there to help with the woman. She told herself that she was unhappy about seeing Norma again the next day, rather than disappointed that she wouldn't be seeing Mark, although she fell asleep before she'd managed to convince herself of that.

On Wednesday morning Norma seemed to be feeling more confident. Lisa sat quietly in the corner and watched as she dealt with several customers, printing tickets and processing payments easily.

"I think you've got it all worked out," Lisa told her when there was a lull in tourist traffic.

"I suppose so," Norma said cautiously. "And Ginny knows the system better than I do, so I can always ask her for help if I need it."

"I'm going to head over to the Laxey Wheel," Lisa told her. "I have to check how the system is working for them. Please ring me if you need anything."

Lisa stopped for an early lunch on the short drive to Laxey. She ate a jacket potato with cheese and bacon, which left her feeling as stuffed as the potato had been.

At the Lady Isabella, everything was running smoothly. Lisa spent a few minutes chatting with the staff there and then headed back to her car. She was considering driving down to Cregneash to install the system there when her phone rang.

Lisa was surprised that it wasn't Norma ringing, but instead, there was a small glitch at the museum with the reporting system. With nothing else planned for the day, she was happy to head into Douglas to deal with it.

She spent the afternoon sorting out the problem and then working through a few other minor issues that had arisen. On her way out at five, she stuck her head into Mark's office.

"You look miserable," she told him as he looked up from his chair. Really, he looked tired and stressed and Lisa had to force herself not to rush over and give him a hug.

"Actually, things are looking up," he told her. "I think I may have just sorted out the last little detail." He glanced at the clock. "Now I just have wait for them to ring back to be sure."

"What did you have for lunch?" Lisa asked.

Mark frowned. "I don't know if I had lunch," he said. "I can't remember."

Lisa shook her head. "Do you have to stay here and wait for that call?"

"Yeah, pretty much," Mark shrugged. "It will probably be a little while, maybe an hour or so, but they could ring earlier if they have questions."

"So I'll go and get pizza," Lisa told him. "I'll be back as soon as I can."

Mark looked like he was going to protest, but Lisa smiled and waved and then walked away before he spoke. Half an hour later, she was back with pizza and a large bottle of fizzy drink.

"That smells wonderful," Mark groaned as she set the box on his desk.

"I know," Lisa laughed. "I almost stole a slice on my way back."

Mark laughed. "I probably wouldn't have even noticed," he told her.

The pair ate in silence for a while, both hoping the phone would ring. Eventually, the pizza was gone.

"Do you want me to stay and keep you company while you wait?" she asked Mark as she tidied up the plates and napkins.

"No, you go and do something fun," he replied. "It won't be long now, and you spent the morning with Norma. You deserve a break."

Lisa thought about arguing, but just then Mark's phone rang. He answered it and gave Lisa a thumbs up. She quietly left the office and headed for home.

It wasn't until the following morning that she realised she and Mark hadn't agreed on what to do next. She thought about ringing him, but then decided to just head to Cregneash herself. It was a long drive and she wanted to get there before they opened for the day. She locked her front door behind her and walked towards her car. A horn honked, and she felt a silly grin spread over her face as she spotted Mark's car behind hers.

"I meant to ring you last night," he told her as she climbed into his car. "But I ended up on the phone with London for over an hour and then I had to make a bunch of follow-up calls. By the time I got home, I just went to bed."

"Never mind," Lisa told him. "I was planning on doing Cregneash today, if that's okay with you."

"That's perfect," he told her. "I need to do a few things down there anyway with one of the exhibits. I've been putting them off, but this is the perfect opportunity."

Lisa spent the drive telling Mark about the time she'd spent with Norma, while Mark filled her in on what he'd been doing for the previous few days. By the time they arrived in Cregneash, Lisa felt better than she had in days.

The installation took longer than usual, mostly because Lisa had to keep fielding calls from Norma at the Grove Museum, but eventually she finished.

"It's pretty much time for lunch," Mark told her when she was finally done. "Why don't we grab something here?"

"That works for me," Lisa told him. "I'm still not sure if we should try to fit the Grammar School in today or not."

The small café on the site was crowded and lunch took longer than Lisa expected. A phone call from the museum in Douglas was what finally made up Lisa's mind for her, though.

"Another glitch in reports," Lisa told Mark with a sigh. "I think I'd better go and get that sorted for today. The Castletown sites will have to wait for next week."

Before they headed north, Mark checked his emails.

"I have to go to London tomorrow," he told Lisa on the drive north. "I'll probably be gone all weekend, sorting out this stupid exhibit."

Lisa laughed. "No one will loan you anything if you start calling exhibits stupid," she said, ignoring how disappointed she felt at the thought of not seeing him for a few days.

"I've told Jack at Cregneash to give you the full tour tomorrow," he told Lisa. "Once you're happy everything is working correctly, have him take you around. There's a lot to see down there."

Lisa nodded unenthusiastically.

"Anyway, I talked to Darcy last night and she'll be back a week tomorrow. I have your next blind date all arranged, and it's going to be a double date with me and Darcy," Mark told her.

Lisa just managed to hold back a sigh. "I don't want to go on any more blind dates," she told him.

"That's why I thought a double date would be fun," he replied. "If you and Andy don't hit it off, you'll still have Darcy and me to talk to."

Lisa forced herself to smile. "Sounds good," she muttered, painfully aware that Mark just considered her a friend. It wasn't like she was falling for him or anything. He was taken. Still, it made her sad that he was clearly excited at the prospect of introducing her to his friend. Obviously, he wasn't at all interested in her himself.

With her feelings seriously conflicted and her brain in turmoil, Lisa struggled through the rest of her day. At home she made herself a tin of soup and forced herself to watch mindless television until she could barely keep her eyes open. She still felt a few tears running down her face as she drifted off to sleep. She wasn't sure how she'd found herself falling in love with her best friend's boyfriend, and she wasn't sure how she was going to deal with it, either.

Friday morning she drove herself to Cregneash, feeling relieved that Mark was away. Now that she'd realised that she was falling for him, she didn't really want to see him.

Everything worked perfectly as the first tickets came off the printer. As promised, Lisa then found herself being given a comprehensive tour of the site. As it was very interesting, she didn't mind. It even managed to distract her from her own problems for a short while.

After another quick lunch in the café, Lisa headed up to Douglas and spent the afternoon playing around with various reports, hoping to ensure that the little glitches that had been coming up were eliminated.

She spent much of her weekend at her parents' house, helping them get it ready for the winter months that were coming. There wasn't a lot to do, but Lisa raked up leaves and helped her mother change summer bedding for winter blankets. Mostly, Lisa enjoyed having something other than her own life to focus on and she took full advantage, even spending Saturday night sleeping in her childhood bedroom.

"I hope everything is okay," her mother said cautiously after Sunday lunch, when Lisa was getting ready to head home.

"Everything's fine," Lisa assured her. "I've just been working really hard and I needed a break."

"You know we're always here," her dad said. "Just minutes from your door."

Lisa laughed. It was true. Her childhood home wasn't far from where she now lived. It felt a world away, though.

Mark rang on Sunday night to make the necessary arrangements for the next morning. "I'll pick you up at nine and we'll head down to Castletown," he suggested.

"Perfect," Lisa answered.

Monday was grey and rainy, which suited Lisa's mood perfectly. She locked up her house and hurried out to Mark's car when she saw him turn the corner. She didn't bother with an umbrella and she was soaked by the time she climbed into the car.

"What a miserable day," she exclaimed.

"It certainly is that," Mark answered.

Lisa peppered him with questions about his weekend while they travelled.

"Over all," he said finally, "I think everything's back on track. It's just a shame it took so much work to get it there."

Mark parked as close as he could to the Grammar School and Lisa dashed inside as quickly as she could.

"I'm not sure why I bothered to brush my hair this morning," she muttered as she tried to force the dripping mess into some semblance of order.

"Hold still," Mark told her. He reached over and finger-combed her hair into place. The gesture felt incredibly intimate to Lisa and she found herself blushing under his gaze. "That's better," he said softly as he pulled his hand away.

Lisa spun away from him and smiled overly brightly at the woman behind the ticket desk. An hour later, she'd installed the new system and was looking out at the rain.

"The House of Keys isn't far away," she told Mark when he joined her. "I'm going to have to make a run for it."

"Take an umbrella," Mark suggested.

Lisa shook her head. "There's no point. It's too windy, anyway."

Mark nodded. "Off you go, then. I'll be right behind you."

Lisa pulled on her raincoat and then ran out into the cold rain. She leaped across puddles, landing in one that covered her shoe. "Yikes," she exclaimed as the cold water rushed inside it.

Inside the House of Keys building, she took of her coat and shook her head. Water splashed everywhere.

"Do try not to get the exhibits wet," the man behind the ticket desk said sternly.

Lisa flushed. "Sorry," she said.

Mark wasn't far behind her and he too brought a lot of water into the room with him.

"Good heavens, please be careful," the man said grumpily as Mark dripped in the doorway.

Lisa and Mark exchanged glances and then they both burst out laughing. Even though they hadn't come far, they were both thoroughly soaked and freezing. Lisa headed to the nearest loo and spent some considerable time trying to dry off and do something about her appearance. After a while she had to give up, however.

The software installation was quick and easy, at least, and once it was finished, Lisa realised she was hungry.

"Is it lunchtime yet?" she asked Mark as she pulled her raincoat back on.

"It is," he told her after a look at his watch. "Let's go next door and get something to eat before we head to the castle."

The restaurant was quiet when they arrived.

"Did you say there's a ghost in Castle Rushen?" Lisa asked after they'd placed their lunch order.

"There is indeed," Mark told her. "But I've never seen her and I doubt I ever will."

"Why not? You need to tell me the whole story," Lisa demanded.

Mark laughed. "It's said that the ghost of Charlotte de la Tremouille haunts the castle," he said in a spooky voice.

"James Stanley, the seventh Earl of Derby's wife?" Lisa asked.

"That's right," Mark grinned. "If you remember, Stanley and Charlotte fled to the island during the English Civil War."

"I remember the story pretty well, especially as Katie Corlett was talking about her at your conference," Lisa said. "The earl left her here, living in Castle Rushen, when he went back to England to fight for the king."

"Exactly, but he was captured and executed and his wife only found out when Parliamentarian forces arrived and demanded that she surrender the island to them."

"So why does she haunt the castle?"

"Supposedly, theirs was a love match rather than an arranged one, and she was said to be devastated when she found out that her husband was dead. They say she haunts the throne room, waiting for Derby to return to her there."

"How sad," Lisa said. "But you've never seen her?"

Mark shook his head. "Apparently, she only appears to women," he told her. "She's supposed to be able to tell you if you've met your one true love or not."

"How does she do that?" Lisa demanded.

"I can't believe you've never heard this story," Mark said, shaking his head. "I thought everyone from the island knew about this."

"I don't know anything about it. Tell me."

"Apparently, many years ago, plenty of young women used the ghost as a test of their relationships. You're meant to visit the castle with the man you're seeing, but go up to the throne room by yourself. If you see the countess and she's smiling, you're with the right man. If you see the countess and she's crying, he's not the man for you."

Lisa laughed. "That's insane," she said. "No doubt lots of girls used the story to get in or out of relationships, but it's totally crazy."

"No doubt," Mark grinned at her. "But it makes a great story for tourists."

Lisa couldn't argue with that. The rain had finally stopped when, after lunch, the pair headed for the castle. As usual, the installation went quickly and smoothly and then Mark took her on a tour of the site.

Lisa sat down in the throne room and sighed. "I can't imagine what it would be like living here in those days," she told Mark. "Or sitting and waiting for news about my husband that would take days to reach me."

Back downstairs, Lisa helped with inventory in the gift shop and answered a few calls from Norma. By five, she was ready to head home. She packed up her laptop and her bag and then frowned.

"What's wrong?" Mark asked.

"I think I dropped my pen somewhere," she said, digging through her bag a second time.

"Is it a special pen?"

"Not really," Lisa shrugged. "I got it from SDDC. It has their number on it for emergencies. I just thought that was easier than keeping a card handy. I suppose I doesn't matter, though."

"Where was it?"

"It was either in my bag or in my pocket," Lisa replied. "I've been sticking it in pockets while I'm working and it probably just dropped out."

"Maybe it fell out when you were sitting in the throne room," Mark suggested.

"Maybe," Lisa shrugged. "It doesn't really matter, though. Let's get out of here."

Mark's phone rang and he frowned at her. "I need to take this. Why don't you run back up to the throne room and see if you can find your pen while you're waiting?"

Lisa nodded and then quickly made her way up the stone stairs towards the throne room. The castle had had several visitors during the day, but it seemed that they had all gone now. Lisa rounded the corner into the throne room and sighed. Her pen was sitting neatly in the centre of the chair she'd perched on. She grabbed the pen and then headed back out of the room.

A sound from behind her had her spinning around. Someone else had come into the room. Lisa stared at the woman who was now sitting on the seat where Lisa had found her pen. She was gorgeously attired in a period costume that looked incredibly authentic. Lisa shook her head.

"I didn't see you come in," she told the woman. "That's a beautiful dress."

The woman smiled and nodded at Lisa, but didn't speak.

"Are you on the staff here?" Lisa asked, sure she would have met the woman if that were the case.

"Last call, everyone out." The voice from behind her made Lisa spin around. They were getting ready to close the castle for the night. She turned back to say something to the other woman, but she was gone. Lisa felt a sudden chill run up her spine.

She headed down the stairs slowly. Mark would never believe her if she told him she'd seen Charlotte's ghost. She didn't really believe it herself. It wasn't until she was nearly back at the castle entrance that she realised why she couldn't tell Mark anyway. Charlotte, if it truly was her, had been smiling. If the legend was right, that meant that Mark was Lisa's one true love. Lisa almost burst into tears as the thought registered in her mind.

She was quiet on the journey home, her mind racing with all sorts of strange thoughts and questions. Mark was equally quiet, obviously caught up in his own thoughts.

"So, I'll see you tomorrow," he said when he dropped her off. "We'll get the last three sites up and running and then the project will be nearly complete."

Lisa tossed and turned all night, and by morning she was dreading seeing Mark again. She was relieved, therefore, when he rang just minutes before she was expecting him to arrive.

"Another day, another crisis," he told her. "I need to start my day in my office, but I'll try to get down to Castletown at some point."

Lisa assured him that she could handle things and then proceeded to do just that. All three sites went live without any complications and Lisa found herself wandering back and forth between the three, answering odd questions and satisfying herself that everything was good.

While she was busy dashing between sites, Mark left a couple of messages on her voicemail, apologising for not getting down to help with the last three sites. There wasn't much he could have done, though, as everything went smoothly.

She planned to spend the rest of the week in her office in the Manx Museum, finalising everything, and by the end of Tuesday, nothing had happened to change her plans.

Lisa spent Wednesday, Thursday and Friday running numerous reports and checking and rechecking everything she could. Mark stuck his head in her office once or twice, but it was clear that he was swamped again and she managed to get through everything on her own. By Friday she was ready to schedule a week of training with MNH's IT department. After that, she would officially be done with the project and she could see what Dan had lined up for her next.

Mark stopped in on Friday afternoon. "So, how's it going?" he asked, sinking into a chair.

"It's going well," she answered. "I need to spend a few days next week polishing up the users' manuals and training your IT guys and then I can get out of your way."

Mark laughed. "You're not in anyone's way in here," he told her. "But I suppose I'm glad the project is wrapping up. Anyway, I talked to Darcy and Andy last night and we're all set for tomorrow night. Darcy said she'll be at your house, so Andy and I will pick you both up there at seven, okay?"

Lisa felt tears filling her eyes. The last thing she wanted to do was go on a blind date with Mark and Darcy. "Sure," she muttered.

"I've booked us a table at *The Outlook*," Mark continued. "It's one of Darcy's favourites."

Lisa forced herself to smile, even if she couldn't quite meet Mark's eyes. "See you tomorrow night, then," she said, grabbing a pile of papers and flipping through them as if looking for something important. Mark seemed to take the hint.

"I'll see you tomorrow night, then," he echoed as he stood up.

Once he was gone, Lisa pushed her office door shut and burst into tears. That stupid ghost didn't know anything, she thought, as she rummaged through her bag for tissues. And tomorrow night she was going to have to spend an evening pretending she wasn't madly in love with Mark so as not to upset her best friend. She sighed and sank back down in her chair. Sometimes life wasn't fair at all.

13

Saturday morning, Lisa woke up from a restless sleep to someone knocking on her door. She frowned at the clock that read sometime just after eight and got up slowly. Before she'd reached her bedroom door, however, she heard her front door opening.

Great, Darcy was here and Lisa had no idea what she was going to say to her. She hadn't seen her best friend in several weeks. Now didn't seem like the time to hit her with "I've fallen in love with your boyfriend."

Lisa shouted a quick "hello" to her friend and then dove back into bed. She buried her head under the duvet. Maybe she could just stay there forever and never have to face Darcy or Mark again.

"I need some sleep," Darcy called from the corridor as she walked past Lisa's room. "Too many late nights, too much champagne. Wake me for lunch."

Lisa heard the guest room door shut. She settled back on her pillows and sighed. It was no use trying to get back to sleep herself. Now she felt wide-awake and miserable. She tossed and turned for another hour, before giving up in favour of breakfast.

Toast and yoghurt did nothing to make her feel better. She showered and got dressed and then headed out for fresh air and maybe some retail therapy. She left Darcy a note in case the other woman woke up while she was gone.

In her favourite bookstore, Lisa scanned the shelves. There was nothing that grabbed her interest. She pulled out a romance novel at random and read the blurb on the back cover. It only made her feel even more miserable.

She finally settled on a new mystery in a series she used to enjoy. No matter how hard she tried, she couldn't remember why she'd stopped reading the series and she was quite desperate for something to take her mind off her troubles.

The promenade was nearly empty under grey skies that threatened rain. Lisa sat on a bench and opened her new book. She was struggling to get into the story when the first fat raindrop fell on her head.

Lisa quickly gathered up her bag and her book and hurried home, feeling as if the weather was a perfect match for her mood. She was thoroughly soaked when she finally reached her front door. Pushing it open, she stomped inside and slammed it shut behind her. Sodden and dripping, she peeled off her T-shirt and slipped off her shoes.

"You know, showers are more useful if you take your clothes off before you get under the water," Darcy drawled from across the room.

"Gee, thanks," Lisa replied. "If only you'd been here to share that wisdom with me earlier."

Darcy frowned. "You're mad at me," she said in a puzzled voice. "I'm sorry I woke you this morning. I'm sorry I've been away so long. I'm sorry I didn't ring more often. And I'm sorry for whatever else you might be mad about."

Lisa shook her head. Darcy would probably also be sorry that she was the one dating Mark if Lisa told her everything, but that wouldn't change anything. No one ever looked at Lisa twice, once they'd met Darcy. She should have been used to it.

"I'm not mad at you," Lisa said, tiredly. "I've been working really hard, that's all. I need a break, I think."

"Mark's been working you too hard," Darcy teased. "I'll have to have words with him tonight."

"It's nothing to do with Mark," Lisa snapped. "Anyway, I think I'll grab another shower. I'm soaked anyway," she said, trying to keep her voice calm.

"Why don't you take a nice hot bath," Darcy suggested. "I brought you some gorgeous truffles from Paris. You can only have a couple, though, since I also brought lunch."

Lisa felt tears fill her eyes. "I think a shower will do," she said. She disappeared into her bedroom before Darcy could reply.

Darcy had brought all sorts of food back with her from her travels around Europe. When Lisa was dressed again, she found Darcy in the kitchen preparing an indoor picnic with all of her goodies.

"Cheese, jam, and wine from France," she told Lisa. "Meats from Italy, chocolate from Belgium...." she trailed off, staring at Lisa. "What's wrong?" Darcy demanded.

Lisa shook her head. "I told you, I'm really tired. I think I have a migraine coming on."

Darcy frowned. "You need to eat something and then take a nap," she told Lisa. "You don't want to miss dinner tonight."

Lisa forced herself to smile. "I'm sure I'll be fine," she said.

She fixed herself a plate and slowly emptied it. Darcy filled the air with stories of her adventures from the past weeks and slowly Lisa began to feel better. She loved Darcy so much. If she couldn't have Mark, she hoped he would be really happy with her dearest friend. At least that's what she tried to tell herself later, as the pair got ready for their date.

"This is like old times," Darcy giggled as she helped Lisa find the perfect outfit, raiding her own pile of clothes when Lisa couldn't find anything she liked.

"We haven't double-dated since university," Lisa said in agreement.

"Why haven't we?" Darcy asked.

"Maybe because every time we tried it, my date ended up trying to get your number instead of mine," Lisa suggested.

Darcy giggled. "It wasn't like that," she insisted.

"Mike Harrison," Lisa said.

Darcy laughed. "He was an idiot and you didn't want him, either."

"Bob Baldwin."

Darcy wrinkled her nose. "Too short and too old."

"Scott West."

"I don't remember him," Darcy said.

"He didn't make it past the starters," Lisa reminded her. "He's the one who picked a fight with your date and claimed the victor would win your hand. You told him to stop being an idiot and then your date flattened him."

Darcy laughed. "Now I remember."

Lisa opened her mouth to name another man, but Darcy held up a hand. "Okay, a few guys have gone for me over you, but they weren't worth your time anyway. Mark swears his friend Andy is perfect."

Lisa shrugged. "They're all perfect, right up until they see you and trip over their tongues."

Darcy frowned. "Would you rather I didn't come along?" she asked in a hurt tone. "I mean, I'm sure I could get Mark to change the booking and just you and Andy could go."

Lisa shook her head. "I'm sorry. I'm being a real bear today," she said. "I'm just really stressed about work. I'm sure tonight will be great."

Darcy grinned. "If he is wonderful and you want me and Mark to leave early, just let me know."

Lisa grinned back. "I can't see that happening, but thanks anyway."

Darcy fixed Lisa's makeup and her own. "There," Darcy announced. "We're perfect. The guys better get here fast before we start to fade."

Lisa managed a small chuckle as she paced in front of her door. She couldn't wait for the evening to be over.

She heard the car pull up and grabbed her jacket. "I think they're here," she told Darcy.

"Wait for them to knock," Darcy told her. "You don't want to look overeager."

Overeager was the one thing Lisa really wasn't. She checked that she had her phone in her bag and waited patiently for the knock. When it finally came, she pulled the door open and then stared. There was a uniformed chauffeur standing in the doorway.

"Ms. Mylchreest? Ms. Robinson?"

Lisa nodded and glanced at Darcy, who was smiling broadly. "That's us," she told the man, grabbing Lisa's arm and pulling her out the door.

A limousine was parked in front of Lisa's house and the driver escorted them towards it. Lisa frowned. "But why? I mean, what? I mean...."

The driver held open the back door to the car and Darcy slid inside. Lisa followed more slowly, still confused by the unexpected.

Mark smiled at her as she settled into her seat next to him. "Champagne?" he asked as he handed her a glass.

Lisa took the glass without thinking and then took a healthy sip. She glanced over at her friend.

Darcy was sitting across from her with her own glass of champagne. "Cheers," she said to Lisa before taking a large drink.

"Lisa, Darcy, this is Andy," Mark performed the necessary introductions.

Lisa studied the man who was next to Darcy. He smiled brightly at her. He looked a bit like Mark, very handsome, with dark brown hair and blue eyes. His suit looked expensive and Lisa immediately felt intimidated by him.

"I thought the car would be a nice touch," Andy told the girls. "Mark was going to grab a taxi, but this is ever so much more comfortable and stylish."

Darcy giggled. "Nothing like travelling in style," she cooed. "But why on earth do you look so much like Mark? I thought you were friends, but you could be brothers."

Andy chuckled. "I don't see the resemblance myself," he said. "But we're first cousins. I can't believe Mark didn't tell you that."

Mark shook his head. "I didn't think it much mattered," he said.

The car pulled up to the restaurant and the driver got out. He held the door open and Lisa and Darcy climbed out carefully, followed by Mark and Andy. Now that they were upright, Lisa could see that Andy was actually a few inches taller than Mark, with the same slender build. Andy said something to the driver, who nodded and then climbed back in the car.

"Shall we?" Andy asked, offering Lisa his arm. Lisa took it gingerly, feeling a bit overwhelmed by the man.

Inside, the foursome was shown to their table and handed menus. Andy insisted on ordering even more champagne.

"I haven't been on a double-date with my cousin since university," he told the girls. "I feel like celebrating."

Darcy giggled. "We were just saying the same thing," she told him. "We used to double-date when we were at university, but we haven't done it since."

After the champagne was poured and everyone had ordered, Darcy smiled at Andy. "So, tell us all about yourself," she instructed him.

"Oh, I'm not very interesting," he replied. "I'm semi-retired from the banking industry. I spend a lot of my time travelling but I still go into the office a couple times a month, if I can be bothered."

"You must have been very successful if you've retired already," Darcy said. "Do you live here on the island, then?"

"Well," he chuckled, "my money lives here, at least. I have a flat here and I live here enough of the year to enjoy the tax advantages, but I have a flat in London as well and that's where my office is," he explained.

Darcy nodded. "I spend a lot of time in London," she told him. "I'll have to look you up sometime."

Andy grinned. "Do that."

Lisa felt her face redden. Darcy was flirting with the man in front of Mark. She looked over at Mark, but he seemed oblivious, sipping his drink.

"How are things with your exhibit going?" she asked him.

"I think I've managed to get everything sorted," he told her. "I'll find out for sure on Monday."

"I didn't realise how complicated your job is," Lisa told him.

Mark laughed. "It isn't usually this complicated," he replied. "Someone dropped the ball somewhere along the line, that's all. Now I'm scrambling to fix it before we have to reschedule our exhibit."

The starters arrived and interrupted the conversation. Lisa sipped her champagne and nibbled on several of the offerings, beginning to feel herself relaxing as the alcohol took effect.

As soon as the starters were finished, the main courses arrived. Lisa was grateful that conversation was limited as everyone ate.

"You look like you're feeling better," Mark whispered to her as she washed down her last bite with her last sip of champagne.

"I'm fine," she told him.

"You looked quite tense earlier," he replied. "I think you've been working too hard."

"Just doing my job," she answered, trying to keep her voice light.

"And you do it so well," he replied with a smile.

"I hope you two aren't arguing about pudding," Andy interrupted. "We definitely have to get pudding."

Lisa opened her mouth to object, but Darcy jumped in.

"Of course we do," she agreed with Andy. "And more champagne, surely?"

Andy laughed. "And more champagne," he agreed.

Lisa frowned. She was quite full and she really didn't want any more to drink.

"Get the crème brûlée," Mark whispered to her. "It's easier than arguing with the pair of them."

Lisa laughed. He was right. She ordered the pudding and then sighed as Andy refilled her glass from the new bottle of champagne.

"You don't have to drink it," Mark whispered to her. "I'm sure Andy and Darcy have a much higher tolerance for alcohol than you and I do. I won't be doing more than occasionally sipping at this glass. The last thing I need to do is get drunk."

Lisa smiled at him. "The last thing I want to do is get drunk," she told him. Drunk, she might just tell Mark how she felt and she might just tell Darcy to stop flirting with Mark's cousin as well. She sighed again.

"What's wrong?" Andy asked her. "Aren't you having fun?"

"I'm sorry," she said. "I'm just a bit tired. I've been working on this project with Mark for months and I haven't been sleeping well."

"You need a holiday," Andy told her. "I'm flying across to London tomorrow. You should come with me. We can head to Paris or Rome or wherever you like." He grinned at Darcy. "You should come as well," he added.

"I have a few days off," Darcy said excitedly. "And I really could use a holiday. I'd love to come."

"Unfortunately, I don't have a few days off," Lisa told them both. "I'm in the middle of a major project."

"Mark, you'll come with us, won't you?" Darcy asked, batting her eyelashes at him.

Mark flushed. "You know that project that Lisa is in the middle of? I'm in the middle of it as well," he replied. "I can't get away right now."

"You two are no fun," Darcy said, pouting. "I need a break."

Andy patted her hand. "Another time," he told her. "Once this big project is finished, they'll really need a holiday and they'll be able to enjoy it properly."

"I suppose," Darcy said grumpily.

Pudding was every bit as delicious as the previous time and Lisa was glad she had let herself be talked into it. With the last of the dishes cleared, Darcy suggested a quick trip to the loo.

"We just need to check our lipstick," she told the men as she pulled Lisa to her feet.

Lisa followed her through the restaurant, wondering what the loos would be like in such a fancy place. She wasn't disappointed as they walked into the flamboyantly decorated space. Darcy disappeared into a cubicle, while Lisa sank down on one of the velvet couches and studied herself in the mirror. Darcy had done a great job on her makeup, and Lisa knew she looked her very best, but next to Darcy she still felt invisible. No wonder Andy had been flirting with Darcy instead of her.

Darcy plopped down beside her after she'd washed her hands. She dug around in her handbag for a lipstick and then applied it. "So, what do you think of Andy?" she asked Lisa.

"He's way too sophisticated for me," Lisa answered frankly. "He intimidates me."

Darcy laughed. "You can't let him do that," she told her friend. "You're every bit as good as he is and you're probably smarter."

"If I were smarter, I'd be semi-retired at forty, as well," Lisa replied.

Darcy waved a hand. "Never mind that," she said. "He seems really nice and he's gorgeous. You should give him a chance."

Lisa shrugged. "He seems more interested in you than me," she replied.

"He's just a flirt and you weren't flirting back," Darcy told her. "You and Mark kept chatting and leaving me to entertain Andy. When we get back in the car, sit next to Andy and start talking to him. I think he could be perfect for you."

Lisa stood up slowly. "I'll try," she said.

Back at the table, the men rose as they approached. "All set?" Andy asked.

"Sure," Lisa muttered, taking the arm he offered. He escorted her out of the restaurant and into the waiting car. Darcy and Mark followed.

"It's too early to head home," Andy said. "What else is there to do on the island at night?"

"We could try our luck at the casino," Darcy suggested. "Although I didn't bring any money with me."

Andy laughed. "I think I can stake you a few pounds," he offered. "Let's give it a go."

Lisa exchanged glances with Mark, who shrugged. She opened her mouth to object, but Darcy caught her eye.

"Come on, hon, let's go and win some money," Darcy said to her. "Andy will stake us, so we can't lose."

"We'll have to pay him back," Lisa pointed out.

"Don't worry about that," Andy laughed. "I can afford to lose a few pounds here and there. And if you win big, you can keep your winnings as well."

Lisa forced herself to smile. It seemed like the night was never going to be over.

"I've never been to a casino," she whispered to Darcy as they climbed out of the car.

"Just try to have fun," Darcy suggested. Lisa gave her a look that made her stop. "Okay, if you really don't want to do this, we don't have to," Darcy told her. "But if you don't want to try anything difficult, you can just try out the slot machines. Take a few pounds from Andy and get five or ten pence pieces for the slots. If you win big, you'll get about five pounds and if you lose, it isn't a big deal."

Lisa took a deep breath. Darcy and Andy were both excited about the casino and she didn't want to spoil their evening. "That sounds good," she told Darcy, at least a little bit truthfully.

Inside, they all had to sign up for memberships before they were allowed into the casino. All the bright flashing lights and electronic noises made Lisa regret her decision to come. Andy handed everyone a few notes and then grabbed Darcy's hand.

"I need a good luck charm for blackjack," he told her. The pair disappeared towards the gaming tables, leaving Mark and Lisa blinking in the bright lights.

"Well, it seems I'm not lucky enough for your cousin," Lisa said tartly.

Mark laughed. "Don't take it personally," he told her. "Andy's always had a thing for redheads."

Lisa couldn't help but think that Mark was foolish, therefore, to introduce his cousin to Darcy, but she didn't say anything. Instead she looked at the money Andy had pressed into her hand.

"There's a hundred pounds here," she gasped. "I would never waste that much on gambling."

Mark smiled. "Andy can afford to lose it," he told her. "Come on, let's try the slots."

Mark showed her how to change a twenty-pound note into tokens and then they settled in at a pair of slot machines. Lisa dropped a token in and watched the lights flash and flicker. After a few seconds, the machine lit up and a few tokens dropped into the tray below the machine.

"You won," Mark told her.

Lisa picked up the tokens and counted them. "Forty pence," she grinned. "I'm on my way to early retirement now."

Half an hour later, she'd lost Andy's twenty pounds and her forty-pence winnings as well.

"Well, that didn't take long," she laughed.

"Do you want to change another twenty?" Mark asked her.

Lisa shook her head. "I think I've wasted enough of your cousin's money."

"Well, I don't mind wasting a bit of it myself," Mark told her. "Let's see if you can bring me luck at roulette."

Mark purchased some chips and then he and Lisa found a space at a roulette table. "Pick a number," he told Lisa.

"Twenty-eight," Lisa said without thinking. It was her age, so maybe it would be lucky.

She held her breath as the wheel spun around and around.

"Four," the man behind the table announced, collecting all the chips on the table.

Lisa frowned at Mark. "It looks like I'm not very lucky."

"Let's try just picking red or black," he suggested.

That gave them much better odds, but much smaller winnings when they happened to be right.

An hour later they were still playing happily with Andy's money. Mark had occasionally wagered a small amount on various numbers, but none had come up. By betting on red or black, however, they'd managed to win just often enough to keep going.

"We have about twelve pounds left," Mark told Lisa. "What do you say we throw caution to the wind and bet it all on one number?"

Lisa giggled. "Go on then, what number?"

Mark smiled at her. "How about eleven?" he suggested. "That's the number of sites you've converted to the new system for us."

"Sure," Lisa agreed easily.

Mark piled the last of their chips on number eleven. Lisa couldn't watch. She turned away, hiding her face in Mark's chest. The wheel stopped and Lisa held her breath.

"Twenty-eight," the man said loudly.

Lisa blew out a breath. "There goes our chance at a fortune," she told Mark with a grin.

They laughed together as they turned away from the table, his arm draped casually over her shoulders. Lisa stopped laughing when she caught Darcy's eye. Darcy was studying her with a strange look on her face.

Mark spotted her and Andy a moment later. "Hey, cousin, we lost our entire stake. Maybe it's time to call it a night?" Mark said, taking a few steps away from Lisa.

Andy laughed. "I lost a small fortune, too. Neither of our lovely lady friends brought us any luck tonight. At least not here."

"You're just lucky to be able to spend time with us," Darcy told him. "But it's getting late and I think Lisa and I need to get home and get some sleep."

"We are indeed lucky," Andy said, dropping an arm around each of the girls. "And I've had a wonderful time. Let's get you both home, then."

The car ride back to Lisa's house was a short and quiet one.

"Thank you for a lovely evening," Lisa said politely as they pulled up in front of her house.

"It was terrific meeting you," Andy told her. "I'd love to see you again soon and I'm only on the island until tomorrow afternoon. Why don't we all have brunch together tomorrow morning?"

"I love brunch," Darcy drawled. "I get to sleep in and I get lovely breakfast foods. What's not to love?"

Andy laughed. "Mark and I will collect you both at ten, then," he said. "I know a great little restaurant in Port Erin that does the best Sunday brunch."

"Great," Lisa said unenthusiastically. She had enjoyed the evening more than she'd expected to, but that was mostly because she'd spent so much of it with Mark. She really didn't want to repeat the experience, but there didn't seem to be any polite way to get out of the brunch plans.

Mark looked at her quizzically, but she shook her head.

"We'll see you in the morning, then," he said to the girls as they exited the car.

The chauffeur walked them to Lisa's door and then waited politely until they were both inside before returning to the car. Once the door was shut behind them, Lisa kicked off her shoes.

"My feet are killing me," she moaned. "I can't decide if I want to soak them or just go to bed."

Darcy laughed and slipped off her own ridiculously high heels. "You need to wear them all the time. That way you get used to them."

Lisa shook her head. "No way, once in a blue moon is plenty."

Darcy smiled. "Are you very tired?" she asked her.

Lisa tensed. "I am pretty tired, why?"

"I just wanted to talk to you about a few things," Darcy told her. "But it isn't anything that can't wait for morning."

"Before brunch?" Lisa asked.

"Oh, definitely before brunch," Darcy replied.

With that, her friend disappeared into the guest room, leaving Lisa to wonder and worry what she wanted to talk about. Lisa got ready for bed, feeling the now familiar tears pricking at her eyelids as she washed her face. In bed, she tossed and turned, worried that Darcy was angry because of her behaviour with Mark.

Her friendship with Darcy was more important than any man, she reminded herself sternly. If Darcy was jealous of her friendship with Mark, she'd simply stop spending time with Mark. The thought just about broke her heart, but she didn't know what else to do.

After an hour where she couldn't get to sleep, Lisa got up to get herself a drink. On her way to the kitchen, she passed the guest room. She stopped suddenly as she realised she could hear Darcy's voice. Darcy giggled and said something quietly. Obviously she was on her mobile with someone. Lisa puzzled over that while she made herself a cup of tea.

It didn't seem ten minutes after she'd finally drifted off to sleep when someone was knocking on her bedroom door. Lisa forced her eyes open.

Darcy's head appeared around the door's frame. "Lisa, are you awake yet? We really have to talk."

14

Lisa looked at the clock. It wasn't even eight yet. "Brunch isn't until ten," she moaned. "Let me sleep."

Darcy giggled. "Nope, you need to get up. Please?"

Lisa nodded. "Give me five minutes," she told Darcy. Her friend disappeared from the doorway. Lisa stretched and then rubbed her eyes. She had a sinking feeling she knew what Darcy wanted to talk about. Darcy knew her well enough to have picked up on Lisa's feelings for Mark. Lisa sighed. She had no excuse. She knew Mark was Darcy's boyfriend and she knew better than to fall for him.

Reluctantly, she climbed out of bed and shoved her feet into her fuzzy slippers. When she caught sight of herself in the mirror, she gasped and then ran a brush through her tangled hair. It didn't help much. She still looked exhausted and depressed, but at least her hair wasn't standing straight up anymore. She pulled her big fluffy bathrobe off the hook on the back of the door and slid it on. The morning had a definite chill to it.

Lisa opened her door and stuck her head out. She could hear Darcy rattling things in the kitchen, and she could smell coffee. When she reached the kitchen, Darcy handed her a cup of coffee without being asked. Lisa sank down at the small kitchen table and gratefully took a sip.

As her brain began to wake up, Lisa noticed that Darcy was dressed and had her makeup on already. With two hours to go before brunch, that didn't make sense. Maybe Darcy had been called into work and she was worried about disappointing Lisa and changing their plans. Lisa finished her coffee and handed the mug back to Darcy, who quickly refilled it.

"Ready to talk now?" Darcy asked.

Lisa frowned. Darcy was perfectly within her rights to be angry with her, but she hated when she and Darcy argued. "Do we have to?" she asked nervously.

Darcy nodded. "I wanted to talk about something last night, but now we have even more to discuss," she told Lisa.

"Go ahead," Lisa said with a sigh as she sipped more coffee. She braced herself for the accusations, knowing she couldn't deny what Darcy had seen in the casino.

"I know you hate it when I do things impulsively," Darcy began.

Lisa looked up from her mug in surprise. This was not the conversation starter she'd been expecting.

"I do," she said after a pause.

"And I know you think I need to start thinking about settling down and working on my career and all that grownup stuff," Darcy said with a sigh. "But the thing is, life is short and I hate the thought of missing out on things."

"If you're trying to tell me that you're working today, that's okay," Lisa said. "We can cancel brunch and you can go and fly somewhere exotic."

Darcy shook her head. "It's a little bit more complicated than that," she said. "And I feel like you're going to say 'I told you so' and I can't argue."

Darcy sighed and sat down opposite Lisa. She put her elbows on the table and buried her face in her hands.

Lisa wasn't sure what to say. She had no idea what Darcy was talking about. "Darcy, just tell me," she said eventually. "Whatever is going on, we can work it out."

"Did you like Andy?" Darcy asked her. "Because I didn't get the feeling that you two hit it off, really. Maybe it was a mistake, the whole double-date thing. I sort of thought that Andy wasn't quite right for you. What did you think?"

Lisa shook her head. "He's seems like a nice guy, but after brunch today I don't plan on seeing him again," she said. Especially since I'm in love with Mark, she added silently.

"I thought so," Darcy said, her eyes filling with tears. "You know I'd never do anything to hurt you, right?"

Lisa nodded slowly. "Of course I know that. And I'd never do anything to hurt you."

Darcy nodded. "That's the other thing we have to talk about, but first, I need to tell you, well, Andy's going to be here in about half an hour and we're flying to Paris for a getaway."

Lisa sat back in her chair and stared at her best friend. She was beyond stunned. Carefully, she set her coffee mug down and then took a deep breath, trying to work out what she was feeling.

"Are you crazy?" was what popped out of her mouth.

Darcy shook her head. "Probably," she laughed shakily. "We had fun at the casino and we were talking about getting away over dinner, remember? He rang me last night after you went to bed and suggested that we sneak away for a few days. The more he talked, the better it sounded, until I said yes."

"You just met the man last night," Lisa reminded her.

"I know and I knew you wouldn't approve," Darcy said. "But Andy has a flat in Paris with a guest bedroom. I'll be staying in there while we get to know each other. It isn't as bad as it sounds."

"Until he turns out to be an axe murderer," Lisa replied.

"He's Mark's cousin," Darcy pointed out. "I don't think Mark would have fixed you up with the man if he were an axe murderer."

"Maybe Mark doesn't know about it," Lisa suggested. "I can't believe you're serious."

"It's just a little holiday," Darcy said casually. "Andy is rich and gorgeous and smart and funny. Why wouldn't I go for it?"

Lisa sighed. "Do you really want me to list all the reasons why you shouldn't?"

Darcy shook her head. "I really don't," she said. "I know all the reasons why I shouldn't, but there are also a ton of reasons why I should. I need a holiday and Paris is lovely this time of year."

"What happens when it all goes wrong?" Lisa demanded.

Darcy shrugged. "I suppose I'll ring Finlo to come and rescue me," she giggled.

Lisa gasped. "You aren't doing this to make Finlo jealous, are you? I mean, that's just crazy."

"Of course not," Darcy replied.

Lisa stared at her, but Darcy wouldn't meet her eyes. "Darce, Finlo doesn't deserve you, but if you are just doing this to get back at him, that doesn't seem fair to Andy."

"Andy's a big boy," Darcy told her. "He knows exactly what he's getting himself into."

Lisa opened her mouth to argue further, but then had a sudden thought. "What about Mark?" she asked. "You're just dumping him?"

Darcy shrugged. "We only went out a few times," she said. "He's not really my type. He was fun, but it was never a great romance."

Lisa felt tears spring into her eyes. She wanted so much to defend Mark, but she couldn't do it without revealing how she felt about him. It wasn't like she wanted Darcy to stay with Mark anyway, but he must have felt awful when Andy told him.

"I hope he knows how you feel," Lisa said quietly.

"I'm sure he does," Darcy said. "Which brings me to the other point I wanted to discuss."

A knock on the door interrupted their conversation.

"That'll be Andy," Darcy said excitedly. She jumped up and ran for the door. Lisa followed at a more sedate pace. When she arrived at the door, Darcy and Andy were talking in low voices.

"Hey, good morning, Lisa," Andy said, smiling.

"Good morning," she replied.

Andy looked at Darcy and then back at Lisa. "I'm sorry," he said slowly. "I mean, you seem like a really nice person. If things were different, I'd have enjoyed getting to know you better. But Darcy, well Darcy's amazing."

"She is, isn't she," Lisa said dryly.

Darcy flushed. "Lisa, I'm sorry." She turned to Andy. "Give me a minute, I think Lisa and I need to talk some more."

"Take whatever time you need," Andy told her. "The flight will wait for us, right?"

Darcy grinned at him. "It will indeed," she chuckled.

"Oh, don't let me hold you up," Lisa said. "Even if the plane will wait, I'm sure you're anxious to get going. I'm fine."

Darcy shook her head. "You're not fine and we still have one more thing to talk about. Let's go in your room," she suggested.

Andy smiled. "Can I get myself a cup of coffee?" he asked. "I wouldn't normally ask, but I can smell it and it smells wonderful."

"I'll get you a cup," Darcy told him, taking him into the kitchen.

Lisa sank down on the nearest couch and gave herself a mental shake. She should be happy about Darcy and Andy. With Darcy out of the picture, she could make a play for Mark. The only problem was, Mark was probably crazy about Darcy and his heart was probably broken now. This was not the time to get involved with Mark, even if she could work out how to catch his interest. And let's face it, she thought, after dating the beautiful Darcy, Mark wasn't about to give her a second glance.

Darcy returned and gingerly sat down on the couch next to Lisa. "Are you okay?" she asked.

"I don't know," Lisa answered honestly.

"I know we were just talking about how every time we double-date your date ends up falling for me and now this happens," Darcy said. "I swear I didn't mean for it to happen."

"This is the first time you've actually gone after a guy that was meant for me," Lisa pointed out.

Darcy flushed. "I know," she said sadly. "And I feel terrible about it. If you really like Andy and you're going to be mad about this, I won't go," she said.

Lisa swallowed hard to keep from blurting out the wrong words. She knew Darcy meant it, but she certainly wasn't interested in Andy. "I just don't want to see you get hurt," she said finally.

Darcy smiled. "Don't you worry about that," she told Lisa. "I'll be just fine."

"You'd better get going, then," Lisa told her. "Finlo won't hold your plane forever."

"Of course he will," Darcy laughed. "Andy's paying for it."

"I hope you have a wonderful time," Lisa said. "But ring if you need anything or just need to talk."

Darcy nodded. "Oh, and one more thing," she said. "I know you too well. I saw how you were looking at Mark last night. You're clearly crazy about him. Promise me you'll tell him that?"

Lisa flushed. "I'd had too much champagne," she told Darcy. "That's all."

Darcy laughed. "I'm sure you didn't want to say anything to me when Mark and I were together, but we never really were much of a couple and anyway, we aren't together anymore. I suppose I should have seen it coming. You two have been spending so much time together, it makes sense. I've probably just been away too much."

"Mark's crazy about you," Lisa told her sadly. "Even if I do like him a little bit, he's not going to be interested in me."

"You won't know until you ask him," Darcy said. "He's a pretty terrific guy and he seemed to be enjoying your company last night. Talk to him."

Lisa shook her head. "I'd rather not."

Darcy sighed and took Lisa's hands in hers. She waited until Lisa was looking at her before she spoke again. "Lisa, you're my dearest friend in the whole world. I love you like a sister. How do you feel about Mark?"

"I, um, that is, well," Lisa looked down. "I don't know," she said desperately.

Darcy took her chin and tipped her head up until Lisa met her eyes again. "You've fallen hard, haven't you?" she asked.

Lisa felt tears running down her face. She nodded and then let Darcy enfold her in a hug. "I don't know what to do," she sobbed. "He's never going to be interested in boring old me."

"You aren't being fair to yourself or to Mark," Darcy told her. "Talk to him."

Lisa shrugged. "We'll see," she said.

Darcy looked as if she wanted to argue, but just then her mobile rang. She glanced at it and rolled her eyes. She clicked the answer button and Lisa heard her half of the conversation.

"Yes, Finlo, I do know what time it is," Darcy said. "We're just sorting out a few things and we'll be on our way. Be patient."

When she disconnected, she made a face at Lisa. "He's getting impatient. I'm sure he's dying to check out the guy I'm travelling with."

"Darcy, are you sure about this?" Lisa asked again.

Darcy nodded. "I'm more worried about you than I am about me," she told Lisa. "Are you going to be okay?"

Lisa nodded. "I'm going back to bed once you've gone," she replied. "I'll work out what to do later."

Darcy looked unsure, but Lisa stood up and pulled her to her feet. "Come on, off you go," she said.

Darcy grabbed Andy from the kitchen, and with a few final hugs and whispered words of affection, she and Andy climbed into his car and pulled away. The roar of the expensive sports car's engine made Lisa smile briefly. That should be the soundtrack for Darcy's life, she thought to herself as she shut her door.

Sitting back down on her couch, she wondered what to do with herself. She didn't really feel like going back to bed. She'd had too much coffee for that to appeal, but there wasn't anything else that sounded enticing, either.

She'd left her laptop in her temporary office at the museum, so she couldn't even grab that and get some work done. The museum wasn't open on a Sunday, and she didn't want to risk running into Mark, anyway. Tomorrow would be soon enough to see him. Although at the moment, there seemed a good chance she would be calling in sick tomorrow.

She got up and stretched. Maybe she'd feel better after a shower. Then again, maybe today was a stay in her pyjamas all day kind of day. She wandered into the kitchen and checked her fridge. She had plenty of food in, including a bunch of exotic stuff that Darcy had left behind. She could snack all day on the sort of expensive bits and pieces that she'd never have bought for herself. She checked the freezer. She had two tubs of premium ice cream as well. That made it the perfect day to slob around in pyjamas and feel sorry for herself.

She was debating the relative merits of ice cream for breakfast when someone knocked on her door. Assuming that Darcy had forgotten something and rushed back, Lisa crossed quickly to the door and pulled it open. She gasped and very nearly slammed the door in Mark's face.

"What are you doing here?" she demanded.

"Good morning to you, too," he replied with a grin. "I thought we were going out for brunch, but maybe I've come to the wrong house?"

Lisa swallowed hard. Hadn't Andy or Darcy told him? Surely he must have noticed that Andy wasn't around? "I thought, that is, I didn't think," she took a breath. "I thought brunch was cancelled," she said slowly.

"Oh, dear, and I'm starving," Mark replied. "Although I suppose you aren't exactly dressed for going out, are you?"

Lisa glanced down and flushed. Her fluffy bathrobe and fuzzy slippers seemed to triple in size as she tried to imagine how she must look. No wonder Mark had fallen for Darcy instead of her. Darcy always looked gorgeous, even in the oversized slippers and furry bathrobe she sometimes wore around Lisa's house.

"I wasn't expecting you," Lisa said.

"I thought we made plans last night," Mark countered.

"I thought everything was changed because of Darcy and Andy leaving," Lisa replied, waiting for Mark's shocked and hurt response.

"Just because they've gone doesn't mean I'm not hungry," Mark told her.

"So you knew they'd gone?" Lisa asked, feeling confused.

"Andy told me last night," Mark replied. "Do you think maybe I could come in? I mean, it's pretty cold and your heating bill is going to be crazy if you keep this door open much longer."

Lisa flushed. "Sure, of course, come in," she stammered. "I'm sorry, I'm just not thinking this morning."

"It's been a strange morning," Mark said. "I hope you aren't feeling too disappointed," he added as he took a seat in Lisa's comfortable lounge.

"Disappointed? Why?" Lisa felt even more confused as she sank onto the couch opposite him.

"I wasn't sure how much you liked Andy," he explained. "I was afraid you were disappointed when he fell for Darcy instead of you."

Lisa shook her head. "He seems like a nice guy," she said. "But he wasn't really my type."

Mark nodded. "Yeah, he really is more Darcy's type."

Lisa took a deep breath. "I'm so sorry," she said. "I know you really liked Darcy and I'm so sorry that she just took off like that. She can be fickle, but I've never known her to behave like that before. I hope you aren't too disappointed."

Lisa felt like she was holding her breath as she waited for Mark's reply. If he wasn't too heartbroken, maybe he could come to care for her eventually.

Mark chuckled. "I think I've been insulted," he said.

"I know Darcy treated you badly, but I don't think she meant for you take it personally," Lisa said.

Lisa was suddenly desperate to change the subject. She didn't think she could stand listening to Mark talk about how hurt he felt by Darcy's defection. "Hey, you said you were hungry. How about a snack?" she asked.

Mark looked surprised, but agreed readily enough. Lisa led the way into the kitchen and began pulling the various foods Darcy had left from the fridge.

Mark smiled. "You have a real feast here."

"Darcy brought it all," Lisa said, frowning at herself. She shouldn't have mentioned Darcy.

They both fixed plates and Lisa made more coffee. Lisa nibbled uninterestedly at a few things, watching Mark as he did the same.

"You aren't eating," she said finally.

"Neither are you," he pointed out.

"I'm not really hungry," Lisa said, pushing her plate away.

She looked up to find Mark staring at her. She flushed. "I know, I'm a mess," she said. "I need a shower and my hair is filthy."

Mark sighed. "I don't understand women," he told Lisa.

"I'm sorry, I know Darcy's behaviour was awful. I can't apologise enough."

Mark shook his head. "Actually, Darcy's behaviour didn't surprise me at all. It's you that I don't understand."

Lisa felt her cheeks flame. Had he guessed how she felt? "What do you mean?" she asked nervously.

"I'm wondering how stupid you think I am," he told her.

Lisa shook her head. "You're one of the smartest guys I know," she said quietly, knowing he was going to tell her that he knew how she felt and then try to let her down gently. She sighed.

"And yet you're worried that I'm upset about Andy and Darcy?"

"Well, yeah," Lisa said. "She was meant to be your girlfriend."

Mark chuckled. "Darcy just wanted a suitably attractive man to dangle in front of Finlo Quayle. She was hoping to make him jealous enough that he'd come running back to her."

"What makes you think that?" Lisa asked in carefully measured tones.

"Well, that's what Darcy told me the night we met," Mark replied.

"Why did you agree to keep seeing her, then?" Lisa asked.

"She was fun to spend time with and she's gorgeous. Why not go out with her once in a while?" Mark countered.

Lisa nodded. "I see," she said slowly.

"I don't think you do," Mark replied. "If I'm as smart as you seem to think, why would I arrange a double date with you and Darcy and invite my cousin, the rich playboy with a taste for redheads, to come along? He and Darcy are perfectly matched."

"I suppose you just didn't think about it," Lisa said. "You were trying to find the right man for me and you didn't think about all of the possible consequences." She took a sip of coffee and then sighed. When Mark didn't reply she looked up at him.

He smiled at her, and then took her hand. "Or maybe I spent a lot if time thinking about the consequences. Maybe when I realised I knew the perfect man for you, I found that there were obstacles in the way. Maybe I planned last night to clear away those obstacles."

Lisa stared at him, her brain struggling to make sense of his words. "I'm not sure I understand," she said.

Mark sighed. "Let me make myself perfectly clear, then. I've had a wonderful time over the last two months working with you. I enjoyed everything we did together, from exploring sites to sharing meals to struggling to train Norma. No matter what needed doing, it was okay because I was doing it with you. And then I had to spend a bunch of time sorting out the problem with my exhibit and that just drove home exactly how I felt about you."

Lisa pulled her hand away and stood up. She was two steps away from the nearest tissue box. She grabbed a tissue and wiped her eyes and then blew her nose. She knew her face would be all blotchy. She wasn't an attractive crier. Standing with her back to Mark, she was hesitant to turn back around. Her mind was whirling and she was both excited and terrified to think where the conversation might be going.

She heard Mark get up from the table. He came up behind her and touched her shoulder. "Are you okay?" he asked gently.

"I don't know," Lisa said in a shaky voice.

Mark chuckled and then slowly turned her around. "I'll just finish, then," he said staring into her eyes. "When I realised how I felt about you, I wasn't sure what to do. I didn't want to hurt Darcy, but I knew she wasn't really interested in me, so I arranged last night hoping she and Andy would hit it off."

He shook his head. "I must admit, I wasn't expecting things to go quite so well between them," he said. "But Andy's never been shy about going after what he wants and he's never minded taking women away from me, either."

"Really?" Lisa was surprised.

"Why do you think we hadn't gone out together since university?" Mark replied. "He's ruthless when he wants something or someone."

"Maybe I need to warn Darcy," Lisa said worriedly.

Mark laughed. "If ever I met a woman who could handle Andy, it's Darcy," he told her.

Lisa looked at him for a long time, letting her tired brain process what he'd said. "So you were really setting up Darcy last night?"

"Yeah, because I already knew the perfect guy for you," he told her.

He pulled her close and took her chin his hand. "I've been wanting to do this for months," he whispered as he lowered his mouth to hers.

Time seemed to stand still as Lisa felt herself falling into a maelstrom of emotions. She knew she was crying again, but she felt happier than she'd ever felt in her life. When Mark finally lifted her head and she could breathe again, she smiled at him.

"So I need a date for this wedding...." she began.

15

Six weeks later, on Christmas Eve morning, Lisa made faces at herself in her mirror as Darcy fixed her makeup.

"Stop that or your mascara will be all wonky," Darcy said. "I don't know why I bother."

"Sure you do," Lisa laughed. "You fuss over me so you don't have as much time to worry about how you look." Both girls laughed.

"It doesn't really matter how you look, though," Lisa added. "Andy's crazy about you anyway."

Darcy grinned. "He kind of is," she agreed. "But no more so than Mark is about you. When I bumped into him at the grocery store the other day he spent half an hour telling me about your latest project. As if I cared in the slightest about how you're adding the cafés into the existing computer system for MNH."

Lisa smiled. "Mark's like a little kid with a new toy," she told her friend. "He can sit in his office in Douglas and track exactly how many crumpets are being eaten at the café at the Sound. It sounds silly, but it's really useful information for planning and ordering and the like."

"Why don't I think it's work that's put that permanent smile on Mark's face?" Darcy teased. "He's madly in love with you, you know that, right?"

Lisa flushed and sipped the champagne that Darcy had insisted on. "I'm pretty crazy about him, too," she said finally. "I keep pinching myself."

Darcy smiled. "I'm so pleased you two are so happy together," she said. "And I'm so glad we both have perfect dates for today."

Lisa shrugged. "I'm still not sure why we're going," she said grumpily.

"Because Joney invited us and we're her only school friends?" Darcy suggested.

"I don't really even like her," Lisa pointed out.

"She's okay," Darcy said. "In small doses, anyway."

"Well, she should be really busy with her fabulous new husband and his family and friends today," Lisa said. "We should be able to sit in a corner and just enjoy the food."

"And drink champagne," Darcy added. "Lots and lots of lovely champagne."

Lisa laughed. "I'm sure there will be lots and lots of champagne," she told her friend. "It's meant to be the wedding of the year, after all."

Darcy rolled her eyes. "I suppose I'm happy for Joney, but really she's making far too big of a fuss over a marriage that's probably not going to last more than a few months."

Lisa gasped. "You're terrible!" she told her friend.

Darcy grinned and finished her glass of champagne. "What time are the guys getting here?" she asked Lisa.

"They should be here soon," she replied. "We're supposed to be at the chapel for eleven, right?"

The wedding itself was being held in the small chapel in the south of the island. It was to be followed by an elaborate reception at the fanciest hotel in central Douglas. Lisa and Darcy had been surprised to be invited to the ceremony at the chapel, as it only held a small number of people.

Mark and Andy arrived right on schedule in a hired limousine. The girls were ready and watching for them when the car pulled up.

"You look gorgeous, as always," Mark told Lisa as he helped her into the car.

"I can't believe how handsome you look in your morning coat," she replied.

By the time she was settled, Andy had popped the cork on another bottle of champagne and was passing around glasses full of the bubbly stuff.

"I'm going to be too drunk to appreciate the ceremony," Lisa protested as Andy handed her a glass.

"I was talking to Joney last week, and she said they've written their own vows. You're going to need a drink or two to get through that," Darcy said with a laugh, taking a big drink from her glass.

"Oh, dear," Lisa sighed. "If I drink too much I'll probably start giggling."

Darcy laughed again. "I hadn't thought of that."

The drive south was easily filled with small talk. They arrived at the chapel fifteen minutes before the ceremony was due to start.

An enormous red carpet had been spread across the pavement that led from the road to the chapel door. A pair of burly security guards checked their names off a list before pulling open the double doors to admit them. Inside, a large chart, propped against an easel, showed them where to sit.

"We're further up than I was expecting," Lisa whispered to Darcy as ushers showed them to their seats.

"You didn't tell me you guys were such good friends with this woman," Mark whispered as he slid into the seat next to Lisa. "We're practically in the front row."

Lisa shrugged. "Maybe none of her other friends could make it. It is Christmas Eve, after all."

A few minutes after they were settled, the man at the piano began playing softly. Lisa and Darcy exchanged glances as the groom and his groomsmen approached the front of the chapel. The groom was handsome in a strangely artificial way, with a toothpaste-commercial smile and wavy black hair that looked stiff and untouchable. Lisa couldn't resist quickly reaching over and running her fingers through Mark's silky hair. He smiled at her as she pulled her hand back.

"I've never tried styling my hair like that," he whispered to Lisa. "Do you think it would be an improvement?"

Lisa made a face at him that could leave him in doubt as to her thoughts on the subject. He chuckled softly.

People were beginning to get restless, twenty minutes later, when the ceremony had yet to start.

"The bride isn't here yet," someone in the row in front of them whispered loudly. "I hope Joney hasn't changed her mind."

"Ha, she knows she's latched on to big money," someone else whispered back. "She'll be here."

Moments later, a hush fell in the small building. Everyone rose to their feet and turned to the back expectantly. Joney swept in, holding her father's arm. Her hair and makeup were so overdone that Lisa had to believe that it was deliberate. The dark red dress she was wearing had a long slit up the front that was only just decent as she strode down the aisle. Lisa gasped as Joney walked past and Lisa saw that the dress was completely backless. It was much more a cocktail party dress than a wedding dress. She exchanged looks with Darcy and then shrugged. Obviously, Joney could do what she wanted at her own wedding.

The service itself was a civil rather than a religious one and it moved along very quickly. After only a few minutes, Joney and Nigel were invited to share their vows with each other and their guests.

Joney smiled up at Nigel. "When I met you, I knew. I could just picture myself by your side forever. I could imagine our future life together. It was everything that I'd ever dreamt of. I feel happy when I'm with you. I love everything about you. I'm so happy to become your wife. I hope you make me happy forever."

Nigel grinned brightly at Joney. "I've dated a lot of women," he said. "Some of them were smarter than you, or prettier, or sexier, but I never wanted to marry any of them. There was just something about you that made me want to make this commitment. I'm happier today than I've ever been and I hope we have a long and happy life together."

The ceremony wrapped up quickly after that and after sharing her first kiss with her new husband, Joney looked at the assembled well-wishers and grinned. "Let's party," she shouted.

The wedding party piled into a limousine as everyone else headed for their cars. In their limousine, Darcy immediately poured more champagne for everyone.

"Those were the strangest vows I've ever heard," she said with a giggle. "If I'm ever getting married and my husband-to-be tells everyone that he's dated prettier girls than me in the middle of our wedding, I'm dumping him on the spot."

Lisa laughed. "I couldn't believe what he said," she agreed.

"Joney's vows were all about her. How she felt and how happy she was, not one word about how wonderful Nigel was," Mark pointed out. "I don't see this marriage lasting too long."

Lisa shook her head. "I hate to say it, but I'd have to agree with that."

The reception felt over-the-top ostentatious to the point where it wasn't enjoyable. Tuxedoed waiters delivered each course while a band played classical music rather loudly and everyone sat in their assigned seats, unable to do much more than smile and nod at one another.

After dinner, a different band began to play a mix of hits covering a fifty-year range, and a few couples began to dance. The bride and groom began to circulate among the tables, talking to their guests.

When Joney and Nigel finally made it to them, Lisa and her friends had had just about enough. They were talking about leaving when Joney descended.

"Lisa, Darcy, how wonderful that you came," she shrieked. She pulled each of them up into a hug in turn. "You must introduce me to your lovely dates," she said.

Darcy introduced Andy, but Nigel already knew him. "We've worked together once or twice on things in the city," Nigel said. "But I heard you took early retirement, you lucky devil."

"I did," Andy laughed. "I still do a few days a month, at least once in a while, but I'm mostly retired and spend my time travelling and spoiling Darcy."

"I have at least ten years left before I'll have enough resources to do that," Nigel said with a sigh. "Maybe more, if my bride is as expensive to keep as she was to date."

A nervous laugh went through the group before Lisa jumped in to introduce Mark.

"What do you do?" Nigel asked Mark.

"I work for Manx National Heritage," Mark replied. "I'm head of special projects."

"We just bought the cutest little flat," Joney said, clearly uninterested in Mark's job. "Seaside Towers is soooooo expensive, but we decided it was worth the investment. You must come and see it sometime, all of you. We're on the third floor in a little two-bedroom corner unit."

Lisa knew she was supposed to be impressed by that, but she wasn't. "You and Mark are neighbours, then," she couldn't resist saying.

"You live in Seaside Towers?" Joney asked. "I didn't think flats there were allowed to be rented out."

"I bought mine when they first hit the market, off-plan, actually," Mark told her. "I'm on twelve, though, so we aren't exactly neighbours in the strictest sense."

Lisa grinned to herself as she watched Joney's face fall. The twelfth floor was the penthouse level and it housed only four very large flats. While Lisa didn't often think about it, and couldn't have cared less, Mark was actually a very wealthy man.

"Well, thank you for coming," Joney said stiffly. "And Merry Christmas." The pair moved on to the next table while Darcy and Lisa giggled together.

"Oh, I shouldn't laugh," Lisa said. "But she was always so arrogant at school. She was always talking about how rich her daddy was and how she really should be going to a proper school across, but daddy wanted her to understand how the less fortunate members of society lived." Lisa sighed. "I do genuinely hope those two are happy together," she said.

"I don't give them great odds," Darcy replied. "And I don't much care if they're happy or not. She was horrible to you in school, much worse to you than to me. All I really care about is whether you're happy or not."

Lisa looked over at Mark and then smiled back at Darcy. "At the moment, I'd say I'm pretty happy," she told her friend.

The foursome didn't stay long after that. The ride back to Lisa's house was fairly quiet as Lisa sat snuggled up with Mark while Darcy and Andy held hands and sipped even more champagne. Back at Lisa's, the men came in for one last drink.

"It's nearly midnight," Lisa remarked. "It's nearly Christmas."

Lisa was excited about her gift for Mark. She'd tracked down an original copy of a book on Manx myths and legends that had been written in the 1850s. Not only was it in excellent condition, it had been autographed by the author. The museum had a couple of copies, but the print run had been limited and it was rare for copies to become available. Now she gave it to Mark, who was suitably delighted.

"I love it," he told Lisa. "Marjorie will be jealous when I tell her my copy is signed."

Lisa laughed. "Since she's the one who helped me find it and told me what sort of price I should pay for it, she isn't going to be surprised."

Mark laughed. "Good, I'd hate for her to try to make me feel guilty about having it," he said.

"The museum has enough copies. Marjorie said so," Lisa assured him. "I wouldn't have bought it otherwise."

Mark flipped through the pages, stopping at a drawing of the Moddey Dhoo. "Remember when I told you about him?" he asked Lisa.

She nodded. "After you dragged me into the crypt at Peel Castle," she replied.

Mark grinned and turned a few more pages. "And there's the Countess of Derby, Castle Rushen's resident ghost." He held up the picture and Lisa gasped.

"What's wrong?" Mark asked her. "You've gone pale."

"I saw her," Lisa said. "I forgot all about it until right now, but I saw her."

"You saw the Countess of Derby's ghost?" Darcy asked. "I've been down to Castle Rushen with dozen of guys and I've never seen her."

"When did you see her?" Mark asked, suddenly serious.

"When we were installing the new system at the castle," Lisa said in a shaky voice. "Remember, I'd lost my pen...." she trailed off.

"It's just an old myth," Mark said, pulling Lisa close. "Don't let it bother you."

"It doesn't bother me now," Lisa told him. "It upset me at the time, though."

"Why?" Darcy demanded.

"Because Mark was still supposed to be dating you at the time," Lisa replied. "And the Countess was smiling."

Mark just stared at her for a moment and then he started to laugh. "You mean to tell me that the Countess told you I was your one true love all those months ago and you never told me?" he asked.

"I forgot," Lisa said, shaking her head. "So much has happened since then," she tried to explain.

Mark pulled her close and kissed her. "It's all good," he told her as he released her. "And I think it makes giving you your Christmas present even easier."

He reached into his pocket and pulled out a small box. Darcy giggled nervously and Lisa felt her heart race. Mark slid off the couch and got down on one knee in front of her.

"Lisa, my darling, will you marry me?"

Lisa felt tears flood into her eyes as she gasped out a tiny "yes." She swallowed hard and tried again, saying "yes" in a firm voice that made Mark smile. He slipped the ring on her finger and then pulled her into another kiss. It was several minutes later, when Darcy and Andy both began to cough loudly, that the kiss finally ended.

16

Six months later, on a beautiful June morning, Lisa made faces at herself in her mirror as Darcy fixed her makeup.

"Stop that or I'll make a mess of you," Darcy said, reaching for her glass of champagne.

"No drinking until I'm perfect," Lisa told her friend.

"I've been doing your makeup forever and you've never worried about how it turned out before," Darcy challenged.

"It does matter to me today," Lisa admitted. "Today I just want everything to be perfect."

Darcy shook her head. "It won't be," she told her friend. "But that's okay, because whatever goes wrong, and something will, at the end of the day you'll still be Mrs. Mark Blake and that's all that really matters."

Lisa giggled and then reached for her own champagne glass. "I can't believe I'm getting married," she said.

"I can't believe you made Mark wait until June," Darcy replied. "I thought, after his Christmas proposal, that you'd agree to get married right away."

"We talked about it," Lisa said. "And if Mark had really pushed me, I would have agreed. But I'd always wanted a June wedding, and Mark was okay with waiting. This way he was able to clear his schedule at work and I was able to finish a couple of big projects. Now we can have a nice long honeymoon with no worries about work for either of us."

"A month of travelling to various heritage sites around Europe, that sounds like Mark's work to me," Darcy replied.

"But I'm at least as excited as he is," Lisa countered. "It seems like we really are perfect for each other."

"Speaking of perfect for each other," Darcy said. "Andy and I broke up."

"What?" Lisa shrieked. "When? How? What happened?"

Darcy set down her makeup brush and picked up her glass. This time Lisa didn't stop her when she swallowed half its contents. "About a week ago," Darcy said finally.

"But why? I thought you two were really happy together."

"We were," Darcy said with a shrug. "But Andy was getting tired of having to schedule things around my job. He wanted me to quit and just live with him."

"And you didn't want to quit your job?" Lisa asked.

"I do want to quit my job," Darcy replied. "I'm thinking about doing just that. But I want to quit my job for a better one, or at least a different one. I don't want to quit my job to move in with some man."

"Oh, Darce, I'm so sorry," Lisa said, jumping up to give her friend a hug. "I can't believe he wanted you to quit your job like that."

Darcy hugged her back tightly. "It's okay, really," she told Lisa. "I told him I wasn't going to just move in with him, unless he wanted to make it a more formal arrangement, and he declined."

"He's an idiot," Lisa said stoutly. "I won't talk to him today."

Darcy smiled. "It's okay, really it is," she insisted. "We're still friends, even if he doesn't want to marry me."

Lisa smiled. "At least he isn't in the wedding party," she said.

Darcy turned back to her makeup brushes, working on Lisa's eyes again. "By the way," she said, "you know how I feel about attending weddings on my own."

Lisa nodded. "Oh, no, you don't have a date. We can find someone. Let me ring a few people."

Darcy shook her head. "It's all taken care of," she told Lisa. "But I thought I should warn you. I invited Finlo to be my date today."

Lisa made a face. "Really? Please, please, please don't tell me that you're getting back together with Finlo."

Darcy laughed and drank more champagne. "Absolutely not," she said resolutely. "But he understands me better than most men. I rang him last week, right after Andy and I split up and explained about today. He's promised to pretend to be madly devoted to me all day. And I know he'll do a wonderful job of it."

Lisa frowned. "Just don't you start believing it," she told Darcy.

"No worries," Darcy laughed. "I just want to get through the day. Finlo will keep the gossips from thinking I can't find a man and maybe he'll make Andy feel like he's lost out on something special. And before you ask, no, I'm not hoping to use Finlo to make Andy jealous so I can get him back. I'm ready to make some big changes in my life, and Andy isn't going to be part of them any more than Finlo is."

Lisa nodded. "I'm making a few changes as well," she said softly, staring at herself in the mirror. Darcy had done a wonderful job and Lisa marveled at her own appearance. She stood up and fiddled with her dress.

"Don't fuss," Darcy said. "You look perfect."

"Thanks," Lisa said, her eyes filling with tears.

"Don't cry," Darcy told her quickly. "We need to get to the church. I don't have time to fix your makeup again."

Lisa laughed and then hugged Darcy tightly. "Thank you so much for everything."

Darcy hugged her back. "I can't tell you how happy I am for you," she whispered. "You and Mark are perfect for each other. Time for you to live happily ever after."

"I will," Lisa replied solemnly.

GLOSSARY OF TERMS

ENGLISH/MANX TO AMERICAN TERMS

- **bacon butty** — bacon sandwich
- **bespoke** — custom (made to order)
- **bin** — garbage can
- **biscuits** — cookies
- **boot** — trunk (of a car)
- **car park** — parking lot
- **chippy** — a fish and chips take-out restaurant
- **chips** — french fries
- **comeover** — a person who moved to the island from elsewhere
- **crisps** — potato chips
- **cuppa** — cup of tea (informal)
- **fizzy drink** — soda (pop)
- **flat** — apartment
- **full stop** — period
- **holiday** — vacation
- **lift** — elevator
- **loo** — restroom

GLOSSARY OF TERMS

- **midday** — noon
- **pavement** — sidewalk
- **pudding** — dessert
- **queue** — line
- **starters** — appetizers
- **telly** — television
- **tannoy** — public address system
- **trainers** — sneakers
- **Wellies (informal for Wellington boots)** — rain boots

OTHER NOTES:

The UK (and Isle of Man) primary (elementary) school system is similar to the US system, with Reception being the first year of school for children. (Much like a US kindergarten.) After Reception, the years are numbered "Year One," "Year Two," etc. rather than "First Grade," "Second Grade," as in the US. UK (and Manx) students start Reception in the school year that they turn five, so generally speaking, they start a year earlier than their US counterparts.

A wardrobe is a large piece of furniture with rails for hanging clothes in it. Most bedrooms in the UK and the Isle of Man do not have closets as they would in the US, so a wardrobe is needed.

Boxing Day is the day after Christmas (December 26th) and was traditionally a day for giving gifts to servants and tradesmen.

The "TT" is the Tourist Trophy. This motorcycle racing event is held annually on the island and includes two-weeks of racing on closed roads.

If something goes "pear-shaped" it all goes wrong.

Blackpool Tower is a tourist attraction on Blackpool Pleasure Beach. It was built in 1894 and visitors can take a lift to the top as well as enjoy shows and an indoor playground at the site.

A full-English breakfast typically consists of bacon, eggs, toast,

OTHER NOTES:

grilled tomatoes, beans, sausages, and fried mushrooms. There are many regional variations on this, however.

The British say "snap" to mean "same." For instance, if someone says that they are tired, someone could say, "snap" to indicate that they are also tired. The term comes from the card game "Snap" where you turn over cards and, if they match, the first person to shout "snap" wins the cards on the pile.

"A-levels" are subjects studied in the final years of education before university.

Bunscoill Ghaelgagh is a full-immersion Manx language primary school on the island.

When talking about time, the English say, for example, "half seven" to mean "seven-thirty."

A charity shop is a store run by a charitable (non-profit) organisation that sells donated second-hand merchandise in order to raise funds for their particular cause. They are great places to find books, games and puzzles, as well as clothing, knick-knacks and furniture.

When island residents talk about someone being from "across," or moving "across," they mean somewhere in the United Kingdom (across the water).

Irina Dunn was an Australian journalist and politician. She coined the phrase "A woman needs a man like a fish needs a bicycle" in 1970.

ALPHABETICAL LIST OF HISTORICAL SITES VISITED

Castle Rushen: Located in Castletown in the south of the island, Castle Rushen is a gorgeous medieval castle that was later a prison. While most of the castle is now a museum, there are still courts that meet there.

Cregneash Village: Located in the far south of the island, the village is home to several thatched cottages. The site showcases traditional farming methods as well as providing demonstrations of old-fashioned skills like cooking over a fire and spinning and weaving.

The Grove Museum: Located in Ramsey, the museum was once the summer home of the wealthy Gibb family. The museum provides a look at life on the island in the Victorian and Edwardian eras.

House of Manannan: Located in Peel, this award-winning museum showcases Manx history with interactive displays and exhibits.

The Laxey Wheel: Located in Laxey, the "Lady Isabella" is the largest working waterwheel in the world. While the wheel no longer pumps water from the Laxey mines, the site provides a look at the mining history of the island.

The Manx Museum: Located in Douglas, the museum has

exhibits that cover the complete history of the island, as well as an art gallery and an extensive gift shop.

The Nautical Museum: Located in Castletown, the Nautical Museum is home to the *Peggy*, a yacht built in 1790 and later shut up in her boathouse for around a hundred years.

The Old House of Keys: Located in Castletown, the building has been restored to its 1866 appearance and houses an interactive exhibit on Manx political history.

The Old Grammar School: Located in Castletown, the building was built around 1200, originally as a church. It later served as a school until 1930.

Peel Castle: Located in Peel, the site was originally a place of worship before becoming a Viking fort. The ruined buildings on the site date from the 10th and 11th centuries and later.

Rushen Abbey: Located in Ballasalla (near Castletown), the site was once home to Cistercian monks. Now in ruins, extensive archeological excavations have been taking place there for years.

You can find more information on all of these sites on the Manx National Heritage website and also the Isle of Man Government site.

ISLAND CHRISTMAS

Will Darcy find her own happily ever after?

Find out in Island Christmas.

Darcy Robinson couldn't be happier that her closest friend, Lisa, has found the man of her dreams. Now it's time for Darcy to make some big changes of her own. Quitting her job was easy, but finding a new one proves a little bit more difficult.

Gorgeous, sexy, and super wealthy Alastair Breckenridge seems more like the perfect boyfriend, not the perfect boss. But Darcy is determined to keep her personal life and her new career separate. If only she could persuade Alastair to believe her as she begins working on making "Manx Christmas World" an event to remember.

Alastair is the least of her problems, though, once she meets Kerron Kewley, the handsome and muscular farmer who owns the land where the event is scheduled to be held. He doesn't want anything to do with "Manx Christmas World" and he's determined to make Darcy either relocate the event or cancel it altogether.

Can Darcy succeed at her new job and make "Manx Christmas World" a success?

ISLAND CHRISTMAS

Can she resist Alastair's charms, at least until after opening day?

Can she ignore the unmistakable chemistry between herself and Kerron Kewley, even as they argue their way towards the biggest Christmas extravaganza the island has ever seen?

BY THE SAME AUTHOR

Enjoy reading about the Isle of Man?
Like a good cozy mystery?

Aunt Bessie Assumes
An Isle of Man Cozy Mystery
By Diana Xarissa

Aunt Bessie assumes that she'll have the beach all to herself on a cold, wet, and windy March morning just after sunrise, then she stumbles (almost literally) over a dead body.

Elizabeth (Bessie) Cubbon, aged somewhere between free bus pass (60) and telegram from the Queen (100), has lived her entire adult life in a small cottage on Laxey beach. For most of those years, she's been in the habit of taking a brisk morning walk along the beach. Dead men have never been part of the scenery before.

Aunt Bessie assumes that the dead man died of natural causes, then the police find the knife in his chest.

BY THE SAME AUTHOR

Try as she might, Bessie just can't find anything to like about the young widow that she provides tea and sympathy to in the immediate aftermath of finding the body. There isn't much to like about the rest of the victim's family either.

Aunt Bessie assumes that the police will have the case wrapped up in no time at all, then she finds a second body.

Can Bessie and her friends find the killer before she ends up as the next victim?

ALSO BY DIANA XARISSA

The Isle of Man Cozy Mysteries

Aunt Bessie Assumes

Aunt Bessie Believes

Aunt Bessie Considers

Aunt Bessie Decides

Aunt Bessie Enjoys

Aunt Bessie Finds

Aunt Bessie Goes

Aunt Bessie's Holiday

Aunt Bessie Invites

Aunt Bessie Joins

Aunt Bessie Knows

Aunt Bessie Likes

Aunt Bessie Meets

Aunt Bessie Needs

Aunt Bessie Observes

Aunt Bessie Provides

Aunt Bessie Questions

Aunt Bessie Remembers

Aunt Bessie Solves

Aunt Bessie Tries

Aunt Bessie Understands

Aunt Bessie Volunteers

Aunt Bessie Wonders

The Isle of Man Ghostly Cozy Mysteries

Arrivals and Arrests

Boats and Bad Guys

Cars and Cold Cases

Dogs and Danger

Encounters and Enemies

Friends and Frauds

Guests and Guilt

Hop-tu-Naa and Homicide

Invitations and Investigations

Joy and Jealousy

Kittens and Killers

Letters and Lawsuits

The Markham Sisters Cozy Mystery Novellas

The Appleton Case

The Bennett Case

The Chalmers Case

The Donaldson Case

The Ellsworth Case

The Fenton Case

The Green Case

The Hampton Case

The Irwin Case

The Jackson Case

The Kingston Case

The Lawley Case

The Moody Case

The Norman Case

The Osborne Case

The Patrone Case

The Quinton Case

The Rhodes Case

The Isle of Man Romance Series
Island Escape
Island Inheritance
Island Heritage
Island Christmas

The Later in Life Love Stories
Second Chances
Second Act

ABOUT THE AUTHOR

Diana lived on the glorious Isle of Man for more than ten years before returning to the United States with her family. Now living near Buffalo, New York, she enjoys having the opportunity to write about the island that she loves so much. It truly is an amazing and magical place.

Diana also writes mystery/thrillers set in the not-too-distant future under the pen name "Diana X. Dunn" and fantasy/adventure books for middle grade readers under the pen name "D.X. Dunn."

Find Diana at:
www.dianaxarissa.com
diana@dianaxarissa.com

Made in the USA
Monee, IL
20 February 2025

12629035R00125